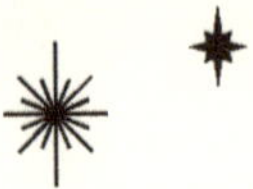

The NEBADOR series:

Book One: The Test
Spring 2010

Book Two: Journey
Summer 2010

Book Three: Selection
Fall 2010

Book Four: Flight Training
Spring 2011

Book Five: Back to the Stars
Fall 2011

Book Six: Star Station
2012

NEBADOR

an epic young-adult science fiction adventure

by

J. Z. Colby

Nebador Archives

Cover art by Rachael Hedges
Illustrations by J. Z. Colby and Amanda Herman

For other print editions, ebooks, dramatic audiobooks, previews, samples, biographies, comments, questions, artwork, writing contests, Ask Kibi advice, deep learning notes, Nebador citizens, and more, please see:

www.nebador.com

Nebador Archives
Kelso, Washington, USA

Library of Congress Control Number: 2009912993
Manufactured in the USA

ISBN: 978-1-936253-00-5
NEBADOR1HCG2: hardcover, 6" x 9", 186 pages,
global/library edition (10-point Georgia type), revision 2

Greetings, young people of planet Earth,

Much adult science fiction is based on the assumption that the human race will be in charge, or at least high up on the pecking order, when we venture to the stars. Young adults have a somewhat clearer memory that when they graduated elementary school, they were not immediately movers and shakers of the world, but instead found themselves in middle school.

Young adults also remember well the training wheels on their first small bicycles. Will-power alone could not propel them to their destinations.

Nebador is about little steps the smallest of us can make from the playpen to the university, from the gutter to the stars.

As you know, your world is changing very rapidly. During times of change, those who are stuck in old, rigid ways of thinking and feeling often don't do well. Those who can see far and think clearly are best prepared to survive, prosper in some way, and find happiness.

Stories like these help by letting us walk in the shoes of those who have lived through similar times. They become our heroes, giving us strength when we face challenges, and whispering their inspiration to us when we must solve problems.

Someday, many years from now, your stories may also be told, and you will become heroes to younger people who are struggling to understand the universe. They will take comfort in your courage, and learn from the lessons you have already learned.

J. Z. Colby
2010

Acknowledgements

Wonderful people throughout the author's life provided unique and irreplaceable lessons and inspirations:

Juniper Russell
Vicky Ball
Linda Dezzutti
Jennifer Carolyn Gates
Rachael Bleich
Paula Wells
Sarah Satterthwaite
Ashley Riddle
Esther Smith
Dottie Frisbie
Martha Higgins
Susanne Koller
Charleen Cox
Meredith Herzog
Patricia Sharp
Antonya Pickard

Valuable readers gave the author feedback after digging through early drafts of the book:

Taia Handlin
Janet Powers
Susan Drake
Karen Oster
Toni Corkran
Katheryn Brunswick
Krista Reichard
Shelley & Jimmy Johnson
Brendan Aragorn
Deborah Meier
Martha Higgins
Aurora WindDancer
Ardith Libby
Dan Clark
Cecelia Harper
Holly Chalcraft
Karen Pihlak
Margaret Brunswick
Jessica Johnson
Elwin Aragorn
Jennifer & Kate Westran
Mike & Ann Bergey
Katie Norris

Excellent critiquers commented on thousands of passages, then provided reactions during in-depth interviews:

Sidney Oster, 8
Sarah Bray, 10
River Lyons, 10
Catherine "Cat" Harper, 10
Aditya Srinivasan, 11
Madison Frasier, 11
Ruth Drake, 12
Jasper W. Romero, 12
Cherish Broker, 13
Hannah Li Powers, 14
Alex Chalcraft, 15
Laurel Koran, 15
Abby Powers, 16
Brie Polette, 17
Winn Barrientos
Beth Littlewolf
Dylan Oster, 9
Joshua Clark, 10
Mitchell Bendis, 10
Kacie Wilson, 10
Courtney Snyder, 11
Thurston Coatney, 12
Jarret Beckoff, 12
Mariah Bruns, 13
Kristen Voie, 14
Patrick Murray, 15
Kathryn C., 15
Stephanie Louie, 16
Abigail Bodley, 16
Rachael Hedges
Elizabeth Renguso

Careful publishing assistants and proofreaders brought the final manuscript as close to perfection as possible:

Sarah Bray, 10
Mariah Bruns, 13
Alex Chalcraft, 15
Amanda Herman, 17
Deborah Meier
Mitchell Bendis, 10
Joshua Utter, 14
Faylyn, 17
Rachael Hedges

Contents

"Personal power is the ability to stand on your own two feet, with a smile on your face, in the middle of a universe that contains a million ways to crush you."

– Nebador Transport Service saying

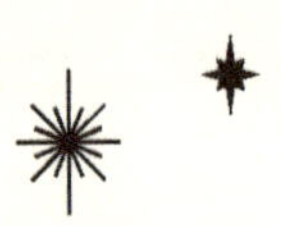

Chapter 1: First Contact

The boot, of some strange, shiny material, made a sucking sound as it pulled free of the sticky mud. One step farther along, water spiders skipped away as the boot plunged back into the swamp.

After several more strides through the watery black ooze, the light-haired young man looked ahead. Bushes and willowy trees covered the higher ground, still many steps away. Green eyes sparkling with curiosity, his face revealed about two decades of life, perhaps a little more.

He teetered for a moment, regained his balance, and wiped the sweat from his brow with a sleeve. Glancing back to where his tracks began, he watched as the large bulge in the swamp sank lower and lower. Shivering, he groped for the wide, dark metal bracelet on his left arm. After fingering it thoughtfully for a moment, he relaxed, took a deep breath, and turned back to his path.

Finally, with only one muddy step remaining, he tossed his shoulder bag onto the grassy bank and reached for a small tree. As he pulled himself onto higher ground, the swamp sucked at his boots one last time, inviting him to join the many creatures whose bones rotted in its murky depths.

*

As soon as the young man stood up, three large four-legged animals grazing nearby raised their heads and made throaty sounds. After a moment of thought, he whispered, "Horse." They shifted positions and returned to grazing, all three female, one close to giving birth.

Suddenly a large, dark-brown stallion bolted from behind a bush, called a threatening high-pitched challenge, and began stomping the ground and moving forward.

The young man stood with his back to the swamp as the huge male animal approached and towered over him. The man's right hand moved toward his bracelet, but the stallion thrashed its head violently and sliced the air with powerful hooves.

The young man lowered his hands and focused on breathing evenly.

After more ear-piercing calls, the stallion began to relax, but did not retreat. Snorting, the horse took in the scent of the puny human it could easily butt right into the treacherous swamp.

The young man began to hum a simple melody while keeping his hands at his sides.

The stallion twitched its ears to catch the new sound, then suddenly opened its mouth and gripped the man's shoulder with powerful teeth. For several heartbeats the teeth lingered, threatening to crush muscle and bone while the young man hummed softly.

With a jerk of its head, the stallion released its grip and leapt away, knocking the man off his feet. The three mares bolted. The stallion paused a stone's throw away, looked back, and finally galloped after the mares into the grasslands that spread out northward, toward the snowcapped mountains on the horizon.

✷

The young man swallowed, let out a long shaking sigh, and closed his eyes as he listened to his throbbing heart.

A minute later, he slowly stood up, and gradually a look of contentment appeared as he scanned his environment. The land everywhere was full of light green shoots and new leaves. From overhead came the cries of winged creatures. Looking up, he saw them circle, dark feathers stretched out to catch the rising air. With few clouds in a blue sky, the new spring day promised sunshine and gentle warmth.

The young man's eyes and ears told him he was otherwise alone. Touching and moving his shoulder carefully, he found it merely bruised and tender. He stood in silence for another moment, just looking around at the plants and listening to the birds and insects. Finally, after taking up his shoulder bag, he put one foot in front of the other toward the grassy hills in the west.

✷

He had only been walking through the damp grass a few minutes when a path offered itself, and he gladly accepted its guidance. A little farther along, the trail skirted a small lake where he paused to rinse the mud from his boots.

As he sat on the grass at the edge of the still water, he noticed shy, careful movement among the rocks and plants nearby. He remained silent and waited, and soon a small furry creature came into view with hops of its hind legs between nibbles of greenery.

"Hello, little . . . rabbit," the young man said softly and haltingly in a language clearly not his own.

The rabbit twitched its nose and kept one bright eye on the newcomer, but continued eating.

"My name is Ilika, and I just arrived in your beautiful land from a place called Satamia, in the greater region of Nebador."

The little creature's long ears turned to the sound as it continued to demonstrate which plants were delicious, and which were not.

"You are my first contact in this land."

The rabbit raised its head for a moment, then went back to eating.

"Well . . . I did meet someone earlier, but the situation was a bit emotional . . . and we didn't get a chance to talk."

Suddenly the piercing cry of a bird of prey filled the sky, and the rabbit vanished into the rocks with one leap.

"Be well, little one. I must continue my journey."

*

Half an hour later, with deep breaths of the crisp air, the young man strode to the top of the highest hill. Standing tall, he looked west. In the small valley below nestled simple farms, little thatched cottages, and people beginning their work in gardens, fields, and animal pens.

Beyond the farms, on a gentle rise of open grass, stood the medieval walled city, its gray stonework glowing in the morning light.

* * *

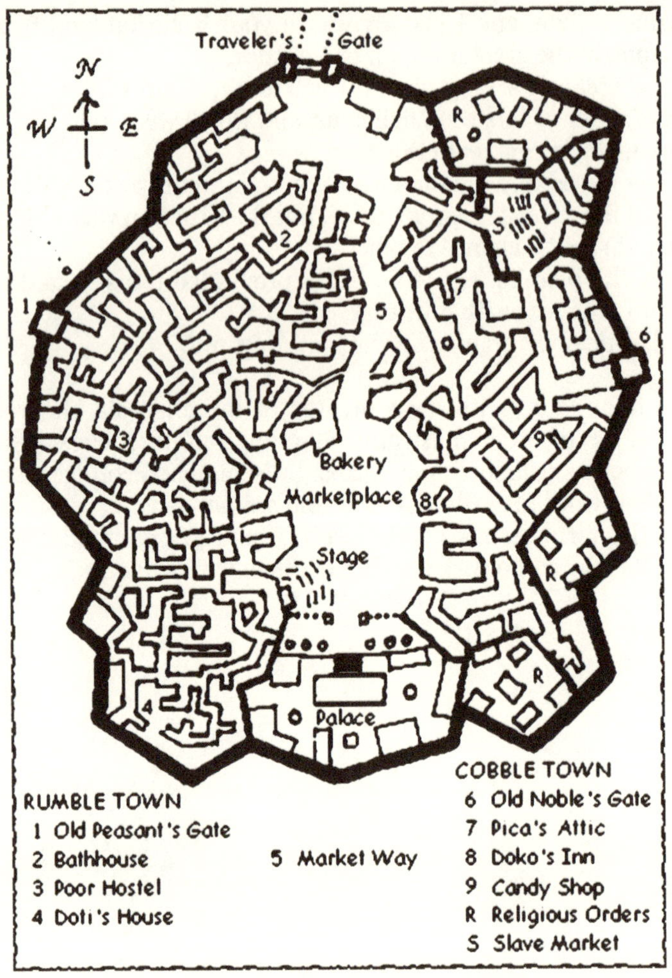

Chapter 2: The Capital City

At the first light of dawn, several hours before the newcomer stepped out of the swamp, the city guards changed duty shifts at the Traveler's Gate and the watchtowers. News and jests were exchanged, and a loaf of bread from the previous day, somewhat stale, was torn and shared.

By that time the bakers, cooks, and innkeepers of the city were already up, prodding children and apprentices who would rather be snug in their beds. With a slice of bread in hand, the young ones blinked and stumbled to their duties.

As morning began to glow on the eastern horizon, wagons approached the city gate, the first few laden with sacks of flour from the mills. Next, carts groaned up the hill, filled with farm produce and craft-wares, bound for the marketplace to sell to those who had coins in their pouches.

Many unskilled laborers, after a quick bowl of mush because they couldn't afford bread, hoisted sacks and crates to their shoulders in the morning light. Strong men unloaded an entire wagon at the large bakery on the edge of the marketplace.

*

The baker's son shuffled loaves in and out of the oven, turning them when necessary, but part of his mind was elsewhere. As an apprentice scribe, he spent long hours working without pay to pursue his dream of someday living the upper-class life of Cobble Town.

The smell of burning bread brought him fully back to the present, and he found the neglected loaf in the back of the oven. He grinned sheepishly at his father and tossed the loaf into a box for the poorest of the people.

*

In a small stable near the bakery, a shaggy gray donkey squealed her complaint, but the stupid man was obviously not going to quit kicking her and calling her "Ka" until she got up. She had tried to tell him her real name, but like most people, he didn't understand. With noises of protest, she got to her feet and allowed him to strap on the harness.

Soon her baskets were brimming with fresh loaves straight from the oven, and she began to follow her owner through the streets of Cobble Town. The hard surface quickly made her legs sore, but she ignored the pain and drifted into a daydream, imagining an owner who would speak kindly to her, learn her real name, and let her walk on the soft earth.

*

Soon after the sun rose, others made way for a noble-born woman who stepped up to the bakery. Her slave girl carried a big basket, soon filled with several loaves of the best bread and a large pie. The girl could smell the delicious pie as she followed her matron around the marketplace.

The noblewoman had plenty of money to spend, but managing her large household took constant attention all day long. Sometimes she glimpsed her two young slaves, late in the evening, when they had finished their duties and retired to their sleeping niche in the back of the kitchen. Laughing and joking, they made games and toys with bits of firewood and pebbles. She would slip away, not letting them see her smile of longing.

*

At the Traveler's Gate, a guard carefully wrote a few words on a piece of rough paper. He gestured to a young boy who stood nearby.

The boy instantly stood before the guard. Other boys watched, ready and willing if the one chosen was too slow or clumsy.

The guard handed him the note and three copper pieces, then looked him sternly in the eyes.

The boy swallowed and glanced at some slaves carrying heavy burdens through the gate, then nodded that he understood the price of failure.

A few minutes later, after dashing up Market Way, the boy handed the note and two of the copper pieces to the baker. He received a wooden shingle bearing six freshly-baked fruit tarts.

To get back to the city gate, the boy selected muddy streets and narrow alleyways of Rumble Town, his home turf, that were not too crowded, and not the regular haunts of thieves and rascals.

*

The high priest had been boring the king with a speech ever since breakfast. It had something to do with priests and monks being exempt from port taxes. Now the king had his chin in his hands, but alas, the speech continued.

At the first pause in the high priest's words, one of the king's advisors interrupted. "If your god is so all-powerful, why do you need special favors from the Court? Other people, even those without an all-powerful god, pay their taxes."

The king lifted his chin. "Good point. I cannot exempt the religious orders from all material contributions to the realm. If the port taxes are becoming a burden, as you say, perhaps it is because your people are traveling too much."

At that moment, a servant entered from the marketplace balancing a large platter of tarts, muffins, and a crock of fresh butter.

"Ahh!" the king breathed. "It is time for the Court to refresh itself."

The high priest bowed low and left the audience hall, an appeasing smile on his face. Once he was outside the palace, the smile changed to a cold frown.

*

As the sun climbed over the hills and city walls on that bright spring morning, those rich enough to have cloaks began to remove them before finishing their breakfast of buttered bread, fruit tarts, or sweet muffins.

Those not so fortunate, still shivering from the morning cold, stood or walked in the golden rays as often as their work would allow, chewing whatever crusts and scraps they could find.

* * *

Chapter 3: Making an Entrance

The newcomer from Satamia in Nebador strode quickly down the grassy hill toward the little cart-road that wound among the farms and cottages. His footsteps brought curious glances from windows and gardens, and to each he smiled and waved. Some waved back, especially the children. Others watched him cautiously.

The road zigzagged between newly-planted gardens, budding orchards, and freshly-tilled fields. As the newcomer reached the last cottage, a young farmer with curly brown hair pushed a cart of old yellow hay onto the road.

"T'sa rat boful di, es'nut?" the lad asked cheerfully.

The newcomer stood silently, his face showing embarrassment. After a few moments of mental effort, he pointed to his ears and made a waving motion with his hands. Then, with palms open, he bowed slightly.

"Oo-kee, g'di t'ya." The young farmer pushed his load of hay toward another farm, the cart's wooden wheels creaking as they turned.

The newcomer stood thoughtfully for a moment, then dug some small silver coins out of his shoulder bag and put them in an outside pocket. He filled his lungs with the cool air, and continued walking toward the walled city.

✷

With every step up the gentle slope toward the city, more and more of the countryside came into view. The cart road from the farming vale was the smallest of the ways that came together at the city gate. Two roads from the north and one from the west brought people, horses, and wagons. More farms lay along the northward roads, with dark forests and white peaks on the horizon. The road from the west emerged from gentle green hills.

When the newcomer came to the meeting of the ways just outside the gate, he paused. An old priest on horseback turned toward the city from the westward road.

The mare stopped walking and turned her head to look at the strange human standing beside the road. She breathed deeply to catch his scent.

The newcomer's gaze met one of the mare's black, sparkling eyes, and they both stood transfixed for a moment.

Finally the priest spurred on his horse, and the newcomer had to blink away a moment of sadness.

A little cart brimming with leafy vegetables, pulled by a farmer and his wife, labored slowly up the road from the north. The newcomer stepped in between the horse and the handcart. As he listened to the words spoken at the gate between the guards and those arriving, a slight smile came to him. When the horse and rider passed through, the newcomer glimpsed the coin that changed hands.

The guards looked at him. "Ye thar! From whence 'n' t'whither?"

"I come here to hire companions for the purpose of making a long journey," he replied, choosing his words carefully. "If you please, direct me to an inn of good quality." He tossed a small silver piece to the guard who had spoken.

The guard caught the coin, squinted at the stranger for a moment, then waved him in, saying, "Hard be t'marchet."

As soon as the newcomer put a few paces between himself and the gate, a long sigh of relief escaped him. He looked around the open area just inside the city walls and saw dozens of people going about their business, four-footed animals tied to posts, wooden buildings two or three stories high with thatched roofs, and little muddy streets going off in several directions.

"Marchet . . . marchet . . ." he mumbled to himself as he picked one of the streets and began to follow it.

* * *

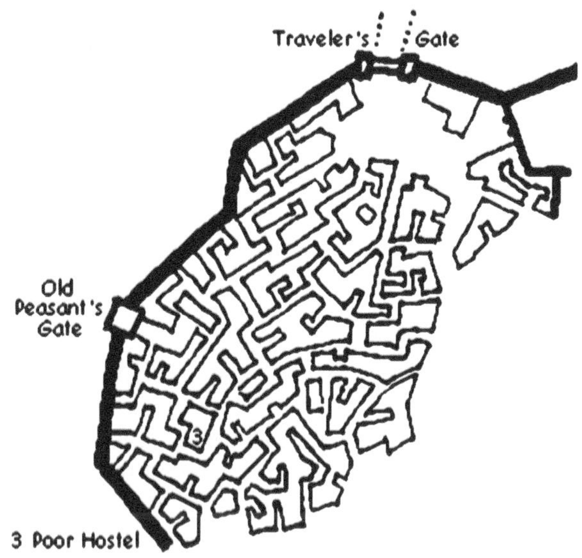

Chapter 4: The City and Its Ways

The young man from somewhere far away began to wander the narrow streets of Rumble Town, crowded with people and carts, and nearly impassable when a wagon broke an axle, or a frightened animal refused to move. On foot and lightly burdened, he found ways around, until faced with a tangle of confused sheep and frustrated people that completely filled the street. A group of children carrying baskets quickly veered toward an alleyway. At the same time, the sound of yelling guards approached from behind. One of the children paused beside a stack of old barrels and looked back at the stranger.

"Git'y on, oh ye be a'slavin'!"

The newcomer heard the key word in the lad's phrase, and on quick feet followed the children into an alley that appeared to go nowhere. After squeezing through a narrow passage between two buildings, they all emerged into another street and the children dashed away.

*

The newcomer looked for written signs, but found no help navigating the featureless maze of winding streets. The ringing sound of metal came from a wide door with an old hammer mounted above. Over another door, a bundle of wheat dangled from a stick, and a man emerged with a sack of grain on his shoulder. A family with hungry looks in their eyes, clutching small coins, entered a doorway marked with an old ceramic plate.

On nearly every street, well-dressed merchants prodded their slaves, and the newcomer cringed as he watched the forced laborers, dressed in rags, staggering under their burdens.

Smells assaulted his nose from every direction. The aroma of animal manure was ever-present, but tolerable. When he came upon the heavy odor of human waste, or the fumes from a smoldering trash fire, he moved away quickly and found something to hold while his stomach settled.

Eventually he came to a hostel that housed its guests in crowded bunkrooms. The only food was lumpy mush. Insects and rodents fought each other for any unattended bit. A sour smell filled the entire building.

The scruffy man stirring a cooking pot looked the newcomer up and down. "Ye need a'hire di strong mans? I ring . . ."

Glancing around, the newcomer saw some of the guests quickly lacing up their boots or slicking back their hair. "I am . . . just looking for an inn."

The scruffy man frowned and turned back to his cooking pot.

*

By now, the newcomer's biggest problem was painfully obvious to him. Having learned the language in classrooms, he could read it, but none of the signs he had seen used words. He could speak it slowly and carefully, but had no experience hearing it in real life.

He clenched his jaw with determination, and from that point on, stopped and pretended to look at something whenever he heard people talking. Then, after they continued on their way, he said the words softly to himself until a smile of understanding came to him. As the hours passed, he began to carry himself with more confidence.

With the approach of mid-day, the desire for something tasty and nutritious made him turn his feet eastward, toward the parts of the city he had not yet explored. He soon came upon a large open plaza with hundreds of people buying and selling in a maze of carts and wagons. The delicious aroma of baking bread made his mouth water. He grinned when he caught the sweet scent of ripe fruit. The odor of raw meat sitting in the sun, however, made him quickly change direction.

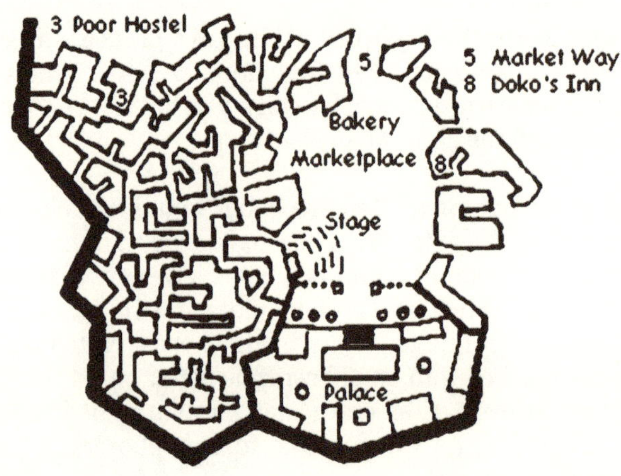

The marketplace filled the northern half of the plaza, and beyond was an open area where men stood talking, women sat on benches, and children played with simple toys. Colorful banners decorated a wooden performing stage, currently empty. At the southern end of the plaza, beyond a low stone wall, lay the palace courtyard with its cleanly-swept stone paving, marble statues, and uniformed guards.

The newcomer let his feet wander through the market, but whenever he heard an argument brewing or noticed a thief at work, he made himself scarce. All the while, he continued to listen to the language as spoken by the people.

Shops and other businesses surrounded the plaza. Wooden signs with words, often hanging from fancy ironwork, brought a smile to the newcomer. He quickly spotted an inn, and perhaps another closer to the bakery.

The first inn, near the palace, was covered with finery from floor to ceiling, wall to wall. A well-dressed man at the door asked his title. The newcomer bowed slightly and departed.

At the next inn, a fire crackled in the common room fireplace, and some merchants and their families sat at tables eating a meal. The newcomer smiled.

⁕

Doko, the large and friendly innkeeper, was able to communicate with Ilika of Satamia without much trouble. Many slurs and contractions still made the young man pause, but the innkeeper sensed when his words had not been understood, and rephrased.

When Doko learned his new guest would be staying for an entire week, he gave the young man a complete tour. Sturdy logs and heavy lumber gave the building a feeling of strength. A corridor separated the quiet common room from the kitchen and reception desk, and at the back of the building, stairs ascended to the upper floors. The innkeeper's plump wife, shy teenage son, and slightly younger bright-eyed daughter, each greeted the new guest, then returned to their work.

Following the innkeeper, Ilika entered a cozy room on the second level, completely paneled with rough boards and roofed with logs. A small window overlooked the plaza. He nodded and dug out five silver pieces to pay for a week's lodging and meals.

"You must understand, Liko," the innkeeper explained, "wine and desserts are not included with basic board."

Ilika ignored the failed attempt at his name, and assured Doko that he understood.

Alone at last, shoulder bag on the small wooden table, Ilika stretched out on the bed. Feeling strange lumps in the mattress, he quickly sat back up. After poking at them to make sure they were nothing alive — or dead — he lay back down and laughed aloud at himself.

⁕

Mosa, the innkeeper's wife, nodded when Ilika explained he ate no red meat, but she burst into a rant when he asked if he could drink fruit juice instead of ale or wine. He soon got the message that basic board did not include special requests. She fell silent when he humbly offered an extra copper piece, and she received it with a grin.

The innkeeper's stocky daughter of ten or eleven years was immediately sent into the marketplace. Ilika soon received a plate of fresh bread, strong cheese, cooked vegetables, and a few minutes later, a mug of freshly-squeezed fruit juice. Seeing the girl shuffle her feet, he brought out another copper piece. Her smile was almost as sweet as the juice.

*

After eating, Ilika stepped back into the sounds and smells of the marketplace. The array of wagons and carts aroused his curiosity.

Spring vegetables filled countless wooden crates. Round cheeses, kept cool with wet cloth, slowly disappeared into shopping baskets. Early fruits overflowed large wooden bowls, and colorful candies nestled in smaller bowls. Wood and iron tools dangled from the sides of wagons, while ceramic plates and mugs rattled as customers examined them.

Catching a whiff of something sweet, Ilika followed the scent to the bakery on the edge of the plaza, and discovered a tray of fruit tarts just out of the oven. He recognized the word "berry" in the baker's words, then discovered that his smallest coin netted him three of the little pastries. He looked around.

A young boy and slightly older girl, very poor by their clothing, sat side-by-side on one end of a log. Ilika sat down on the other end. Soon they were stealing glances at his uneaten tarts.

"I have a problem," he said without looking at them. "I have two more tarts than I need. I wonder if anyone around here would like a tart . . ."

"Yaeg'd sir! We'drilly wantum g'd sir!" the girl announced with sparkling eyes and a grin.

Although Ilika could not follow the girl's rapid speech, her smile communicated the meaning clearly. "Okay, one for each of you."

The three sat in silence, enjoying their berry tarts. The children seemed determined to savor theirs for as long as possible, not letting any crumb escape.

Suddenly both children were grabbed from behind and lifted off the ground by a man dressed the same. The tarts went flying into the dirt, and the children cried as the man yelled at them.

Ilika listened carefully, heard the word "thief" several times, and rose to face the irate parent. "I *gave* them the tarts," he interrupted with the sternest voice he could muster while making solid eye contact.

The father fell silent but didn't release his children.

"I had too many and shared them with these children in exchange for a place to sit," Ilika added.

The embarrassed father struggled to collect himself as people gathered to watch the drama. After a few moments, he released the children, still shedding tears. With a huff, he picked up his bundle and began striding toward the city gate. The crowd parted for him. After several paces, he barked a command without looking back, and the crying children scurried after.

With a heavy heart Ilika turned to find dogs devouring the dropped tarts and the baker standing near, flour-covered hands on his hips. “T’ems ony tarts his child’n see all yer long.”

Ilika understood enough words to gather the baker’s meaning. He looked at the faces of the people around him, sensing only sympathy for the children.

After thanking the baker for his kind words, Ilika made his way thoughtfully back to the solitude of his little room at the inn.

* * *

Chapter 5: The Best and the Worst

For the next four days, Ilika continued to wander the marketplace and the muddy streets and alleys of Rumble Town. Although deeply saddened by the poverty and forced labor all around him, he continued to practice his language skills at every opportunity. At each street vendor and shop, he found a reason to linger or go in, even if just to ask a question.

Braving the insects and odors, he made himself sample the working-class food. Only once did his stomach revolt, forcing him to stay in his room sipping water and nibbling dry bread for the rest of the day.

*

With the dawning of a new sunny day, Ilika made sure he was nicely dressed and began carefully exploring the eastern part of the city. Behind real glass windows, little shops displayed everything a gentleman or a lady could want. The sturdy half-timber houses of Cobble Town were larger, the streets wider and always paved with fitted stones. Walls and dogs protected gardens and patios, both completely unknown in Rumble Town.

No trash or unpleasant odors were allowed. Teams of slaves, supervised by guards, worked constantly to clean up animal droppings and anything else unpleasant.

Cobble Town held one delight the poorer section of the city lacked. Ilika's eyes sparkled every time he heard the simple tunes created by the drums and pipes of street musicians. At other times he would overhear well-dressed children talking about the location of the nearest jester. Following, he too would grin from ear to ear at the juggling, acrobatics, or silent pantomime.

But the entertainment was only for the wealthy residents of the area. Ilika saw peasants quickly arrested and hauled away when caught without a clear purpose or an escort.

On his second day exploring the richer part of the city, Ilika looked carefully at the street signs, carved in block letters but often misspelled. From Doko's Inn, *Jewelers Wey* led to *Heelers Row*. From there, *Scrib Street* branched, unless Ilika got lost on *Murchants Circle*, which he did, twice.

The guild halls and shops of the upper-class professions lined every street. Scribes, accountants, and illustrators seemed to be common. Jewelers and money changers were fewer and always well-guarded. With a frown, Ilika looked askance at the forceps and other crude surgical instruments dangling in the windows of healers.

As mid-day approached, he found an eatery near the old Noble's Gate and relaxed with a bowl of spicy fish soup, fresh bread, and cheese. Around him at other tables sat merchants, workshop owners, and scribes, all discussing business deals, the unreliability of the laborers they grudgingly paid, and the worthlessness of most slaves.

A heavy rain began pounding the streets, so Ilika joined the many customers who ordered custard to prolong their meal.

Eventually, when the rain lightened, he wandered back to his inn to think about all he had seen, and arrange for a relaxing warm bath.

On the third day, exploring far into the southeastern corner of the city,

Ilika was struck by the stillness and quiet. Unlike every other place in the city, these streets were nearly deserted, with no laughter of children nor music of any sort.

He passed houses of the rich, silent as tombs, then came upon a heavy wooden gate set in a stone wall. A metal plaque showed it to be a religious order. With a thoughtful expression, he wandered on.

Soon he passed a headstone sculptor, a coffin maker, another religious order, and the Advocate's Guild with lawyers ready to make wills or manage estates. The gloominess of the area caused his shoulders to slump and his feet to drag.

When another rainstorm began to wash the city, he looked up at the sky, whispered, "Thank you," then happily spent the rest of the afternoon back in the common room of Doko's Inn, sipping warm tea and pondering what he had learned.

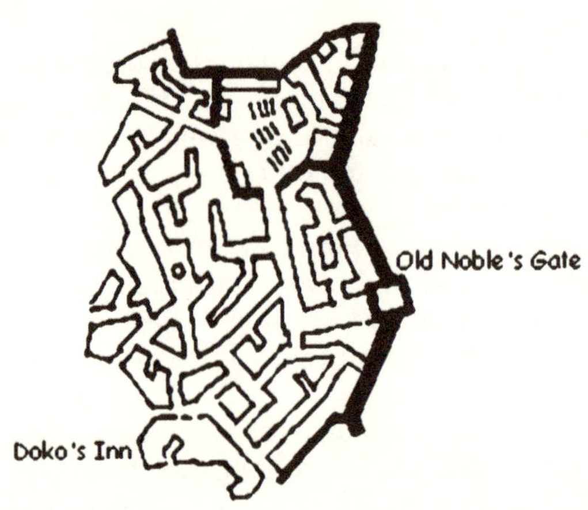

On his fourth day in Cobble Town, after a light morning rain and a bowl of soup, Ilika was slowly walking northward near the eastern edge of the city. The afternoon was passing slowly as his feet carried him from street to street while he glanced at guild halls and anything else that piqued his interest. As the sun came out and the wet streets began to dry, the rising vapors created an eerie feeling of unreality throughout the city.

Suddenly he heard shouting somewhere ahead that snapped him back to full attention. Some of the people around him on the street continued walking toward the sound, apparently anxious to get there, while others were moving casually away. After a deep breath, he walked on.

The street ended at a small open square. Guards on both sides of the entrance watched people coming from the square, but not those entering. The space was like a theater, with many benches and an elevated platform similar to a stage. Ilika entered the open area behind the benches and looked around.

A young girl, maybe five years old, stood on the auction block wearing a ragged burlap sack. Tears stained her face, but she stood silently with downcast eyes. The auctioneer shouted about the good housekeeper she would make, and the bidding was opened at one small silver piece. Even though the man coaxed and goaded his audience, she finally sold for only three small silvers. The buyer grumbled about the cost of feeding her as he came up to claim his purchase.

Ilika, nearly white, staggered back out of the square. One of the guards made a jest as he passed, something about a missing portion of his anatomy, but he wasn't paying attention. Soon he found a bench and nearly fell onto it, closed his eyes, and breathed slowly.

Ilika could still hear the auctioneer. In contrast to the little girl, a healthy grown man caused heavy bidding and brought between five and ten small gold pieces. A lad of about twelve or thirteen went for three small gold. Obvious health problems generated little interest, but females would sometimes command a high value.

After Ilika regained his color, and the shaking in his knees passed, he dragged himself slowly back through the streets of Cobble Town toward the plaza and the comfort of his room at the inn.

*

That evening, Ilika discovered that Mosa, the innkeeper's wife, made a pot of stew every day, of small beans and root vegetables, for use when the meat ran out. A slight smile came to him for the first time in several hours.

Without being asked, Mosa sent her daughter to the market for fresh juice. He gave a copper to the matron and another to the girl, who glowed with happiness and ran off to stash away her prize.

Ilika watched and listened to the other guests as he dipped bread into the savory stew and sipped his tangy fruit juice. A moment of sadness passed over him when he saw blood oozing from a large piece of red meat at the next table.

After praising Mosa on her stew, he strolled into the marketplace where most stands and carts were packing up for the day. The bakery was sold out of bread, but still had some pies and tarts, and the baker himself was tending the counter while preparing to close.

"Loki!" the baker said in greeting.

Ilika smiled. "A berry tart, please, Tori," he said, sliding over a copper coin. When four tarts appeared, he chuckled.

The baker shrugged. "A copper buys a lot at closing time."

"Please, give the others to some children. I just ate dinner."

Without pause, Tori whistled and shouted a pair of names toward the market. Two young peasant girls, helping to load a cart, came running over. "Ye'sir? Ye'sir?"

"Take a tart each, and one to your brother."

"Ye'sir, tank'u sir!"

Ilika nibbled at his dessert while watching the drama that turned out much better than his own act of kindness a few days earlier. Then he suddenly looked at the baker, busy brushing out his oven, and a sparkle of understanding came to his eyes. "Tori, if I wanted to hire some . . . smart people," he asked, choosing his words carefully, "where should I go?"

"Depends. Street smarts or book smarts?"

Ilika was silent for a moment, his mouth twisted in thought. "That's a very good question. Mostly street smarts, I think, but also the ability to . . . um . . . learn new things, and . . ." For a moment he was at a loss for words. "And inner strength."

Tori nodded. "How old?"

"Fairly young and adaptable, maybe . . . fifteen to twenty?"

The baker was silent as he considered the question while scraping his kneading board. "Hmm . . . maybe . . . no. Maybe the religious orders. Probably not the college."

"College?" Ilika prodded with interest.

"There's a school for rich kids over by the Jeweler's Guild, but I don't think they're what you want."

"Oh. Thank you very much. I guess I should go talk to the religious orders."

"Good luck. That's a rare thing you're looking for."

"Yes, I know," the younger man replied, and left another copper piece on the counter.

* * *

Chapter 6: Heavy Wooden Gates

After a cold night, the sun was climbing into a clear sky as Ilika knocked on a large wooden gate deep in the southern part of Cobble Town. No response came from within. He knocked again, harder.

Finally, perhaps a minute later, the gate opened with a creaking sound, and a large, round-faced monk filled the opening and gave the visitor a blank stare.

"Hello . . . I would like to see if there are some people, in your order, whom I might be able to hire."

The monk continued to look at the visitor as if no words had been spoken.

Ilika was about to try a different question, but the gate was pulled open wider. A priest, judging by his robes, stepped forward. The monk shrank away.

"Greetings, young sir! Do I understand correctly that you wish to hire someone? You must forgive my brother. He takes his vows very seriously."

Ilika glanced at the monk, whose eyes were downcast, then looked at the priest. "I was told I might find some . . . good workers here."

"Come in! Let us walk in the garden while we discuss your needs. Thank you, brother," he said to the monk still standing nearby, "you may resume your duties."

The monk looked at the ground as he shuffled off toward a stone shed.

With an ominous click, the wooden gate was closed and locked. Ilika shivered for a second. After a deep breath for courage, he turned to look at the garden.

Plants crept over the ancient stonework everywhere. Cobbled paths led to religious statues, often with a monk or two kneeling in prayer. As the young visitor and the older priest ambled along, no sound penetrated the sanctuary from outside the walls.

"I am looking for people who are able to travel," Ilika explained, "and are flexible enough to deal with different cultures and . . . different types of people."

The priest paused a moment to direct his visitor toward an archway. "The brothers make good use of every opportunity to travel. It gives them a chance to spread the Word."

Ilika furrowed his brow for a moment as they entered a stone building filled with wooden tables and benches. "How much time do the brothers need each day to . . . practice their religion and . . . spread the Word?"

"We pray for an hour in the morning, at mid-day, in the evening, and before retiring," the priest said as he led his guest toward a door where several monks could be seen working in a kitchen. Two mugs of tea were quickly poured for them. "But we practice our faith constantly, looking for words or deeds that violate our beliefs wherever they arise."

The tea was bitter, but Ilika sipped it slowly. "The work I am talking about has specific duties . . . and the people I hire would not be able to do religious work at the same time." He followed the priest along a covered walkway into another building. Many monks sat at tables reading aloud from different books. None of them appeared to be listening to any of the others. Ilika cringed at the resulting noise.

"Our scribes and illustrators are good at getting their assigned work done, by candlelight if necessary," the priest said loudly so the visitor could hear him. "At the same time, they are constantly watching for violations of our faith in their work, and in the people around them. Some of them can copy as many as five pages a day!" the priest said proudly.

They left the reading room and stepped into another garden. A slapping sound, followed by occasional moans, came from the far end of the yard, and made Ilika's hair stand on end. As they approached, he could see two monks with bare backs flogging themselves with short whips and trying to deal with the pain silently, but not always succeeding. Ilika swallowed hard and struggled to keep his feelings from showing on his face.

"As you can see, the brothers practice self-discipline," the priest said with a pleasant smile.

"Yes, I . . . I see."

They entered a building, climbed a stairway, and came upon several monks working at desks near open windows. Precise lettering, sometimes brightly colored, slowly formed under their pens and brushes.

"What do they do if they notice a . . . violation of faith?"

"The usual. All copies of the work must be burned. If it arises from the words or actions of a person, he must be whipped and given the opportunity to repent before being stoned."

They descended a narrow staircase, single file, so the priest didn't notice the painful look on Ilika's face.

"We can also offer cooks and gardeners," the priest said as they returned to the order's main gate.

Ilika bowed slightly to the priest and handed him a small silver piece.

"Thank you for your time. I will consider your brothers for the work I have."

When the wooden gate had been closed and locked behind him, Ilika let out a huge sigh and a long shiver.

For the rest of the day he ate soup, wandered already-familiar streets, and sat on a bench near the marketplace, all the while wearing a thoughtful expression. Sometimes silent tears came to him, and much later in the day, a smile of acceptance.

*

The following day, after a good breakfast of hot porridge and fruit, Ilika wandered over to the bakery to buy a tart.

"Delicious, Tori!"

"The wife gets the credit for tarts and pies."

"Please tell her. Tori . . . I was wondering . . . are the three religious orders different in their beliefs and practices?"

"Yes, but I couldn't say exactly how. It's not a topic people discuss when buying bread."

The younger man thanked the baker and set his feet to the streets of Cobble Town. Not far from the marketplace, some street musicians caught his attention. Pipes and a stringed instrument created a lively tune that caused several of the children to dance in circles. Half an hour later, Ilika left a coin and dragged himself away.

Finally he arrived in the southeastern corner of the city, but his feet became heavier and heavier as he approached his destination. He gazed at fancy book pages in a scribe's window while attempting to gather his courage.

Out of sheer force of will, he eventually arrived at the wooden gate, even larger than the one he had knocked upon the previous day. He stood a full minute, touching the plain, dark bracelet on his left arm.

When Ilika finally tapped, the gate quickly opened and a priest with a short sword on his belt looked the visitor up and down.

"I . . . I wonder if it might be possible to hire . . ."

"Come," the priest said, and rapidly escorted the visitor through a small yard and into a large timber building, up a steep wooden stairway, and into a tiny room with a simple bench. "Wait here."

Ilika looked around the featureless room. The small window could not be reached without a ladder. It could have been a prison cell, except that the door was not yet closed. He fingered his bracelet thoughtfully as he sat down on the bench and tried to relax.

"You wish to hire someone," a man about fifty said from the doorway a few minutes later. He was not wearing the robes of a priest, nor was he armed, but his bearing revealed high status and extreme self-confidence.

"Yes," Ilika said as he rose. "I am looking for companions for a journey . . ."

"Where will you be going?"

"To many different far-off lands, so the people I hire need to be adaptable and . . ."

"What will you be doing in these foreign lands?"

"Um . . . sometimes just visiting . . . at other times bringing supplies . . ."

"Will these supplies ever include books, writings, or art works that have not been approved by the order?"

Ilika's eyes opened wider, but he suppressed several other emotions. "I would not want to violate the beliefs of the order. You have a list, I presume . . ."

"Of course. To what order do you give allegiance?"

As the interrogation continued, Ilika somehow found vague answers to the high priest's pointed questions. At the same time he slowly walked back toward the order's gate, forcing the older man to walk with him if he wished to continue the questioning. Eventually they arrived in the small yard near the gate.

"Will you submit your records to the order for review each year?"

"I never hide my activities from anyone. Thank you for your hospitality," Ilika said with a slight bow to his host, then handed him a small silver piece.

"You still must declare the types and numbers of workers the order shall send."

"I will consider your workers," Ilika said. Facing the gate, he waited for it to be unlocked and opened while his heart pounded in his chest.

The high priest was silent for a moment as he glared with hostile eyes at the young man. Then he abruptly gestured for the armed priest to open the gate.

As Ilika walked down the street away from the religious order, he knew the gate had not yet been closed, and could sense he was being watched. He touched the reassuring bracelet he wore. Slowly, as he turned corners and put distance between himself and the wooden gate, he began to breathe more freely.

Finally, back in the marketplace, surrounded by the aromas of ripe fruit and baking bread, he let himself smile for the first time that day.

* * *

Chapter 7: No Stone Unturned

The following morning, when all of his guests but one had finished breakfast and departed, the innkeeper was in the common room collecting dirty dishes. He knew something was wrong, as his guest from another land had never before picked at his porridge for an entire hour.

"My wife makes a good porridge, does she not?" Doko asked with worry.

Distracted from his thoughts, Ilika looked up. "There's nothing wrong with the porridge, Doko. It's very good, as always. It's just me. I should do something today, but I'd rather do something else . . . scrub floors . . . anything."

"I have been in your shoes, my friend. Anything . . . I can help you with?"

"Perhaps you could. Are you familiar with the religious orders?"

"Just a bit . . . things I hear, you know."

"I have visited two of them, and found them far too rigid to supply the kind of people I am seeking. I haven't yet seen the one near the Traveler's Gate. Do you know anything about it?"

"It's the strictest one. I hear you shouldn't go in unless you plan to stay and never come out."

Ilika breathed a huge sigh. "Thank you, Doko! You just saved me a frustrating and useless day."

"Glad to be of service. You have become Mosa's favorite customer, you know, with your compliments about her stew and the coins you give young Sata for fetching your juice."

As the large man carried a stack of dishes toward the kitchen, Ilika smiled and leaned back against the wall. Once he was alone in the common room, he closed his eyes.

A few minutes later the innkeeper's daughter set a cup of fruit juice on his table. "Sorry, sir. The fruit man was late getting to market."

"Thank you, Sata," he said, and dug out a copper piece.

"Sir, what's that?" she asked, pointing at the bracelet on his left arm.

"Just some jewelry that comes with my profession."

She grinned, glanced at the bracelet again, then dashed off to add the coin to her growing stash.

Ilika found the girl's youthful joy and carefree attitude quite contagious. He soon finished his breakfast and strode out the door.

*

Ilika let his feet carry him that day, and allowed the world to reveal itself to him in its own fashion. Every time he passed a guild hall or a shop that looked interesting, he went in and asked about adventurous young people who were smart enough to learn new skills. He received a wide variety of reactions.

In some shops there were simply no young people. Aging workers with bent backs and shaking hands looked up from their workbenches.

In the craft guilds, only the master craftsmen were allowed to do any training, and then only for the guild's apprentices.

But in a few shops he did spy bright-eyed young people, his age and younger.

"Now don't get me wrong," one shopkeeper said after Ilika explained his purpose. "My three sons and two daughters are not slaves, and if you ran into them on the road, made them an offer, and they decided to go on this journey with you, well that would be their choice — all but the youngest one who is just eight, of course. But seeing as they are at work right now, I'd have to take offense. It would hurt the family business for them to disappear just now, it being springtime when we need the most hands." The man pulled out a dagger and started sharpening it with a flat stone. "If you take my meaning."

"I do," Ilika replied. "Thank you for your time."

In three other shops he received a similar answer, although it was usually given with many fewer words. The dagger, or something similar, was almost always present.

*

Toward mid-afternoon, Ilika noticed the Jeweler's Guild, remembered something the baker had said, and circled the area several times before finding what he sought. The sign was small and easy to miss, set beside a modest wooden door.

As soon as Ilika stepped inside, a wrinkled clerk slowly rose from his cluttered desk to greet the visitor with a slight bow. "Welcome to the College of Nobles, young sir."

"Hello. Do you have students who might be available to learn highly-skilled professional work?"

"Um . . . well . . . most of them are destined to carry on the occupations and inherit the estates of their families. But a few, second and third sons mostly, sometimes apply to the guilds. May I show you around?"

"Yes, that would be wonderful. How old are your students?" Ilika asked as they ambled along a gloomy wooden corridor.

"Usually twelve to fifteen or sixteen, although we can make exceptions for families of high status. In this room, they study labor management."

Four nicely dressed young men goaded, sometimes whipped, half a dozen slaves who carried bricks from one end of the room to the other, then back again. A guard with sword stood by the door. Ilika closed his eyes for a moment but said nothing.

"And over here is where the girls learn the womanly arts to prepare themselves for marriage," the clerk said, pointing to another door.

Seven or eight young ladies worked on dresses or applied makeup, all the while talking and giggling among themselves. A matron helped one girl with her dress.

"I think I have a good idea of what you teach in your college," Ilika said. "I should be going."

"But . . . um . . . what kind of professional work did you say you had available?" the clerk asked anxiously as he followed his visitor back to the entrance.

"Oh . . . it really isn't the right kind of work for these fine young men and women. They would be better off on their estates, or in the guilds."

"I see," the clerk said with disappointment. "Thank you, sir, for visiting."

Ilika avoided showing his frustration until he was outside, but he was soon smiling again when he rounded a corner and discovered street musicians and dancing children.

As he resumed his wandering along the streets of Cobble Town, Ilika became aware that another man, wearing the robes of a religious order, was ambling in the same direction, always just a little way behind. Ilika's heart pounded in his chest and his mouth became dry.

After gazing into a shop window for a moment to consider the situation, he began a slow, zigzagging course through the streets, a course that no one else could possibly take by coincidence. After half an hour, the man from the order was still near, pretending to peer at some flowers blooming in a window box.

Ilika glanced around. A little candy shop caught his eye, so he casually crossed the street and entered.

The girl tending the counter wore her wavy yellow hair loosely about her delicate shoulders. Her blue eyes sparkled as she made eye contact with the handsome young man who had just entered the shop.

Ilika immediately forgot why he was there. The girl smiled as she answered his clumsy questions about the candies on display. Soon he too was smiling.

"Do you know you are being watched?" she asked in between their glances at each other.

Jarred back to full awareness of his situation, he somehow resisted the temptation to turn around. "Yes, I know. A goon from one of the orders. I don't think they like me."

"There are two of them."

A shiver coursed through Ilika's body. "Would you make me an assortment of candies, about a dozen of your favorites?"

"Okay," she said, still smiling and glancing at him as often as possible. "After I make up your box, would you like to go out the back door into the alley? It comes out on Scribe Street."

He looked into her eyes for a long moment. "That's . . . a good idea. But . . . can I come back and see you again?"

With a glowing smile she set the little wooden box of assorted sweets on the counter between them. "I would be very happy if you did!"

"Is this enough?" he asked, holding out a great silver piece.

"Several times over!" she said with wide eyes.

"In that case, the rest is for you."

She grinned and blushed. "There are three priests now. They are talking among themselves and not looking. If you go quickly, they might be confused and not try to follow."

After a moment of indecision, he scooped up his box, dashed into the kitchen, and slipped out into the alley. A round-about series of streets brought him to Doko's Inn without, as far as he could tell, anyone following.

* * *

Chapter 8: Making a New Plan

Ilika barely slept that night, awakening to every little noise in the marketplace, every creak and knock elsewhere in the building. As dawn crept into the sky, he lay awake, hands behind his head, brow wrinkled in thought.

Suddenly, just before the sun rose, he hopped out of bed and dressed quickly, slipped what he needed into a pocket, and bounded down the stairs.

Stepping into the kitchen, he motioned for the innkeeper and his wife and children to gather around. Sata set down her knife, and her older brother looked up from stirring the porridge.

"I do not know exactly why, but one of the religious orders is looking for me. I don't like them, and don't want them to find me." He pulled four small coins from his pocket. "If I could finish my business in this city without them finding out where I am staying, it would be worth these coins to me, one for each of you, on top of my payments for your services."

All four pairs of eyes were big and round. Smiles and nods told him they planned to earn the gleaming gold pieces.

*

Before leaving the kitchen, Ilika got a bowl of porridge to take up to his room. His cup of fruit juice arrived soon after, and Sata was as happy as ever to receive a copper piece for her errand.

As he took thoughtful spoonfuls of his cereal, he slowly began to relax and unwind from his restless night. The fruit juice was sweet and red, and as he swirled it in his mug, a mischievous smile replaced his frown.

After eating, he padded down the stairs and slipped out the back door of the inn. His knowledge of the streets and alleys allowed him to arrive at the large clothing shop on Market Way without being seen by anyone but a pair of laborers carrying wooden crates.

After picking out a common design worn by many merchants, and selecting a fabric, he left to give the tailor time to make his new garments.

Following directions given by the tailor's wife, he soon found the hairdresser and asked about getting his pale hair dyed a darker color. When they informed him it would take several hours, he smiled and sat down in the chair.

✷

Shortly after the noon hour, a black-haired young gentleman stepped up to the bakery counter wearing a deep blue tunic, wide belt, and matching pants, all framed by a sturdy brown cloak. As his new clothes had no pockets, he pulled a copper piece from a leather money pouch. "A tart please, Tori, and two for the children."

Recognizing the voice, the baker gave his customer a second look, then burst out laughing. "Your own mother would not know you!"

"Good. It was time for a change."

"Plum tarts today, fresh out of the oven."

Ilika took a bite of the warm pastry. "Excellent, as always! May I ask you another question about the people of this city?"

"Of course! A good customer is welcome to what little knowledge I have."

"This might be a question without an easy answer . . . perhaps without any answer. But I'd value your opinion."

"Ask away!"

"If there were some adventurous young people who were so smart they wouldn't like the strict policies of the religious orders, couldn't stand the narrow structure of the guilds, refused to be hidden away in the back of a shop, and weren't rich enough to attend the college, where would they be found?"

The baker thought about the question for a long time. His wife brought him a large ball of bread dough and he began silently kneading.

Eventually Ilika opened his mouth to rephrase the question, but the baker spoke first.

"You are right — it is a hard question. But here's my answer, for what it's worth. People like that would easily get into trouble, and quickly wind up as slaves."

An expression of utter astonishment came to Ilika for a moment, then he burst out laughing.

The baker, dividing the dough into loaves, spoke without looking up. "I knew my answer to your question wouldn't be worth much."

"Actually . . . I think you might be right, and I would not have realized it without your help. Thank you!" he said, and laid a silver piece on the counter.

"That'll buy many tarts, Master Loki!"

"For the children!" Ilika yelled happily as he dashed off across the plaza.

✷

His mind was elsewhere as he entered the front door of the inn, but the look on Mosa's face, from behind the reception counter, instantly caused him to freeze. Beside her, Doko was talking to a man who had his back to the door, a man wearing the robes and symbols of a religious order.

". . . and it is very critical that we find him, as he left something of great value at the order . . ."

Ilika shook his head with a frown, and the matron's slight nod told him she understood. His right hand moved toward his bracelet for a moment, then retreated. Instead, he took a deep breath and walked right past the man and strode down the corridor toward the stairs.

"Please send word to the order at once if you should see this man. We would be most appreciative."

"We would be happy to help, but he doesn't sound like anyone we have seen," the innkeeper said as he glanced at the dark-haired man in blue rapidly vanishing up the stairs.

Once Ilika was safely in his room, stretched out on his bed, he sighed as his racing heart slowly relaxed, then started chuckling.

Not much later, Doko came by the room to compliment Ilika on his excellent and timely disguise.

*

Ilika spent the remainder of the day asking questions about slaves, about the circumstances that could lead to slavery, and about the slave market. He asked the innkeeper when he was served lunch in his room. He asked the tailor when he went to pick up his extra tunic and pants. He asked a friendly guard in the marketplace. And he asked the baker when he stopped by for a tart.

The situations that could land a person in slavery were almost too many to remember, but few of them had anything to do with criminal behavior. The poor were in greater danger, as their poverty itself was nearly sufficient. Being alone for almost any reason could be used as an excuse. Even just clumsiness in the wrong situation might do the trick.

He looked around for slaves he could talk to, but whenever in public, they were always pressed into continuous work, and well guarded.

* * *

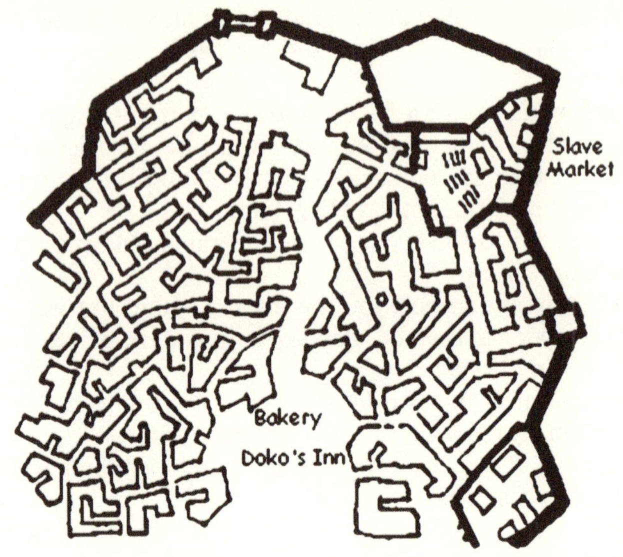

Chapter 9: The Place of Dread

The following morning, Ilika gave the common room a glance before entering, then arranged for a lunch he could carry with him.

He again used the door to the alley, slipped through the crowded marketplace, and made his way along the dirt streets of Rumble Town toward the Traveler's Gate. After crossing Market Way, he easily found the street that led directly to the slave market.

The day was still young and cool as the audience began to gather. Ilika of Satamia, with more than a little shame, found a box to sit on near the back where he could see and hear everything of importance, but not be seen from either entrance.

His heart went out to every person who stepped onto that block, especially the old, the women, and the children. Tears threatened to come, but instead he made himself look at each and every one of the slaves, look into their eyes, into their very souls if possible.

An old man, good with horses, said the auctioneer, went for a few silver pieces. Ilika whispered farewell.

A girl of about eight years who walked with a limp brought only one silver piece. He looked at her intently, but saw only dullness in her eyes.

A strong-looking lad of sixteen stepped onto the block, but he twitched from some disease. Still, he was purchased for two small gold pieces, and Ilika overheard talk of putting him to work in a mine.

A woman of about twenty received whistles and cat calls. She was, at first glance, very attractive. Then Ilika looked into her eyes and saw hatred from many years of abuse. He had to close his eyes until she was gone, bringing an entire great gold piece for her future services.

After several more slaves came and went, a freckled lad, twelve or thirteen, stepped onto the block. He stood calmly, confidently, with almost a smile. His eyes gleamed as he slowly scanned the audience, ignoring the auction process itself. The auctioneer said he had a tendency to daydream and didn't respond to punishment, but got lots of work done, and never ran off.

Ilika could barely stop himself from jumping up and making a bid. There, before his eyes, stood the sort of person he wanted and had not been able to find anywhere else in the city.

✷

Ilika ate his lunch slowly and stayed until late afternoon, learning all he could about the people who had fallen into slavery, and the customs of the slave market.

Every type of unfortunate person he could imagine was paraded before his eyes that day. If their reason for being unable to live in free society was physical, it was usually obvious. If psychological, it was sometimes obvious in their behavior on the block. At other times Ilika saw hints in their eyes or their posture, but couldn't be sure. But often the brief display did not reveal anything that justified captivity and forced labor.

During the afternoon, two more slaves caught his attention, both showing a bit of the same otherworldly detachment, and a certain rebelliousness. Again, he waited.

As the slave market prepared to close with the approach of dinnertime, Ilika strode along Market Way with a determined look on his face.

✷

After a hearty breakfast the next morning and another walk through the streets of Rumble Town, Ilika entered the slave market again. He explained to three different guards that he had a profitable business deal to discuss with the slave master, and only the slave master. The last guard grumbled and showed him to a waiting room.

Comfortable furniture and brass fixtures reminded Ilika of the upper-class inn near the palace. He heard muffled voices from the inner chamber, sometimes talking calmly, at other times yelling.

Suddenly the door burst open, and the visitor backed out saying, "I will do my best to get what you want at that price . . ."

"Succeed or do not return!" an aggressive voice responded from within.

Ilika stepped into the office and quietly seated himself in a chair facing the massive wooden desk.

The slave master, a large burly man with little hair, continued to look at some papers. "Profit is down, people just aren't bidding like they used to."

"Profit . . . is something I can provide," Ilika said softly but clearly.

"Speak."

"You have a certain type of slave that doesn't generate much interest, but I have a use for several of them. They are fairly young, say . . . twelve to twenty. They might be smart, but not in ways that fit into orders or guilds, and maybe so smart they tend to get into trouble. They are often spindly and not strong workers. Perhaps they are daydreamers, and not easy to discipline. Do you know the sort I mean?"

"I certainly do. Hardly worth taking up auction time."

"I did not buy one such slave who was for sale yesterday morning, at about the eleventh hour, because I could not tell enough about him on the block. I need to test and interview as many as possible to find the ones I want, so I am coming to you as a middleman. You know where they have gone if they have been on your block in recent months. I am prepared to pay all your expenses to gather as many of this sort as you can. I will pay their owners for a day of their time, and then I will give their owners, and you, a handsome profit for the ones I select."

The slave master rubbed his chin. "Rounding them up will be time-consuming. I will have to send agents to many different farms and shops. There will be travel time and expenses. Let's say . . . a great silver for each one you test, and a small silver for each of the slave's time."

Ilika took a slow breath. "I can handle that. About how many do you think you can gather?"

"Mmm . . . twenty-five. No, thirty. And I'll need a week to do it. How many are you buying?"

"As long as you can find me ones like the lad who was sold yesterday, I'll be buying at least five, maybe more."

The slave master shuffled through some papers, found the one he wanted and studied it. "About the eleventh hour? Okay, I see who you are talking about. How much profit can I promise the present owners?"

"I think a small gold over what they paid should motivate most people."

"True for boys. Girls may take two," the slave master said, making solid eye contact for the first time.

Ilika held the eye contact. "As long as they fit my description."

"And what about *my* profit, beyond expenses?"

After a pause, the younger man said, "You tell me."

The slave master rubbed his chin again, but did not break eye contact. "Two small gold for boys, three for girls."

Ilika let a long moment pass while looking at the slave master. "Done."

"I will need my expenses in advance."

Ilika nodded. "I will have thirty great silver pieces in your possession by the end of today. At what hour should I return?"

"Come at dinner and share my table."

Keeping a friendly smile on his face, instead of his true feelings, Ilika shook the slave master's hand and departed.

After agreeing to give a huge amount of money to one of the most evil men in the kingdom, Ilika arrived back at the inn shaking like a leaf. He ate a good lunch, arranged for a bath, closed his window, and curled up for a nap.

*

By late afternoon, Ilika of Satamia stood tall again with fresh clothes and a great gold piece in his pouch. After visiting the money changer, he left the marketplace as shadows began to consume the streets. The evening was warm, and people everywhere were ceasing work and turning to food and drink.

About half-way to his destination, Ilika noticed two men talking in slurred voices outside a lower-class eatery. He started to touch his money pouch, much heavier than usual, but stopped himself. As he approached, their words nearly chilled his blood.

"Wheres we gonna git some money fer dinners, huh?"

"Du'nasks me, I ain't got none!"

"Maybes we could borrows it from somebodies . . ."

Ilika's heart pounded in his chest, but he forced himself to breathe slowly.

"Hey, there's somebody who's got plenty o'money!" one of the men said, pointing at the young man in blue tunic and pants.

"Yeah, look at them *pretty* clothes!"

Ilika kept walking but focused all his attention on the two men, seeing how slow and clumsy they were in their drunken state. One of them began making fists. Just a few paces away, Ilika quickly veered to the left and strode right into the eatery.

"Come on in if you want to eat!" Ilika called over his shoulder.

It took the confused men several moments to get inside. By then, Ilika had placed a small silver piece in the owner's hand and pointed out the two men, just coming in the door.

"Hey, boys, it's your lucky day!" the owner called to them. "Meat and wine for dinner, and dessert too!"

They turned to each other, trying to understand what had happened. "Did you hit him? I didn't hit him . . ."

"Enjoy your meal, fellows," Ilika said as he passed them, returned to the street, and continued his journey.

*

"The slave master is expecting me for dinner."

"We know. Straight down the hallway."

The guards did not see the cringe of utter shame that crossed Ilika's face.

The slave master's dinner table could easily seat a dozen people. Ceramic plates and silver utensils were set, candles lit, and five men were already sipping wine and talking. Ilika seated himself at an empty place to one side.

As soon as the slave master entered, he caught Ilika's eye, pointed to a seat beside him at the head of the table, and drained a glass of wine.

"These are my regulars, most of them work for me," the master said as soon as Ilika sat down. "You and I have business to do."

Ilika took the thirty large silver pieces from his pouch and set them on the table.

The slave master laughed. "Three small gold would have been easier to carry." He scooped up the coins and handed them to one of his employees.

"Thieves can spot a bulging pouch a mile away."

Ilika smiled with embarrassment, but said nothing.

The master began to fill his plate from the serving dishes coming out of the kitchen. "I am going to search the land to find just what you want. I have already sent out two agents, and will have reports in three or four days. Let us meet again at that time to finalize plans. I'm sure I can have them all here by evening, six days from now, so they will be yours on the seventh day. Where and when do you want them delivered?"

After reluctantly taking a small piece of some roasted bird he couldn't name, Ilika discovered a bowl of cooked vegetables no one else seemed to want. "I will rent a space and tell you when I return. I need them very early, and will feed them all day long. Can you provide three guards?"

"They will cost a silver piece each."

"No problem. The daydreaming lad who was sold yesterday — he is your model. I want the ones who don't seem to be . . . quite part of this world."

The slave master laughed and took another bite of red meat. "I already have that lad, and two others like him who were handy. Whatever do you want them for?"

Ilika spread soft cheese on a chunk of bread. "To go on a long journey, and possibly never return."

The slave master made a rude noise and began talking with his employees about the trading and profits of the day.

For the rest of the evening, Ilika sipped his wine carefully as he listened to the conversations around him, learning more about slave traders and their business. Eventually a custard with fruit sauce was served. He bid his host good-night after that, as the other men were starting to light pipes and cigars.

* * *

Chapter 10: Asking the Impossible

Ilika awoke late the following morning clutching his head from the effects of the wine. A small table in the darkest corner of the common room welcomed him.

Sata quickly fetched his fruit juice, a truly welcome sight. After accepting the usual copper piece, she hesitated. "Sir?"

"Yes, Sata?"

"How many of these would I have to save to make a small gold piece, like the one you might give me?"

Ilika forced his brain to work. "One thousand."

"One . . . *what?*"

"Do you know what a hundred is?"

"Yes! Ten tens."

"A thousand is ten hundreds."

With a look of happiness and awe, the girl pranced back to her chores. Soon Mosa brought his porridge.

"I would like to talk to your husband about some special arrangements," Ilika said.

"He is upstairs, but will be down soon."

As Ilika savored the nutty taste of the porridge, he looked over the common room with a new purpose in mind. It seemed right for the task, with no windows to the street. The little storeroom beside the fireplace might be useful.

He counted the stools — twenty at the two long tables, another sixteen at the four small tables.

The innkeeper sat down across from him.

"I want to rent your common room for an entire day. Is this possible?"

"Well . . . I guess we could serve other guests in their rooms for one day."

"It will be six days from now. I also want you to serve breakfast, lunch, and dinner for about . . . thirty-five people."

Doko's eyes grew large. "We will have to stock extra supplies!"

"And I need curtains put up over the two doorways, and three seats out in the corridor for the guards . . ."

"Guards? Why guards?" Doko asked suspiciously.

"I will be testing thirty young slaves."

"Um . . . we have never allowed slaves in the common room before."

"There will be no other guests in the room, I am prepared to pay you well, and the guards will make sure there is no trouble. I will look elsewhere if you prefer."

The innkeeper's expression shifted several times. "Well . . . I think . . . it would cost about one great silver for the food . . . and another for the room and the preparations."

Ilika smiled and nodded. "Also, I would like to look at your largest sleeping room."

"It's free now, has eight beds, but we could bring in more ."

*

The cold, overcast day created a sense of brooding throughout the city. Ilika entered Cobble Town, spent two hours talking to seven different healers, and was told each time that they would not, under any circumstances, practice on slaves. He headed west across the marketplace.

As he wandered, he searched for any symbol a healer might use. The sign over a dentist's office, a wooden tooth with twisted roots, caught his eye. Even as he was passing, a painful moan came from within.

During the next hour, Ilika visited five more healers, but did not hire any of them. In each case, after discussing what should be included in a general health exam, he was not convinced they knew any more about the human body than he did.

Growing more and more frustrated, he was somewhere deep in the southwestern corner of the city when he noticed a young mother step out of an unmarked doorway. She spoke reassuring words to the weak little girl she carried.

"Good woman, is there a healer within?"

She looked him over. "I . . . don't know if this is the kind of healer you want. The witch who lives here will sit with you all night long while your only child fights with the Fever Demons, tossing magical herbs into hot water, or placing a drop of potion on the child's tongue, until finally at morning light your little one returns from the gates of Death with sparkling eyes and is ready to eat and drink again. And when you have nothing to give but two potatoes, the witch takes only one and sends you home with the other to make a good meal for your child. I don't think you are looking for this kind of healer."

Having poured out her testimony, she bowed slightly and walked down the street, holding her precious little daughter close.

With tears threatening to roll down his cheeks, Ilika spoke to no one but himself. "Yes, I think I am looking for this kind of healer." He knocked on the unmarked door.

After a few moments, a man opened the little window.

"I was told there is a healer within, one of great skill."

The man, still saying nothing, opened the door. Well-muscled and about forty, he wore a long tan robe with a belt of animal fur.

Upon entering, Ilika found himself in a simple, dark room made comfortable with old furniture, pillows, and hanging fabrics. The man gestured for the visitor to sit, then left through a heavy curtain.

The room was like a living being, fully intent on comforting anyone who might linger. A dancing candle drew the attention and the faint aroma of incense relaxed the mind. Symbols woven into the fabrics seemed to speak directly to the heart. Ilika's eyes grew heavy.

He had no idea how long he rested, but slowly became aware that another person sat near, watching him. He opened his eyes. The black material draped about her slender frame shimmered with subtle streaks of color.

"You are a healer," Ilika said with certainty.

"You are *not* a nobleman, even though you wear their clothes. You have had experiences far beyond your years. I have rarely seen a man, much less a young man, able to descend into trance as you did. There is something very, very unusual about you. You are far from home, or I am no witch."

Ilika nodded. "I am looking for some special companions, and have discovered they can only be found among the slaves. The slave master will send me thirty young slaves six days from now, and I will test them in many ways, but I need a skillful healer to examine them. Might you be available for this work?"

She was silent for a moment. "I am Doti. I work with my man, Tibo, who is also a healer. He will examine the boys, I the girls."

"I like that. They would be more comfortable that way. Can you write?"

She smiled. "Three languages, and all the old symbols."

"Please, will you both examine me? I will pay you for your time, and be assured of your skills."

"Come."

They passed through a much larger room, illuminated by a window in the west wall, where several tables and many shelves held books, instruments, and jars. Passing through another curtain, they entered a small room with a low examining table.

Ilika undressed, and the man probed his body with sensitive hands. The woman also examined him without touch, feeling for subtle energies only she could detect.

"You broke your left arm many years ago, and it was set by a skillful healer," Tibo said. "You fear failing at what you must do. You are otherwise very healthy."

"You keep most of your fear in your shoulders," Doti said. "You ate something yesterday – meat and wine, I think – that your body didn't like. Otherwise, I agree, you are sound."

Ilika nodded. "I am completely satisfied. Please, will you examine the thirty young slaves six days from now?"

"We will."

"What may I pay you for your time today?"

Doti laughed. "Our people seldom have a copper to spare."

"Here is a small silver for your time, and another for the little girl who had a fever. Will a great gold piece be enough for the thirty examinations, with written notes?"

Doti smiled, and Tibo began to massage Ilika's tight shoulder muscles.

* * *

Chapter 11: Finding Help

Shortly after breakfast the following morning, while sitting on his bed making notes about the upcoming event, the puzzled look on Ilika's face suddenly changed to a smile. He dashed downstairs and into the streets of Cobble Town.

He entered the first illustrator's shop he found. "I am looking for an artist, one who can sketch faces quickly."

"Oh my, I'm sorry, but our illustrators work slowly and carefully. If you want to commission a portrait, the Painter's Guild is just down the street. I hear they have students who can do something small and simple in a month."

Back outside, Ilika paused to take a few deep breaths for courage, then set off down the street. When he stepped into the reception room of the Painter's Guild, an aged man with wild white hair looked up from the picture frame he was carving.

"It would be worth a silver piece to me if you could steer me to an artist who can quickly sketch faces."

"Hmm. How many such faces?"

"About thirty. And it must be done in one day."

"Just sketches?

"Yes. I just need an image that will help me recall each of the people I will interview that day."

"Hmm. Yes. When do you need this artist?"

"Five days from now."

"Hmm. Yes, we can supply such an artist. A one day job . . . that is rather unusual . . . let us say . . . four great silver pieces?"

"No problem. But I must meet the artist and see his work before I decide."

"Well . . . um . . . the artist is actually a . . . well, you'll see," the old man said hesitantly. "Namo!" he called over his shoulder.

A young lad ran out of the back room.

"You know where Pica lives?"

"Yes, sir!"

"Fetch *her*. Tell *her* I have a customer for a small job. Tell *her* to bring her sketch box." As he spoke, his eyes shifted back and forth from the apprentice to the visitor.

Ilika sat down in a comfortable chair, closed his eyes, and relaxed.

✷

The female artist soon arrived. Her outgoing personality filled the reception room with merriment as she gave the old man, then the boy, warm hugs and friendly kisses. Then the old man gestured toward the visitor.

She greeted Ilika with a smile and a warm handshake. He described the situation and his need for sketches.

"That would be great fun! There is rarely any call for quick sketch art."

"Your guild master said it would cost four great silvers."

"Jobi? The guild master?" she questioned with wide, smiling eyes as she turned around and looked at the old man. He cringed.

To Ilika she said, "If you can't afford that, I can do it for less, but I have to give one quarter to the guild."

"No, I think I'm getting my money's worth. I just want you to sketch me before we finalize the agreement."

She found paper and a drawing board. Ilika sat, and estimated she finished in about twelve minutes.

"You're hired!" he said, looking at the sketch and handing her a small silver piece. "I'll make it five great silvers if you'll come early to help me set up, then give me your impressions at the end of the day."

She smiled and nodded.

✷

Ilika strode down the street to his next stop, the papermaker Jobi and Pica recommended. A bell above the door jingled as he entered the shop.

"Good morning, young sir!" the woman in charge said in greeting.

"Good morning. May I see your paper samples?"

She led him to a table by the window.

He found the one Pica had described, a fine-textured drawing paper.

"Expensive, and not stocked in large quantities," the matron said.

Ilika also selected a rough paper he had seen used for writing in many shops. "I need to commission something a little unusual. I need thirty pads of paper, each with a sheet of this drawing paper on top, and then twenty sheets of writing paper underneath."

"Sir, I have never heard of a *pad* of paper. We can *bind* sheets. Is that what you mean?"

Ilika looked worried for a moment, but soon relaxed. "You have some kind of glue?"

"Of course, the best cowhide."

"Get me a few sheets of scrap paper, but with one straight edge, some glue, and I'll show you how. I'll let you name your price when you see what I want."

She quickly ordered her son to heat up the glue pot, then spread the word that a demonstration was about to take place. Soon the materials had been assembled and the workers had gathered around.

"First I put all these straight edges together," Ilika said. "I hang this edge off the end of the table and weight it down." He looked around.

An iron weight was quickly located and handed to him.

"Now I take the glue brush and coat the edge lightly like this. As soon as it dries, it's done. Then it's easy to tear off a sheet whenever you need one."

The matron took charge. "This is called a *pad* of paper. Practice it, but make sure you use scraps!"

*

To Ilika's delight, the pencil had already been invented.

The little shop the paper-matron recommended was tucked away on a side street not far from the plaza. As Ilika looked over the possibilities, he noticed a thick, easy-to-hold pencil with a soft, black center. As he was testing it on a scrap of paper, he suddenly frowned.

"Sir, what is the black material in this pencil?"

"Soft lead from the northern mountains. All pencils use it. The very best!"

After a moment of thought, Ilika smiled. "I need forty."

"I will have them by tomorrow," the clerk said with a grin.

*

Ilika located a large woodworking shop not far into Rumble Town. After listening to his need, the journeyman walked with him to the inn and measured the tables.

"You want these partitions to be about four hands high, you say?"

"Yes, just enough so a seated person can't see a piece of paper on the table anywhere but right in front of him."

The journeyman sat at a table and experimented with his measuring stick. "Okay, I have it. Without any finishing work, let us say . . . four silvers?"

"Good, as long as they can be done in three days."

"I will deliver them myself!"

* * *

Chapter 12: A New Candidate

Ilika woke early, got his morning porridge and juice, and returned to his room.

All of his preparations for testing the thirty slaves had been relatively easy so far. He had rented a space, hired a pair of healers, found an artist, requested pads of paper, bought pencils, and ordered wooden partitions so his candidates couldn't cheat. Now it was time to begin the hard part.

Ilika pulled a small, thin, rectangular device from his shoulder bag. As he set it on the crude wooden table beside his hand-made ceramic bowl of stone-ground porridge, its display screen glowed slightly, and strange symbols on tiny keys shimmered. He touched several keys, causing words in another language to appear on the screen and keys to change color. As he ate his cereal, he began to scan the hundreds of subjects and tens of thousands of test questions the little device contained.

It wasn't long before he laughed out loud, seeing how few of the questions, even after translation, could be used with the people he needed to test. After a minute of thought, he grabbed paper and pencil and started writing his own questions, in the local language, occasionally glancing at his device for inspiration.

*

As lunchtime approached, Ilika looked over the questions he had created to test raw intelligence, and the drawings to go with them. The sound of knocking and the voice of the innkeeper's son announced the arrival of lunch.

"My mother wants to know if she should stock meat for that big group."

Ilika was silent for a moment, and his expression revealed an inner conflict. "Just a little, a small piece for each of them."

"Are you . . . really preparing for a long journey?"

"Yes, far beyond the borders of this land. Have *you* ever thought of traveling?"

"Me, sir? No, I'm . . . I'm afraid of the water," the lad said with downcast eyes. "I don't even like going outside the city."

Ilika gave the boy a copper piece.

✷

That afternoon, keeping the vocabulary and grammar as simple as possible, Ilika translated a series of questions to reveal the slaves' personalities. As dinnertime approached, he set aside his work and walked to the little pencil shop, where he found his pencils waiting. On his way back to the inn, he strolled by the bakery.

"I haven't seen you in a while," Tori said.

"I've been preparing to test my candidates. You wouldn't believe how hard it is to write questions for uneducated slaves who have no reason to trust you."

The baker thought about it for a moment, then shook his head. "I don't envy you."

"Can you have three dozen fruit tarts ready after dinner four days from now?"

"They will be fresh out of the oven!"

✷

Ilika got a bowl of stew on the way back to his room. To bring out the slaves' ethical values, he had to translate both the language and the situation. After tossing four sheets of paper, he finally created a discussion question that looked promising.

Later, he wandered down to the common room to see what was available for dessert. Sata was the only one in the kitchen, busy cleaning up.

Her eyes didn't quite meet his as she handed him a dish of custard. "Sir, are you going to consider girls for your traveling companions?"

"Y . . . yes. Girls are just as welcome as boys."

"The people you are going to test . . . are they all slaves?"

"At the moment, yes."

"Is that for some reason, or just because they were handy?"

He took a bite of custard to buy time to think. "I tried the religious orders, the guilds, the College of Nobles, and many workshops. The people I want might be in those places, but the strict rules won't allow me to talk to them and test them, like I can with slaves."

"If you discovered someone who wanted to be tested, but they weren't a slave, would you let them?"

He took another bite of custard, trying hard not to smile. "Is the person who might want to be tested named Sata?"

"Um . . . yes," she said in a tiny voice.

Ilika took a slow, deep breath. "Maybe. It would have to be okay with your parents, and I would have to tell them what I'm about to tell you."

"Okay."

"The truth is, Sata, I am a ship's captain, and I'm looking for a crew. It's a small ship that doesn't need big, strong men like most ships. It needs smart people who are willing to learn many, many new things."

"I like learning new things," she said with hopeful eyes, looking up for the first time. "You taught me what a thousand is, and I taught my brother!"

"Good. But here's the part I want you to listen to very carefully. My ship and its crew will be leaving this kingdom and going far, far away. We might not be back for years, so you would have to say good-bye to your family and friends, your city, and your kingdom."

Her eyes lowered and she remained silent.

He let a few moments pass. "You still have three days to think about it. Good night, Sata."

*

When Ilika awoke the following morning, the sun was rising in a clear sky, and he could hear the sounds of the marketplace as it came to life. Getting his breakfast, he tipped Sata for his fruit juice as always. She flashed him a tiny smile, but said nothing.

The morning passed as he completed the translation of questions about the mental health of his candidates, and several drawing projects to tell him how well their brains worked. With a sigh of relief, he looked back over the questions and projects he had prepared, all inscribed on sheets of rough paper spread out on his bed and table.

While relaxing in the common room at lunchtime with soup and grilled bread, Sata wandered by. She glanced around, then whispered, "I'm still thinking about it."

Ilika nodded, and tried to keep his surprise from showing.

*

Still dressed as a merchant of the city, Ilika made his way out into the sunshine and northward through the streets of Rumble Town. When he arrived at the slave market, he was again, to his shame, recognized and waved right in.

The slave master leaned back in his chair. "My good friend! Come in and sit. Wine? Ale?"

Ilika tried very hard to conceal his discomfort. "A glass of cold water would be nice."

A servant left the room to fulfill the request.

"You are going to be amazed at the line-up I have for you, and hard pressed to not buy all thirty! If you'd like, I could get you more . . ."

Ilika nearly choked. "I think thirty is all I can handle."

"Suit yourself. I did run into one additional expense . . ."

"Yes?"

"Since you want me to hold them until noon the following day, I cannot send them back to work that morning, so we must pay for one and a half days of their time."

"Not a problem."

"Okay, so you owe me forty-five silver for the slaves' time, and three for the guards."

Ilika placed five great silver pieces on the table.

The slave master grinned. "Ah! You've finally learned how to carry money, I see."

Ilika smiled. "Of course, if you have indeed found more than thirty, you may be able to increase the number I purchase by making sure the ones you send are what I want."

"I will personally double-check the list the evening before. Where do you want them delivered?"

"Doko's Inn, on the east side of the plaza."

"I know it, have eaten there several times. Good cooks. Are the rooms okay?"

"Simple but clean. I want the slaves there as soon as possible after sunrise."

"It shall be done!"

"And the ones I select the following day need to be in the same condition as I leave them."

"I guarantee it. I never let the guards play with merchandise that has good sales potential."

Ilika shuddered, but disguised it by draining his cup of water, rising, and extending his hand.

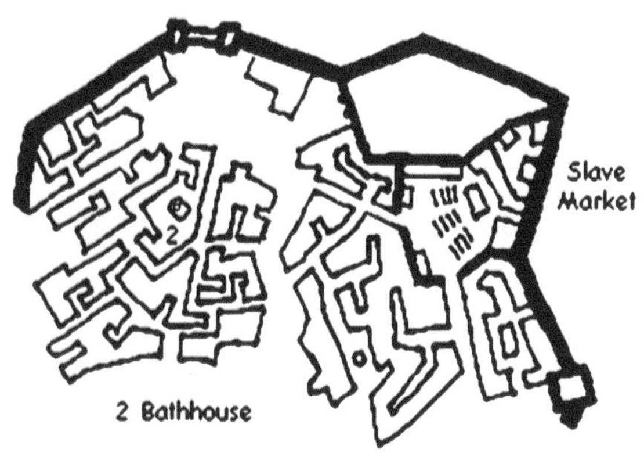

After leaving the slave market, he wandered into Rumble Town and had not gone far when a public bath house caught his eye. The man at the counter, his body twisted from some disease, looked at Ilika with wide eyes. "Sir, this is not a bath house for you."

"I can bathe at my inn, but I will soon be buying some slaves, and I want to get them cleaned up right away."

"Fresh warm water, with soap and towel, is one copper each."

"How many people can you take at once?"

"Six. Or we have a big outdoor pool."

The attendant hobbled through the inner door and Ilika followed. The man pointed out the rock pool, large enough for ten people.

Ilika grinned. “Perfect! Can you fill it with fresh, warm water?”

“If you tell us ahead of time. It costs a small silver and comes with soap and towels.”

“I want it at noon four days from today.”

The twisted man nodded and hobbled back toward the reception counter.

✷

Back at the inn, Ilika spent the entire evening pondering what to say to the young slaves when they first arrived, early in the morning, knowing nothing about who he was or why they were there.

✷ ✷ ✷

Chapter 13: A Matter of the Heart

Morning light revealed a sprinkling of cold, white powder on every roof and street. The common room was crowded with guests who wished they could find an excuse to stay indoors all day, but after a prolonged breakfast, most had to leave on business or journeys.

Doko assured Ilika that a snow this late in the spring would quickly melt, and there was little chance it would affect his upcoming event.

As Ilika was nearing the bottom of his bowl of hot porridge, Sata wandered near his table and continued to wipe other tables as she spoke. "I think I'm going to ask my parents. Is there anything else I should know before I do?"

"The important thing to realize, Sata, is that you would be going off on your own . . . following a profession on your own . . . succeeding or failing on your own. If your parents are not ready to let you take your own chances, then I cannot consider you."

She swallowed. "I think I understand. I have to sink or swim on my own, and they have to say it's okay."

"Right."

She busied herself with her work, and Ilika headed out into the cold.

*

His instincts told him to be wary as he approached the candy shop, even though several days had passed. He stepped through the door, tracking in as little snow as possible.

"Today's batch is not yet ready," an older woman said as she worked in the kitchen, "it being so early and the supplies were late because of the snow, but I have many things left over from yesterday that are half-price."

"An assortment of left-overs sounds good. Also, I'm looking for the young lady who was tending the counter when I was last here, six days ago, in the afternoon. Will she be in today?"

"Oh, my. I'm sorry, but the owner booted her," the woman explained in a kindly voice, coming up to the counter. "She offended some priests, and they complained."

Ilika turned red with anger and guilt, then slowly took on a softer and more forlorn look.

"I'm sorry," the woman said with genuine concern. "I can see she was special to you."

Ilika had to swallow several times and breathe slowly and deeply before he could speak. "Do you . . . know how I can . . . contact her?"

"No, I'm sorry, I don't. She is not a noble's daughter. She lives somewhere near the Traveler's Gate, I think."

"Please, what is her name?" he pleaded with a sad tone. "I was . . . rushed and didn't have a chance to ask her."

The woman looked into his moist eyes. "Her name is Zini."

"Thank you," he whispered, a great depth of sadness coloring his voice.

"Here's your candy."

He looked down at the box of assorted sweets. Somehow, he had lost his appetite, but paid for them and left the woman an extra silver piece.

Stepping out into the cold air, Ilika felt an emptiness that he didn't know how to fill. He wandered slowly down the street, not knowing or caring where he was going.

✷

Ilika of Satamia stayed away from Doko's Inn for several hours. For lunch, he half-heartedly nibbled on something he bought at a street-side stand somewhere in Rumble Town.

Eventually he wandered back to familiar territory, and found himself sharing his sad story with the baker. Without tasting it, Ilika ate a tart while Tori kneaded dough for the last batch of the day.

"Why don't you find her and ask if she'd like to spend some time?" Tori asked.

Ilika was silent and thoughtful for a long moment. "Like I said, I only know her name."

"The crier's office is right up the street."

Ilika almost choked on the tart. "You mean . . . they could find someone?"

"Sometimes you seem like a smart young man, and other times I think you were born just last week!"

A half-smile crept onto Ilika's face for the first time in several hours.

✷

"I need to find someone urgently," Ilika explained to the little round man behind the counter.

The crier took paper and pencil and carefully wrote as his customer spoke. "I can find her, if she's in the city and wants to be found. The message to give her?"

Ilika composed a message that invited her to dine with him at the inn.

"I've lots of work waiting. I can start this one in four or five days. Cost is a small silver a day until I find her or you say stop."

"I understand you are busy, but if you happen to find her today, I will give you a small gold piece, and if tomorrow, five great silvers."

"Well . . . um . . . yes, these other jobs aren't so important," the crier said, reaching for his coat and bell.

*

Just before he stepped into the inn, Ilika could already hear the crier heading up Market Way toward the gate. *Zini, who worked in a candy shop! Zini, who worked in a candy shop!*

With mid-afternoon slowly passing, Ilika found only one other guest in the common room, nursing a mug of ale. A fire crackled in the fireplace, and someone occasionally rattled pans in the kitchen. Ilika selected a small table.

Suddenly, Sata entered, followed closely by her mother.

"Well, see what the good captain Liko would like to eat or drink!"

Sata approached his table a bit shyly, but was grinning from ear to ear. "Hello, sir. I told them! What can I get for you?"

"Can you get fruit juice at this hour, Sata?"

"I think so."

He handed her two copper pieces, and she dashed for the door. The innkeeper's wife came near, but was reluctant to sit down.

Ilika gestured at the chair across from him. "Please, Mosa, sit and speak your mind."

"We are so very happy that you might let Sata be tested. We have long seen that she is too full of smarts and curiosity to stay cooped up in this little inn. Our son is probably going to take it over when we are old, but we have been at a loss to know what to do with Sata, other than marriage. For the life of me I don't understand how a girl could work on a ship, but we are thrilled that she might be able to get some training and see the world."

While Mosa spoke, Ilika's expression changed several times as he discarded his earlier assumptions. "There are several jobs on my ship that Sata could possibly do. For example, there is a steward who takes care of the passengers, and a navigator who has to be good with numbers."

At that moment Sata came in with the cup of juice and set it on the table.

Mosa grinned proudly at her daughter. "Sata, you could be a steward or a navigator!"

The girl acted shy for a moment, but couldn't conceal her excitement.

Ilika took a pull of the tasty juice. "Can I assume that Doko feels the same as you?"

"Oh, yes," Mosa said. "If anything, the parting will be harder for me."

"Come, sit with us, Sata," he said. "I already know you are a good worker, but there are many things about you I don't yet know. You both must understand that I will have to be fair. If you score well on the tests, and have the right qualities, I will offer you a place on my crew. But I won't take you just because I've known you longer than the others."

Sata looked indignant. "I want to do all my own work, fair and square."

"Good. I've already seen that you like learning. So . . . I guess you have a seat in this room the day after tomorrow."

"Hurray!" the girl cheered, jumping up and dancing around in circles.

"Shush!" her mother said. "There are other guests!"

"Sorry."

*

Zini failed to arrive that evening for dinner, and the crier's office remained shut.

Ilika waited as long as he could. When the innkeeper's son announced he had to wash the pot, Ilika accepted the last bowl of stew. He sat in a dark corner, ate slowly, and sipped on a small cup of ale.

Finally, when everyone else turned to drinking and smoking, he dragged himself up to his room. The emotions of the day and the ale left him without energy or clarity, so he lay on his bed and let himself doze.

At what seemed like midnight, he was awakened by a knock on his door.

"It's Doko! The crier says he has urgent business with you."

Ilika opened the door. The crier looked very pleased with himself.

"I found her at about the eleventh hour. Very pretty girl. Her response is that she will come to dinner tomorrow. She also said something about the back door, hoping you wouldn't have to use it. I didn't understand that part."

Ilika smiled, lost in a sweet memory until he realized the crier was clearing his throat.

"It's very late, sir, and I'd like to be heading home."

Ilika produced a small gold piece from his pouch, and the crier bowed and departed.

"Shall I set a table in the common room tomorrow evening, and see if Mosa has something special she'd like to make?"

With an effort, Ilika focused his mind. "That would be wonderful, Doko. Will this cover a nice dinner for two?" he asked, handing the innkeeper a couple of silver pieces.

"It will cover it very well, sir. And thank you for letting Sata be tested. She is so excited, I don't think she'll sleep tonight or tomorrow night."

"I know how she feels."

* * *

Chapter 14: The Hardest Decision

Rain fell and the snow melted that night, leaving the marketplace and Rumble Town ankle-deep in mud. A clear sky and a bright sun, however, promised to dry them in record time.

Sata came by Ilika's breakfast table, nearly bouncing up and down with excitement. "When does it start?"

"Soon after sunrise. Remember, you will not be able to help your family with any of the food and drink tomorrow."

"I know. My brother has a friend who's helping."

"Something else to keep in mind – the others are slaves. They'll be dressed in rags and smell bad. But that isn't their fault – they just have no other choice right now."

Sata shriveled her nose for a moment, then caught herself. "I understand."

"I want you to wear your poorest clothes, and follow all the same rules I make for the others."

"Okay. I think I can see why."

"Good."

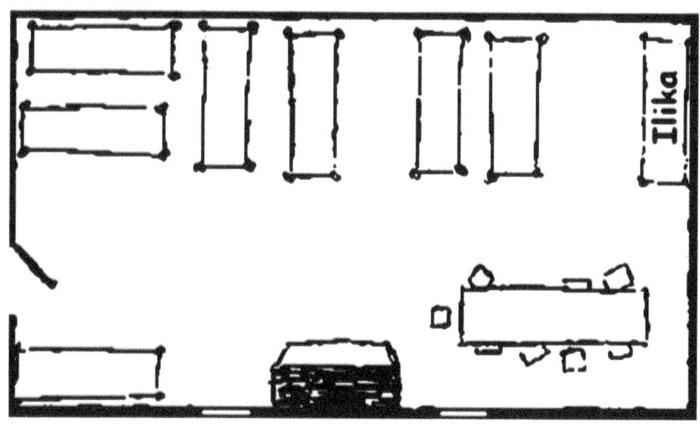

Ilika began his last day of preparations by moving into the inn's largest sleeping room.

"When will you know how many beds you need?" Doko asked.

"By late morning, day after tomorrow."

The innkeeper made sure plenty of firewood was stacked on the hearth and blankets on the beds, then departed. After finding a hiding place for his extra gold coins, Ilika spread out his notes on the large table. During the next few hours, he copied all the illustrations for the tests onto big sheets of paper.

Before getting lunch, he made a quick trip to the papermaker to request another pad for Sata. The matron promised it that afternoon, and two apprentices helped him carry the first thirty pads back to the inn.

As Ilika ate lunch in the common room, he saw the innkeeper's son cleaning out the storeroom beside the fireplace, and Mosa hanging curtains over the doorways. With only a few hours remaining before his dinner date, he arranged for a bath and headed out into the plaza.

*

First he visited the healers. Doti was working with a sick woman, but Tibo was free, and they reviewed their plans for the following day.

Next, he wound his way through the streets of Rumble Town to the public bath house near the slave market. An extra silver piece brought promises from the twisted man that the water would be as clean and warm as they could make it.

At the woodworking shop, the table-top partitions were finished, and delivery at sunrise the following morning was guaranteed.

Back at the plaza, Ilika stopped at the bakery to grab a tart.

"I hear Sata is one of your candidates," Tori said.

"Yes. What do you think of her?"

"Solid, reliable girl. Grown up beyond her years. She has moods, but never lets them affect her work."

"She's younger than I was planning to consider, but I can't argue with you, from what I've seen. By the way, the crier found that girl I met, and we're having dinner tonight."

"Congratulations! Should I bring over a couple of tarts?"

"I think Mosa is making a pudding."

Tori laughed deeply. "I can't compete with that!"

Finally, Ilika entered Cobble Town and stepped into the Painter's Guild. The apprentice led him to Pica's room, where Ilika found her working on a painting, but glad to take a break. They talked for nearly an hour about everything that would happen the following day.

After saying good-bye to Pica, he briefly returned to the guild hall to borrow two easels. A few minutes later, back at the inn, Ilika lowered himself into a tub of clean, warm water and didn't think about slaves or test questions for the rest of the day.

*

On the front porch of the inn, dressed in his nicest tunic and pants, Ilika glowed with happiness when he saw Zini approach on foot. Her dress was simple, revealing her youthful feminine beauty. Pink ribbons trimmed her yellow hair, slightly curled for the occasion. She smiled brightly and took the hand he offered.

Ilika's heart beat faster as he inhaled the floral scent of her perfume. "I'm so glad the crier was able to find you. I hope he didn't come too late."

"I didn't mind. It's not every day a girl is called by the crier with an invitation to dinner with a handsome man."

For a moment he stood grinning, and had trouble finding words. "Um . . . there's a table waiting for us . . ."

Still holding his hand, she let him guide her into the inn. The new curtains over the doors to the common room, currently tied back, added a touch of elegance. Their table, in the quietest corner, glowed with a pair of tall candles. Ilika seated her, and himself beside.

The innkeeper's son brought delicate cups and poured from a bottle of wine.

"This is very special," she said with sparkling eyes. "I've never had a fancy meal before. I must tell you . . . I am not of noble birth."

"That makes no difference to me – I have no use for titles and social status. I am so sorry that I was in such a hurry when we first met."

"The moment that high priest came in the door, I knew he was bad. I didn't tell him anything, and never will."

"He tried to find me here too."

A small plate of appetizers – crackers with soft cheeses and herbs – was placed between them.

Zini smiled and looked into Ilika's eyes. "You seem like a kind and gentle man. I would like to marry a gentleman. What do you do when you are not buying candy or slipping out the back door?"

Ilika smiled. "I have been in training to be a ship's captain since I was ten years old. Now I have my own small ship, and for my final test, I have to find and train my own crew. It's a lot harder than I expected."

"So you would be away from home some of the time? I guess that would be okay."

Her obvious interest in a serious relationship made him blush. A moment later, bowls of creamy soup were placed before them, which they savored in silence for a minute.

"What sort of life do you dream of having with that gentleman of yours?" Ilika asked.

"I want a nice house somewhere. I don't really care if it's in the city. Maybe since you're a captain, it could be at the seashore. And I want to have four beautiful children, maybe five!" she said excitedly.

Ilika had to swallow to keep from choking. Their main course arrived – a baked fish and cheese casserole covered with tasty white sauce, and buttered green beans on the side.

Zini chuckled. "I can tell you love the sea."

"Do you . . . like it?" he asked hesitantly.

"Oh, yes, I have always loved seafood."

He smiled pleasantly.

"And since you'd be away some of the time, I want to have a good slave," she said casually. "Two would be better."

Ilika cringed, but hid it well by taking a sip of his wine. "Would you ever consider traveling with me?" he asked when he recovered.

"I couldn't do that! Traveling isn't good for a girl when she's with child or nursing. Of course . . . you'd be there for part of it!" she said with an appealing smile.

They glanced at each other often as they ate, occasionally asking simple questions, or sharing little memories from their lives. Once their empty plates were removed, dishes of perfectly cooked pudding, covered in tart berry sauce, were placed before them.

"Zini," Ilika began with a dry throat, "you are a beautiful and wonderful girl, but I'm not the right man for you."

"I know," she said in a sad voice. "I can tell."

"I'm glad you see it too. I'm sure you will find just the right man very soon. But there's something I want to help you with. You lost your job because of me."

"Yeah. I live in a little room in a boarding house, and I don't know where I'm going to find my rent for next month. Some girls have to . . ." She shuddered, and didn't complete her sentence.

Ilika brought three great gold pieces out of his pouch and set them on the table next to her dessert. "These will take care of you for a long time if you are careful."

"Wow! I could buy a house!" she said with a grin.

"Yes, but you wouldn't have much left for food and other things."

"You're right. Besides, I'd only feel good in a house if it came from my husband."

"And you have so many wonderful things to offer a man, I'm sure a good husband will be at your side very soon."

"I shall buy a fancy dress and shoes, and start going to the upper-class social events. As long as you're dressed right, they don't check."

"That sounds like a good plan. I wish I could come to your wedding, but I will probably be far, far away."

"I understand. You are the nicest, sweetest man I have ever met, and I hope I can find a husband like you . . . except, maybe one who isn't a ship's captain."

They both laughed, then took bites of their delicious pudding.

✴

Savoring their desserts and sipping their wine, Ilika of Satamia in Nebador, and Zini who once worked in a candy shop, lingered in the cozy atmosphere of their candlelit corner. She talked about the names she was going to give her children, and he shared all the places he had looked for possible crew members.

When they finally rose from their table, Ilika gave both the cook and the server generous tips. Zini was impressed with his kindness, and as they slipped out into the night, she held onto his arm and looked longingly into his eyes.

He walked her all the way to her boarding house, and kissed her on the cheek as they said good-night.

She turned and went inside before he could see the tears gathering in her eyes.

Somehow he managed to get back to the inn and up to his room without letting anyone see the moisture in his own eyes.

* * *

Chapter 15: The Longest Day

With so many emotions lingering from the evening before, Ilika experienced a moment of dread when dawn light and sounds in the plaza woke him.

Then he remembered what day it was.

He quickly dressed and bounded down the stairs a quarter hour before sunrise, where he found the entire innkeeping family, and one extra lad, hard at work. A few trips up and down the stairs brought the easels and other materials to the common room.

As the eastern horizon began to glow, Pica arrived with her drawing supplies. They worked together to arrange the tables and stools so all the candidates could see the easels at the front of the room. Then she set to work building a fire in the fireplace.

Somewhere east of the city the sun rose.

Soon the healers arrived, and Ilika showed them the little storeroom where they began setting up their examining table.

The woodworker and several apprentices carried in the wooden partitions, two long ones for the big tables, three more in the shape of a simple cross for the small tables. Ilika pointed to a corner and paid the agreed-upon price.

About half an hour after sunrise, Sata entered wearing a tattered old dress, and carrying a tray with four mugs.

"Thank you, Sata," Ilika said, taking a big swallow of the sweet, warm tea. "It's about time for you to take off your apron and sit down in here."

Ilika introduced everyone, and they chatted about the upcoming tasks. Doti agreed to take charge of getting the slaves seated.

Suddenly the sound of many bare feet pounded across the wooden porch of the inn. Ilika quickly strode to the entrance and directed the roped line of slaves, led by a guard, into the common room.

A few of the slaves made searching eye contact with the strange man in a blue tunic. At the very end of the line, a girl of about thirteen years hobbled along with a crutch, not tied to the rope but trying hard to keep up with the others. As she passed, she gazed into Ilika's eyes for the longest time of all. Two more guards brought up the rear.

As soon as the guards untied the rope from the slaves' wrists, Doti took charge. Ilika ushered the guards out into the corridor, untying the curtains so they would close behind him.

"I have paid the slave master for your time, so you work for me today. With luck, it should be an easy day for all three of you."

"Did we hear right that you would feed us?" one guard asked with concern.

"Yes. Here's a table and stool for one of you to watch the front curtain. Down here . . ." he said, walking with them along the corridor, "is a table for the other two who will guard the rear curtain and the toilet room."

When all three men understood their duties, Ilika left them to decide how they would arrange themselves.

*

The strange young man in a blue tunic, with unusual pale skin and sparkling green eyes, stepped through the front curtain into the common room.

From the two long tables in the middle of the room, twenty pairs of eyes looked at him. Eight more faces turned in his direction from the two small tables at the back. The girl with a crutch and one other had joined Sata at the small table near the front. In all, thirty-one candidates awaited whatever was about to happen.

Pica sat on the hearth, tending the fire, and the healers stood beside the open door to their examining room. Both curtains to the corridor were closed.

The young man standing at the front of the room took a slow, deep breath. "Good morning. My name is Ilika Imni Zalara Sim. You can call me Ilika."

Someone in the room giggled.

"That's right, my name sounds like a girl's name to you because it ends in an A. Truth is, I come from far, far away. In fact, the entire language in my . . . kingdom . . . is different from yours. My kingdom is known as Satamia, in a greater region called Nebador."

He began to stroll among the tables. "I am the captain of a small but very fast ship, and I'm looking for a crew of five special people. It's a new kind of ship that a slender lad . . ." He tapped the shoulder of the thirteen-year-old freckled boy he had first seen on the auction block. ". . . a lad like this could pilot. Or a girl," he said, gesturing at a head of tangled brown hair. "Or maybe even someone who has trouble walking," he said as he returned to the front of the room.

"You are here because I believe some of you might be the sort of people I want for my crew. If I select you, I will give you your freedom. That means you would never again suffer any mistreatment you couldn't walk away from."

Murmurs of amazement spread throughout the room.

Ilika waited until silence returned. "Also, I will give you an education in reading, mathematics, chemistry, logic, ethics, and many other things. I will give you the training you need to work on a ship like mine, and an honorable job doing skilled work on one of the most beautiful vessels in existence."

"Hell no!" a boy of about fifteen blurted out in a whiney voice, standing up. "I don't wanna work on no damn boat!" Even though boldly expressing his feelings, he was also cringing, expecting a blow or a lash to strike him.

"No problem," Ilika said softly. "I won't take up anyone's time who doesn't like the idea. Anyone else feel the same?" he asked the entire room.

"Me . . ." a younger boy said, much more timidly.

"Okay, follow me, you two."

They started to move toward the rear curtain when suddenly a shaggy black-haired girl of about sixteen years hopped up and ran to the departing boys, hugging one of them. "Bye, Toki!" Then she hugged the other. "Bye! I'll miss you!"

"Bye, Kibi. Watch your back."

Ilika observed from the curtain, but said nothing. Then he took the boys through and one of the guards rose from his stool. "These two can go back. I've paid for their time, so they should not be punished or put to work today." As soon as the guards had the task in hand, Ilika returned to the common room. Kibi was already back in her seat.

"So . . . I guess the rest of you are still interested. Here's the deal. For me to consider you for my ship, you have to let me test you all day today. They are paper and pencil tests, so you just have to think about each question and do your best to figure out the answer.

"Also, you have to let this pair of healers examine you for medical problems. They are gentle and respectful.

"And this is Pica, an artist. She's going to sketch each of you so I can remember you after you leave tonight."

He glanced at his notes to see what else he needed to say. "There's a toilet room through the rear curtain, one person at a time." He scanned the room to see who was paying attention and who wasn't. "Any questions?"

"Can I use the dump hole?" a squirrelly-faced girl of about fourteen asked.

Ilika squinted as he figured out her meaning, then smiled. "Just poke your head through the curtain, and the guard will let you through. But for any other questions, I want to see a hand in the air before you speak."

She nodded and dashed for the curtain.

Ilika saw excited looks on about half the faces in the room. Another eight or ten appeared to be merely putting up with the situation. The rest . . . he couldn't be sure.

"Okay, let's have breakfast!"

*

The front curtain immediately opened and large trays came in, first with mugs of tea, then with steaming bowls of porridge.

Sata started to hop up, then caught herself and settled back onto her stool with an embarrassed grin.

Ilika made sure the guards and his three helpers had been served, then ate while sitting on his table and observing the candidates.

"Honey!" someone whispered loudly. "I haven't seen any in years!"

"By the way," Ilika announced, "it's okay to talk to each other during meals."

A buzz of amazement broke out. Soon Ilika overheard a comment from one of the long tables. "Eat it slow, it's probably all we get today."

Ilika smiled, but said nothing.

*

As soon as the breakfast dishes were cleared, Ilika and Tibo lifted the wooden partitions into place. Then, while Pica distributed pads of paper and pencils, Ilika spoke.

"You each have your own private space that no one else can see. Everyone has to find their own answers to the questions. Cheating will get you kicked out."

He stopped talking. Two of the slaves sitting next to each other, a boy and a girl, had begun a poking match under the table. Ilika waited a moment to see if it would pass. Finally he walked over and tapped them on the shoulders. "You two are in the wrong place."

"Aaaawwwww!" the boy moaned as he reluctantly stood.

Again Kibi hopped up to say good-bye, sharing a tender moment with the girl about her age.

"Hang in there, Kibi," the girl said. "I know you can do this."

As soon as they departed with a guard, Ilika returned to the front of the room and picked up a pencil. "The black part of these pencils is a metal called lead. It's a slow poison that can make you blind. Putting them in your mouth or writing on your skin . . . maybe isn't such a good idea."

He noticed Pica's eyes grow wide with worry, almost fear.

"Okay, here we go. Your first sheet is expensive drawing paper for Pica to use. Tear it off and set it aside."

A tremendous noise filled the room as twenty-seven sheets were ripped off at the same moment. Pica began her first sketch in the back of the room.

"I know most of you can't write, so I got these thick pencils that are easy to hold. You always have to put the question number before each answer, and this is what the number one looks like.

"Question one. What is your name? When I point to you, tell me your name and I'll write it on this sheet. You remember which name is yours and copy it to your paper beside the number one. I'll go first."

He pointed to himself, and the room exploded with laughter. "Ilika." He wrote and spelled aloud, "I-L-I-K-A."

He pointed to the girl with the crutch.

"Mati," she said shyly.

"M-A-T-I."

"Gema."

"G-E-M-A."

He continued around the room, putting the names on the sheet in the same pattern as the candidates were seated.

The slaves, with few exceptions, gripped their pencils like daggers. Many noises of frustration revealed the effort that went into making, for the first time in their lives, the four letters of their names. Ilika heard strong words he had never heard before, even on the streets of Rumble Town.

Occasionally, after Ilika spelled a name for them, he scribbled the name on a piece of paper on his table. Mati's name went there, along with Sata's. Kibi had already caught his attention. The slender, freckled lad was Rini. Miko, about sixteen, looked at the world with penetrating eyes.

Suddenly a snapping noise made everyone look at the large, muscular boy, about fourteen, at one of the back tables. "S . . . sorry. My pencil . . . broke."

"I have more," Ilika assured, tossing one to Pica.

"Question two. How old are you?" He wrote the numbers ten through twenty on another large sheet, calling them out as he went.

A boy's hand went up. "What if we don't know?"

"Hmm. Make your best guess. Compare yourself to your friends. No harm if you're off by a little."

The boy seemed satisfied.

"Question three, is there anyone else in this room that you are close to, whom I must accept if I accept you?"

A hand went up, and a pair of intense, smiling eyes looked at Ilika.

"Miko?"

"My dear sweet Neti!"

Chuckles and giggles filled the room. The girl seated beside him grinned with pride. Ilika pointed to Neti's name on the name list, and Miko began carefully copying it, letter by letter, onto his answer sheet.

"Anyone else?"

Neti raised her hand, still smiling.

The room filled with laughter again. Ilika pointed to Miko's name, then added Neti to his list of interesting candidates.

No other claims were made.

"The healers will start the exams now. Don't worry if you miss a question or two."

While Doti called in the first slave, Ilika got his easels ready.

✷

"Okay, a little bit of number work. We'll pretend we have only five fingers," he said, holding up an open palm, "instead of the way people in this kingdom really do numbers. That way, the next few questions will be just as hard for those who already know their numbers."

Sata's frown would have curdled new milk.

"We'll use the digits you might already know — zero, one, two, three, and four." He wrote the digits, and the same number of dots, on a sheet.

A hand went up. "Why are there no dots after the . . . um . . . zero?"

"Zero is the number of horses in this room."

They all looked around. Most smiled with understanding. A few didn't.

"Now to make a number, we need more than digits. We need place values." He drew three boxes. "On the right side of the number is the one's place. In the middle is the five's place, our base. And on the left is the number we get when we make a square five by five. Don't count the number of dots in this square. It won't help, and it might confuse you."

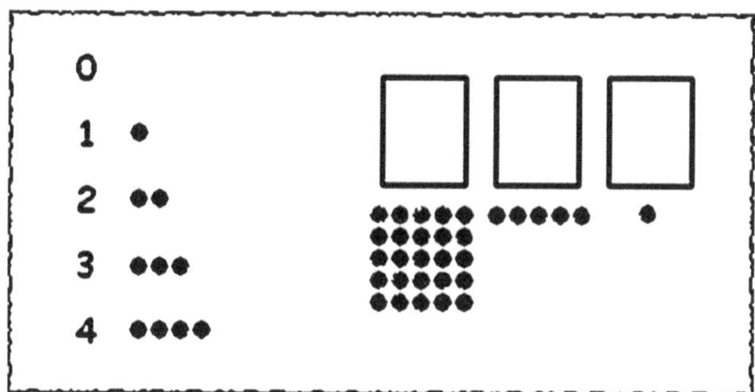

"Here's an example." He put a large sheet of paper on the other easel, and again drew three boxes.

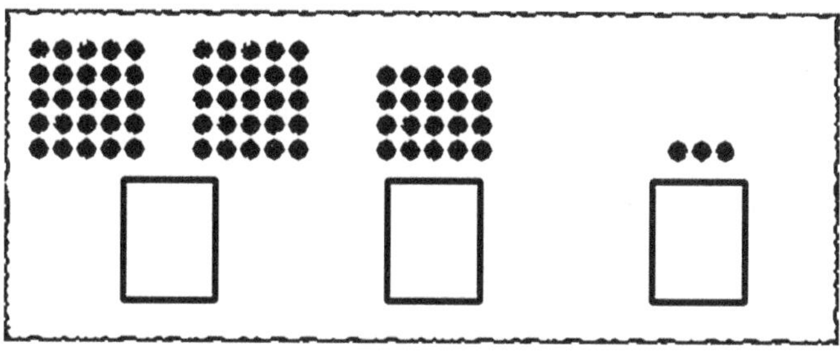

"We start with the largest place value. First I see *two* complete squares, so I put a two in the left box." He could see many eyes flashing back and forth between his example and the list of digits. "Next I see *four* lines of our base, so I put a four in the middle box. Finally, I see *three* left-over ones that aren't part of anything else, so a three goes in the right box. The answer is two-four-three.

"Now it's your turn. This is question number four." He put up another sheet, but left the sheet with the digits and place values showing.

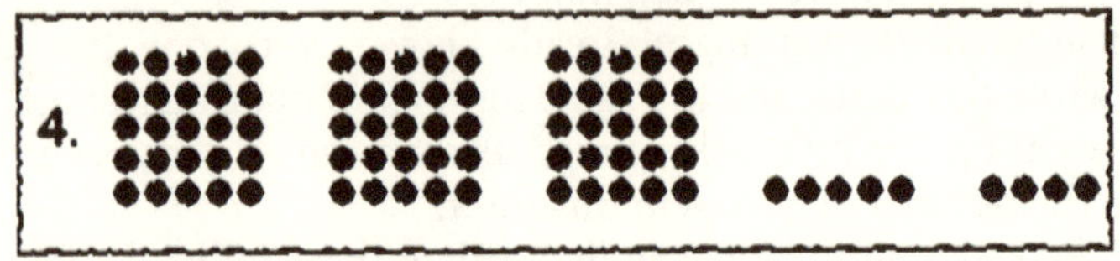

During a minute of silence, he scanned the room for cheaters. A few tried, but the partitions made it too difficult.

Suddenly, a boy stood up and whined, "I can't do this!" Looking around like a frightened animal, he knocked over his stool and started to bolt.

Pica tossed down her drawing board and grabbed the lad. She wrapped her arms around him as he wilted into tears and sobs.

"I always do my work!" he poured out. "I never goof off!"

Ilika stayed at the front, seeing that the artist was doing all that could be done. A guard poked his head into the room, but Ilika waved him away.

"You know what?" Pica asked when the lad had finally gained some distance from his feelings.

"What?"

"This isn't work. We all have work we have to do, but today, you can sit all day long, not answer any of the questions, and just eat the good food."

"You're sure?" he asked with disbelief.

"She's right," Ilika said from the front. "Everyone, even the smartest of you, will find questions you can't answer. Not everyone on my ship needs to be good at numbers. Just do what you can, and you might find that some questions are easy for you, even if this one is not."

As Pica led the sensitive boy back to his place, Ilika looked at the name chart, and put Pomi on the special list, somewhat separate from the names already there.

"I did a lot of the work for you on that last question by making it all neat and organized. The real world isn't always like that."

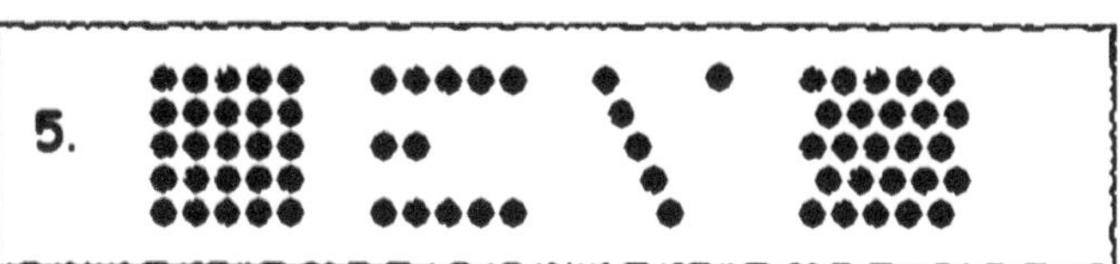

Several of the slaves moaned when they saw the new sheet. Ilika also noticed two or three who wrote down the answer quickly, including the squirrelly-faced girl with tangled hair. While the rest were working, he added Buna to his private list.

"For question six, I'll give you the number, you answer with dots. The number is one-four-two," he said, and wrote it on a large sheet.

Ilika strolled around the room as some of them carefully made rows of dots, others fidgeted. Eventually everyone appeared to have answered, or given up. Just then, the innkeeper entered.

"Tear off a sheet," Ilika said. "Pica will collect them, and we'll take a break for a snack."

The room filled with cheers at the mention of food. Trays of assorted early fruits arrived, and the slaves were amazed that they could choose any piece they wanted.

*

"Now we'll do some questions that don't have right or wrong answers, but will help me know what kind of people you are. Question seven. When you are with your friends, with no masters or parents around, do you (A) mostly talk, or (B) mostly listen to others talk? Here's what an A looks like, for mostly talk, and here's a B, for mostly listen."

He gave them a few moments.

"Question eight. Which is more interesting to you, (A) the thoughts and feelings inside you, or (B) the people and things outside of you?"

While doing this part of the test, Ilika was also paying attention to the personality factors he could directly observe, and making little symbols next to their names on the chart.

"Question nine. When making big decisions, do you most often (A) think them through, or (B) follow your heart?"

A girl's hand came up timidly. "Is it *really* true there aren't any wrong answers to these questions, and no matter how we answer them, it won't make any difference?"

"It's really true."

"So . . ." the girl continued, "that means we don't have to do them!"

Ilika grinned. "You're right!" As he looked around the room, he saw plenty of others rolling their eyes. "Question ten. Do you (A) make decisions quickly and easily, or (B) like to think about them for a long time?"

The rest of the personality questions were just as painless, although two or three slaves spent the time cleaning their fingernails.

*

"Okay," Ilika began, putting up a new sheet. "If I rotate the drawing at the top, which of the other four drawings can it become?" He demonstrated rotation with a small piece of paper, just to be sure they understood. "Only one answer is right."

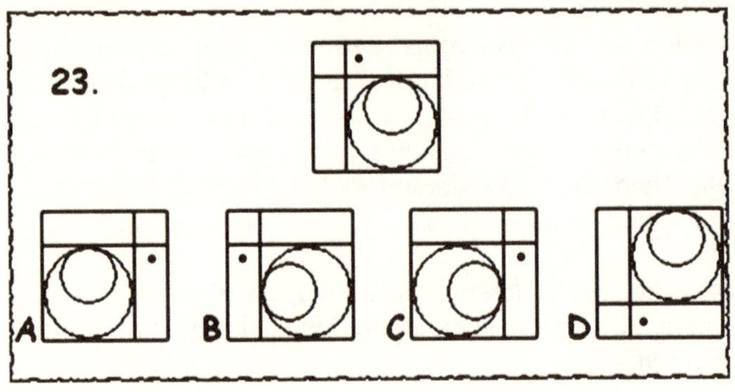

Pomi looked much happier, and his pencil approached his answer sheet.

"If I look in a mirror at the drawing on top, which of the other four drawings can I see? Your imaginary mirror can be placed anywhere you want."

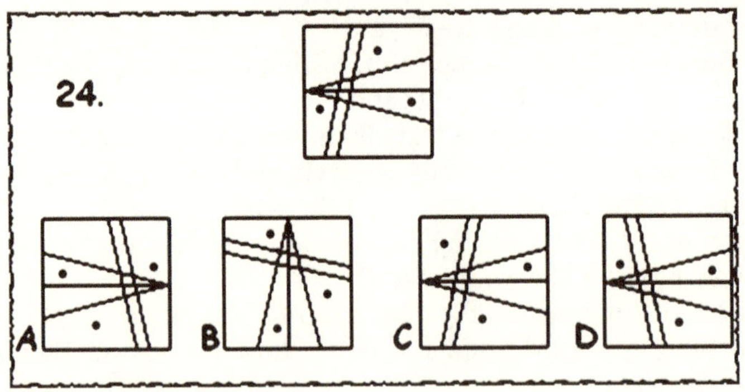

Ilika noticed several of the slaves who weren't making much of an effort, including those who skipped the personality questions.

"Which of the four drawings at the bottom of the sheet can be found somewhere *inside* the drawing at the top?"

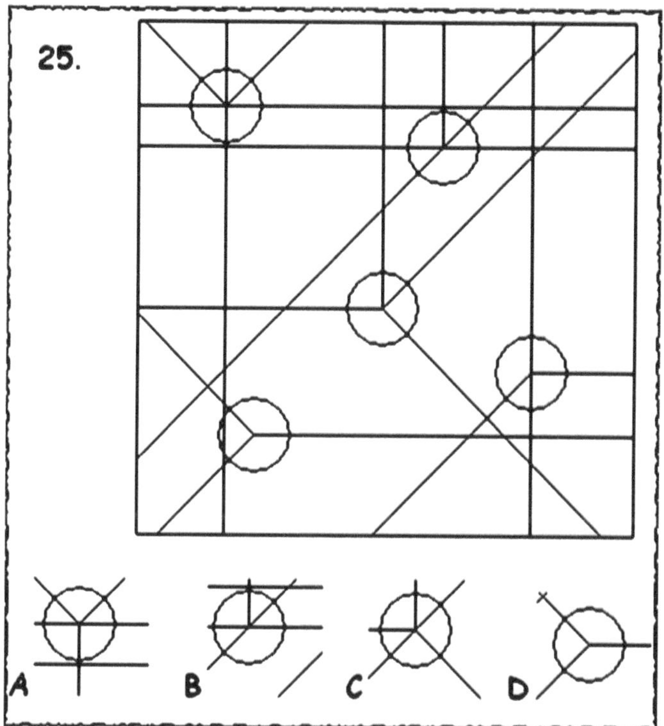

Sata appeared to be finding answers to most of the questions, even though she often squirmed on her stool.

"Which of these four drawings is completely contained inside *itself* at a different size?"

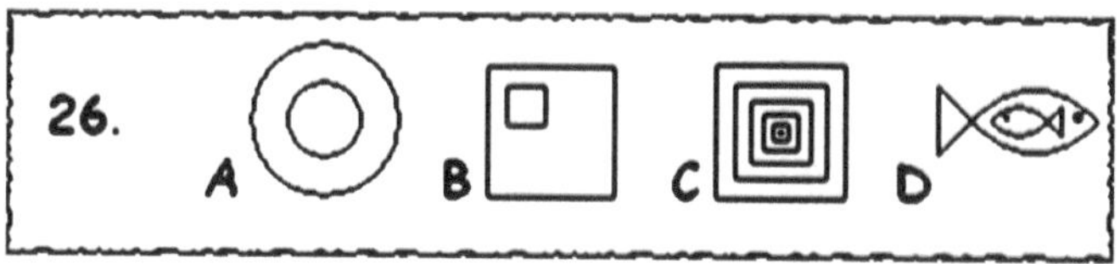

After a minute of troubled silence, several candidates had moments of insight that made them laugh out loud.

Ilika checked with the guards, occupying themselves with playing cards. They reported no problems. He poked his head into the kitchen, and Mosa nodded.

Ilika returned to the common room. "Shall we eat lunch?"

"Yeah!" they all cheered at once.

✷

Pica and Doti collected the pads of paper, and as soon as the partitions were lifted off the tables, a lively chatter began.

Some of the slaves were in a very lighthearted mood because they had already given up.

A few, including Sata, were very quiet at this point. They had started with high hopes of earning a place on Ilika's ship, but had been shocked by the difficulty of the questions, and were now beginning to rethink their chances.

A few looked confused. They had never before excelled at anything, but to their amazement, the answers to Ilika's questions were coming to them, and quickly.

Bowls of hearty stew came out of the kitchen, followed by fresh bread and sticks of hard cheese, then mugs of sweet, fruity tea.

As the eating and chatting continued, Ilika conferred with his helpers. The healers hadn't found anything too terrible, except Mati's knee, but mentioned that head lice were common. Ilika shrugged with ignorance, so they laughed and promised to explain it to him later.

*

Ilika and Tibo lifted the partitions back onto the tables as Doti and Pica passed out the pads of paper.

"I want Mati, Luba, Tiko, and Boro to come sit at my table," Ilika announced. "The rest of you get to copy this drawing."

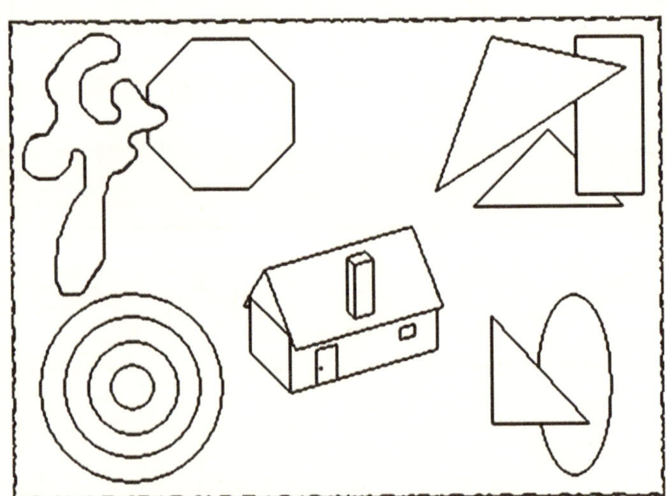

Some faces in the room showed excitement, others dread.

Once the four slaves settled onto stools at the front table, Ilika grabbed an extra stool and squeezed in at the corner.

"I'll give you a situation, you talk about it and decide what you would do. If you disagree with others, you can try to convince them you are right. No one's ideas will be right or wrong to me. I'm just going to listen."

The four looked at each other.

"You are in a room, doing your work. There are two doors into the room, and some empty crates. A little girl runs in, yells, 'Help me!' and hides in one of the crates. A moment later an ugly man runs in the same door, holds up a big, bloody knife, and grumbles, 'Where is she?'"

Ilika fell silent and leaned back.

The four looked at each other again and the silence lengthened. They looked at Ilika, but he said nothing.

"Um . . ." Boro began. "Our masters always want us to tell the truth. But we don't, except when it doesn't really matter."

"That's because they always use it against us," Mati added, "or against one of our friends."

"He's obviously going to kill the girl," Luba said, "so I'd tell him she went out the other door."

"I'd just kill *him*," Tiko said.

They stopped and glanced at Ilika. He continued to listen.

"Yeah, and you'd get beheaded for murder!" Luba burst out.

The arguments went on for another ten minutes, and Ilika was very happy with the information he gained about the ethical values and communication skills of the four slaves. He released them and returned to the front of the room.

"Buna, Sora, Miko, and Kodi are at the table. The rest of you will be doing another fun drawing," he said, and put up a large sheet. "You have only these lines and shapes to work with, and you need to make something artistic, something expressive. You can turn the lines and shapes any way you want, even connect them or overlap them."

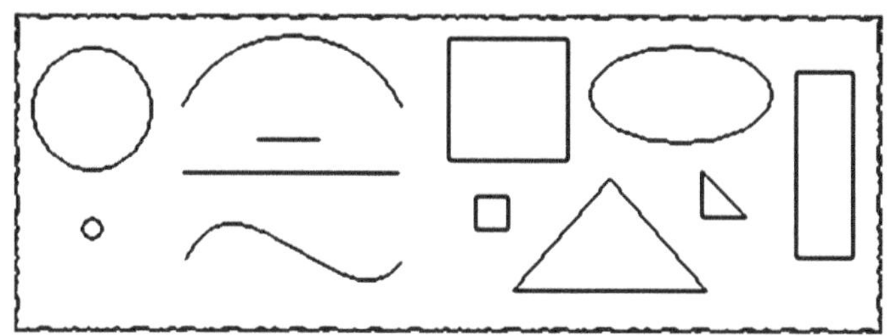

"That sounds like fun! Can I do it too?" Pica asked with a big smile.

Everyone laughed.

"After you get your sketches done," Ilika replied with a grin.

He gave the second group the same ethical situation and leaned back to listen.

*

Not one single slave, in any of the groups, thought a person should tell the truth in any situation, regardless of the consequences. Sata started out with that opinion, but the others in her group were able to convince her that life wasn't that simple.

Most of those on Ilika's special list gave thoughtful answers, communicated well, and made some attempt to help the girl. Mati and Kibi both had trouble sharing their views with those who had a different opinion, but were willing to risk their own safety for the little girl.

A few made the mistake of revealing where the girl was hiding in an effort to protect her. Others pointed out that they had just condemned her to death.

Rini suggested that the man was her father, he was angry because she hadn't done the dishes, and he was carrying the bloody knife as an example. This led to a lively debate, but Ilika could see his tiny smile.

When everyone had returned to their seats, Pica ran to the front of the room and cried, "Help me!" in a little girl's voice, then hid behind an easel. Everyone laughed as trays of sweet biscuits arrived from the kitchen.

*

Ilika returned to the front of the room. "Everyone know what a relationship is?"

Miko and Neti raised their hands.

Ilika laughed deeply. "I'm using the word in a general sense." He started drawing on a sheet at the easel. "This is a hand, and this is a glove. They have a relationship. A hand goes in a glove, and the glove protects the hand." He scanned the room to see if they were following him, then started to draw again. "This is a foot . . ."

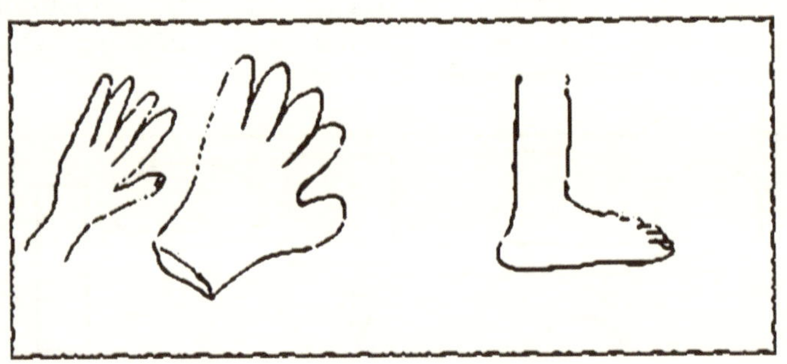

Six hands shot up, closely followed by five more, with another ten coming more slowly.

"Wonderful! Hand is related to glove, as foot is related to . . . shoe or boot. That one was easy. Now we will get a little more serious.

"Question thirty-four. Rider is related to horse, as crate is related to (A) donkey, (B) wagon, (C) nail, or (D) cargo." He drew simple sketches of the four possibilities, then repeated the entire question.

"Question thirty-five. Shovel is related to mine, as broom is related to (A) dust, (B) handle, (C) house, or (D) cat."

Ilika judged he had chosen about the right difficulty level. Many were getting answers, but not too easily.

The loud snapping sound came from the back of the room again, and Boro grinned with embarrassment. Ilika tossed him another pencil.

"Question thirty-six. Flame is related to wick as wheel is related to (A) circle, (B) cart, (C) axle, or (D) wood."

The questions continued, becoming more and more difficult. Soon, few pencils were touching paper.

"Question forty-one uses drawings instead of words. These first two drawings are related to each other, as this one is related to A, B, C, or D."

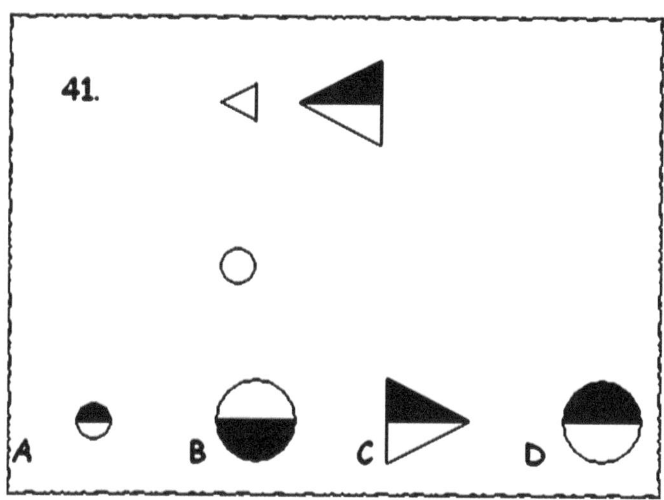

When enough time had passed, Ilika took a deep breath. "Let's do something that doesn't have right or wrong answers, so you can rest your brains. These are all T for true, or F is for false, in your opinion." He drew a smiling face next to a T and a frowning face next to an F. The room filled with chuckles.

"Question forty-two. Crying is just for babies."

Several of them appeared thoughtful. Pomi looked like he would rather be under the table.

"Question forty-three. If you make a mistake, you are bad."

Many of the slaves cringed at the thought.

"Question forty-four. Life is good."

"Have *you* ever been a slave?" Buna burst out, not even bothering to put up her hand.

All the other slaves held their breath.

"No, I haven't," Ilika replied thoughtfully.

"Then how can you ask a question like that, and expect us to answer it honestly? That's not fair."

"Okay . . ." Ilika began. "I think I see your point. It wouldn't be fair for me to judge your answers without having had a life experience similar to yours. Do I understand you correctly?"

Buna's mouth opened with surprise. "Uh . . . yeah."

"Let me try to clarify and see if that makes you comfortable with the question. I am not asking if the details of your present lives are good. They are not. I am asking if you think that life, in general, is a good thing to have, even though it is sometimes wonderful, and sometimes terrible."

Buna swallowed. "Okay . . . I can answer that."

After a moment, Ilika continued. "Question forty-five. If you feel angry, you should hit someone."

A couple of boys swung fists in the air, obviously delighted by the idea. Ilika wasn't worried, as neither had put much effort into the test, nor were they on his private list. The true or false questions continued for another quarter hour.

"Question eighty-one. Every person, regardless of status, deserves respect."

They all answered that one easily, and Ilika was not at all surprised.

*

"You guys are fantastic!" Ilika said. "I thought I'd come to this part of the afternoon, and most of you would be asleep. You have certainly earned this day off work and the good food we are sharing.

"This last part is about language. You have all done the hard part — you have learned a spoken language. Even though you have not yet learned to read and write, we're going to play with some words by translating from one language to another. Here's your word list."

BLUE	WOG	DOG	FOTOR
GREEN	PIL	FISH	JIKIL
RED	TIM	TREE	DILEM
RUNS	KEES	SLOWLY	TU
SWIMS	ROOP	FAST	WI
GROWS	DEEK	DEEP	ZO

"While you are translating, it doesn't matter if you remember what the words mean. I'll do one for you." He put up another sheet. "RED DOG RUNS FAST. First I look for RED and find TIM, then DOG and find FOTOR. RUN gives me KEES, and FAST is WI. So the answer is TIM FOTOR KEES WI."

The room erupted with laughter at the strange words.

Buna's hand shot up. "Is this how you talk in your kingdom?"

Ilika smiled. "No, but my language would sound just as strange to you. Okay, question eighty-two. Translate this." He put up another sheet and read aloud, "BLUE FISH SWIMS DEEP."

He waited. Scanning the room, he could see that only four or five candidates were working on the translation. Pica finished the last sketch. A few minutes later, a boy emerged from the examining room, and the healers sat down on the hearth.

"Question eighty-three. Try the other direction, the foreign language into your language. PIL DILEM DEEK TU."

Ilika quietly strolled around the room for several minutes so they would have plenty of time. "Long enough?"

"No!" Kibi barked, concentrating on what she was writing in crude block letters.

Ilika took another minute to organize the stacks of paper on his table. "How about now?"

"Almost," Sata declared, scratching out a word.

Doko peeked through the front curtain, so Ilika went over and whispered with him for a moment.

"Now?" Ilika asked, addressing the room again.

"Okay!" Kibi and Sata both said. Everyone else had already put down their pencils.

"We are done."

"HOORAY!" twenty-six slaves and one innkeeper's daughter cheered all at once.

*

Doti collected the pads for the last time, and Pica gathered the pencils. The partitions were lifted and set in the corner. Several slaves lined up to use the toilet room, or stood just to stretch.

Bowls of hot soup arrived, then plates with grilled bread and melted cheese, a little sliced meat, and a good serving of cooked vegetables. Smiles lit up their faces, replacing all the tension and frustration of the test. Their amazement reached a peak when small cups of ale appeared.

With the test out of the way, the slaves were more talkative than ever. They had begun their own testing of this strange ship's captain with a weird girl's name, and many impressions were shared in words spoken too quietly for any of the adults to catch.

*

As the dishes were cleared and the tables wiped, Ilika sent Pica to the bakery. Everyone received a tasty plum tart, still warm, and the room fell very quiet as the pastries were lovingly savored. Once fingers were licked clean, an anxious mood settled over the entire room.

Miko raised his hand. "When will we know?"

"Tomorrow at about noon," Ilika replied.

After a long moment of silence, Pica began wandering around the room, looking into the eyes of the candidates, sharing a hand clasp, a shoulder pat, or an embrace, and speaking a few words of good wishes for the future. Her example prompted Ilika and the healers to do likewise.

After Ilika had shared a parting moment with all the rest, Kibi stood before him. Their eyes met for a long moment, then she slipped her arms around him and held him close.

His heart leapt inside him and he held her shaggy head tightly to his shoulder. After a few moments, they parted and looked into each other's eyes again.

When Pica saw them part, she opened the rear curtain to the corridor. The guards entered with their rope and began herding the slaves into line. Kibi was shaking as she let go of Ilika and went to join the rest.

After blinking a few times, Ilika joined his helpers and Sata on the hearth.

None of the slaves looked back. The human chain filed out, one guard at the front, two at the rear where Mati hobbled along with her crutch, trying desperately to keep up.

Their feet pounded once more on the wooden porch of the inn, then there was silence, save for the crackling of the fire and the muffled sound of someone doing dishes in the kitchen.

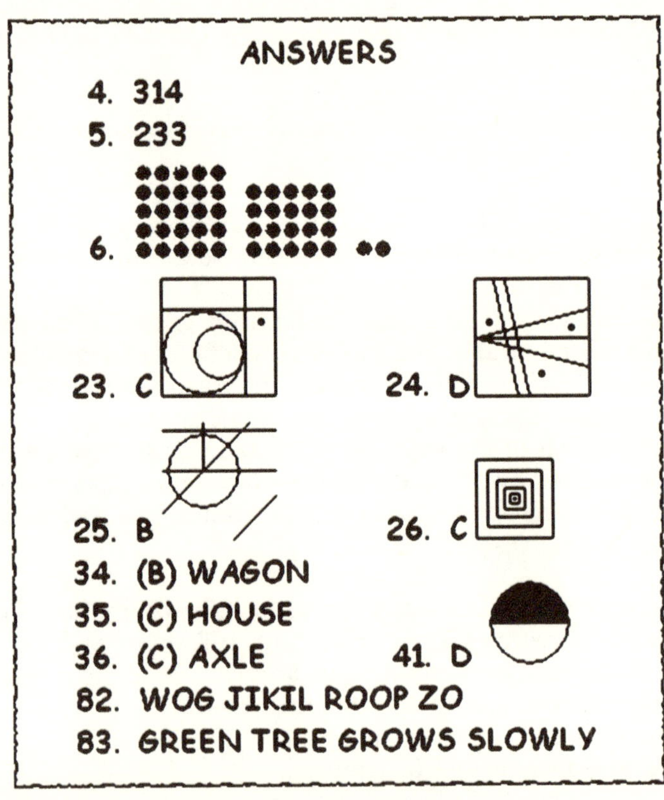

* * *

Chapter 16: Making Sense of It All

"Head lice are little bugs that live in your hair," Doti explained. "Most of the slaves have them. Kibi is the worst. That means *you* now have them, Ilika."

He laughed out loud.

"I saw Sata and Pica doing some hugging too," Doti continued, "so I'm talking to both of you, also. Do you want me to take care of the little critters, or can you sleep and scratch your heads at the same time?" she teased with a smirk.

Ilika grinned back. "Yes, please, and any other health problems you can treat in the ones I select."

"That starts tonight. My dear partner will fetch me the potion I need. Then I'll treat the ones you buy once a week for four weeks."

Chuckling to himself, Tibo strode out the door.

"I have a pool of warm water reserved at noon tomorrow," Ilika said.

"The bath house near the slave market? I know it. I'll be there."

Ilika looked around the common room. "Let's organize these papers, and when Tibo gets back, you can treat Sata first so she can go."

They all set to work spreading out the sheets on the big tables, one pile for each group of questions.

The bottle of lice potion soon arrived, so Doti took Sata aside and started combing the dark green oil into her hair, and instructing the girl on what to do with her clothes.

When they finished the sorting, Ilika excused Sata, asking her to arrange for his bath an hour later. Pica planned to bathe at home, but was glad for the potion that Doti combed into her hair.

Once Sata was out of the room, Ilika placed the stacks of paper before him and began turning pages until he came to someone he wanted to talk about. "Mati. Thirteen, no attachments, worked really hard on the tests. Medical?"

"No lice," Doti said, "and no specific ailments other than the knee, but a number of signs of poor nutrition."

"What can you tell me about the knee?"

"She says it's been like that all her life, so it must have happened in early childhood. It's an injury, not a deformity, and can't support any weight. She says she knows how to keep it from hurting, but any pressure causes pain."

"The other knee is good?"

"Yes, but over-worked because of the bad one. It might fail early in life."

"Could she ride a horse?"

The healer thought for a moment. "I think so, although she might need help mounting."

"Okay. General impressions, anyone."

"A little shy," Pica said, "but full of feelings that she'd love to express."

Ilika made notes as his helpers spoke.

"Yes, she wants to do something with her hands, I think," Tibo said.

"And very determined to succeed," Doti added, "although she hasn't the foggiest idea how."

"Got along well with Sata," Pica observed.

There was silence, so Ilika turned a few more pages.

"Toli, nineteen, no attachments. Medical?"

*

Ilika's helpers confirmed most of his observations about the candidates. During the discussions of the last few, he submitted to having the green oil combed into his hair.

Pica's work was done. Ilika paid her five great silver pieces, and she thanked him for the information about lead, sharing that most of her pencils and some of her paints contained the metal. Then she collected her sketch box and coat, and headed home.

Ilika thanked the healers for their skills and insights, and paid them for the exams and the lice treatments. They took up their examining table and walked back to their home in Rumble Town.

*

After the healers had departed, Doko entered. "Is all your business done?"

"Yes. These wooden partitions may be broken up for firewood."

"Thank you. I don't think Sata will sleep tonight. She took a bath, with lots of soap, as instructed. Your bath is ready as soon as you are."

"Good. Let us sit so I can settle my account with you."

"What shall we drink?" the innkeeper offered.

"Tea. I still have hours of work tonight."

The innkeeper left, and soon returned with two mugs of hot, sweet tea. He added up the charges, and Ilika counted out the coins.

"I will cover any other problems that arise because of the lice . . ." Ilika began.

"Bah! We have had lice around many times and know what to do. Your slaves were not much dirtier than some of our guests."

They both laughed, then drank their tea in silence for a moment.

Suddenly Sata bounced into the room. "Do you know yet if I can be on your crew?" she asked excitedly.

"Is it tomorrow yet, at the eleventh hour of the morning?" Ilika asked, giving her a stern but kindly look.

"Sorry . . ." she said and scurried out of the room.

*

Ilika took his bath and plunged his clothes into a kettle of hot, soapy water, just as Sata had done before him.

Up in the large sleeping room, with all the stacks of answer sheets spread out on the beds and a fresh mug of tea on the table, he began by making a scoring chart on a large sheet of paper. Each row began with the name of a candidate he was still, in any way, considering. A column for their ages came next, then columns for each of the groups of test questions.

For the next three hours, Ilika of Satamia dug his way through stack after stack of answer sheets. Some of the groups of test questions were easy to score — the answers were either right or wrong.

The personality questions took more time, but mostly agreed with what he had observed. When they did not, he put down both symbols.

The psychological questions gave him the most trouble. A separate chart allowed him to scan the answers for patterns. An hour later, he felt he had extracted what he could from them. Some of the slaves had developed some very dark attitudes about life. He just had to decide which of those dark attitudes ruled them out as potential crew members . . . and which made them even more interesting.

When he finally completed his scoring chart, he pinned it to an easel and looked at it. The chart, his notes, and his memories were all he had. If he could not make the selection, he would have failed, and all his efforts and expenses would be for nothing.

He stared at the chart for another quarter hour. Still nothing came to him. He had no idea how to pick five crew members out of the twenty-seven possibilities.

Then he realized what was happening. His eyes were barely focusing, and his eyelids were starting to close against his will. He had been awake for nineteen hours, but now he was losing all ability to think clearly and creatively. He might be able to stare at the chart and his notes awhile longer, but it would do him no good. No insights would be forthcoming, no decision possible.

So he left the chart on the easel, crawled into bed, and was instantly asleep.

* * *

Chapter 17: Clarity

Only minutes later, it seemed, a soft knock rattled Ilika's door. He poked his head out from under the blankets, but his face showed confusion.

The knock came again.

"Hello?" he called out in a groggy voice.

"It's Sata," she said through the door. "My father thought you might want breakfast in your room. I got juice, too."

Still wearing his clothes, he stood, yawned and stretched, and opened the door. Sata stood holding a tray, but looked fearful.

"Good morning, Sata. Thank you very much," he said pleasantly.

She relaxed. "Is there anything else I can get you?"

He looked at the tray, brimming with porridge, honey, cream, two pieces of fruit, and a mug of juice. "This is a feast!" he said, handing her two copper pieces. "There is one more thing you can do for me. Come and knock again at the tenth hour so I'll know it's time to . . . finish what I came to do."

"Okay!" she agreed. "See you then!"

After drinking deeply of his fruit juice and sweetening his porridge, Ilika looked up. The scoring chart on the easel looked back at him, representing the hopes and fears of twenty-six slaves and one innkeeper's daughter.

He grabbed blank paper and pencil, and started writing down names, letting his heart jump from name to name on the list. He quickly had eight names, all of whom had touched him in some way. Kibi was at the top, but Sata, Mati, and Rini were there also.

After a few bites of porridge, he set that sheet aside and started a new one, this time ranked by intelligence scores. Toli headed the list, but he smiled when he saw that all eight from his first list were near the top.

Next he tried the same thing with the language scores. The first ten were the same as the first ten on the intelligence list, and Kibi and Sata were at the top.

Ilika became excited. Next he looked at the psychological symbols that worried him the most. Seeing none of them beside the names of the top ten, he breathed a sigh of relief.

Then he looked over the names on the chart who had not touched him emotionally and were not among the top ten on the other lists. None of them spoke to him strongly. With a slight cringe, he let them go, marking them out completely on the scoring chart.

*

An hour later he finished several more lists based on personality types, the drawing projects, and the ethics discussion. Each list was different, but each felt complete with the ten who had survived the first cut. None of the others were threatening to return.

Ilika sighed. There appeared to be no way to choose five crew members. Any five he chose based on one or two lists would leave out some of the best in other categories. But he could choose ten and get the cream of the crop in all ways.

What would happen, he wondered, if he couldn't narrow it down from ten? Would that be the same as failure?

In a sense it would, he admitted to himself. His ship only had places for five crew members. He could not begin training until he had only five.

What if he . . . added a step? What if something came between the initial selection and the serious training? Something . . . that would allow him to get to know them better? He lay back on his bed, trying to imagine what he could do that wouldn't require the ship.

The answer nearly slapped him in the face. His candidates were almost completely illiterate and uneducated. Before he trained his crew, he would have to teach them many things. He could use that time to get to know them better.

A great weight lifted from his shoulders. He looked at the list of ten names again, then copied it in large, clear letters to another piece of paper, leaving off Sata.

His heart made him go back through the sketches again, taking one last look at all the faces he would not be choosing, all the young people he would allow to remain in slavery.

Ilika suddenly remembered gut-wrenching exercises from his own training, emergency simulations in which the captain could only save part of his passengers and crew.

But he was not, he told himself, condemning the other slaves to death. He was simply leaving them where they were, where their own people had put them.

*

Not much later, his door rattled again. "It's the tenth hour, even a little past," Sata's voice called.

He opened the door. "Thank you, Sata. Please tell your parents I will be down in a few minutes with my decision."

"Okay!" she squeaked with a broken voice full of excitement and fear.

Six great gold pieces, and several smaller coins, came out of hiding and into his money pouch. The final list of nine slaves was placed in a side pocket of his shoulder bag.

Ilika of Satamia found a small table in the common room. The two innkeepers and their daughter joined him.

"I thought I could choose my five crew members after all the tests yesterday. I was wrong. I cannot make my list any smaller than ten. I have decided to take the next several months, all during this summer and early fall, and give those ten a good education. I will then hopefully know them well enough to choose my five. The ones I do not choose will receive three great gold pieces each to help them get started in life."

Sata shook like a frightened animal, barely holding in the burning question Ilika had not yet answered.

"If this situation is okay with all three of you, Sata is invited to be one of those ten."

She squealed, clapped, and bounced up and down on her stool.

"Where will you do the teaching?" Doko asked.

"We will be here for a little while, long enough to get clothes and other gear for everyone, then we will buy horses and wander about the kingdom."

"I want to know my daughter won't be . . . forced into anything," Mosa asserted with a worried look.

"I will make sure of that. I will not allow any . . . intimate relationships during the learning time, although I'm sure close friendships will develop. Anyone who wants out will be free to leave at any time. In the case of Sata, I would deliver her back here.

"But," he said pointedly, "there are always dangers in the wide world. I can protect her from harm by anyone in our group, but I cannot guarantee her safety from all mishaps."

Doko nodded. "Are you comfortable with all that, Sata?"

She smiled and nodded excitedly.

"And you, good wife?"

Tears were close, but Mosa nodded also.

"Okay, Sata," Ilika said. "I want you to come with me to get the others, wearing your old dress. There won't be any differences in routine between you and the other nine. Some of them are just as smart as you, and a couple are even smarter at some things, although you were one of my highest-scoring candidates."

She grinned. "Wow!"

Her parents glowed with pride. They had both listened at the curtains to the common room off and on during the previous day, and knew how difficult some of the test questions were.

Sata dashed to her little room behind the kitchen to change into her old dress.

"My son and I will bring in the extra beds before you return," Doko promised.

✷

The sun brought warmth to the cool spring day as the pair, appearing to be master and slave, began their journey up Market Way.

"The girl with the crutch is also in the group," Ilika mentioned.

"Mati's nice. I think we could be friends."

"I bet she'd like that."

They entered the clothing shop. Ilika found the stacks of simple, ready-made tunics and pulled out his list to guess the sizes he needed.

"When do you want me to change?" Sata asked as Ilika paid for the tunics.

"When the others do. Is it okay if your old dress gets tossed along with their rags?"

They headed back into the street. "Yeah. If the others can leave their old lives behind, I can too."

They walked in silence awhile.

"You and I have something in common," Ilika said.

"What's that?"

"I was ten years old when I started training to work on ships."

"So when I'm your age, I could have my own ship!"

"It's possible. I did have some advantages you don't have."

"Like what?"

"I had had a good education already."

"But you're going to give us that this summer, right?"

"Yes, but it's always easier when you start younger. Where I come from, education starts at about seven."

"I started working at the inn when I was five."

"My first job was like yours, serving food at an eating place."

Sata smiled with pride. "We do have a lot in common."

"It's okay that we have these little secrets, but I have to give you a warning."

Sata lost her smile.

"There is no place for boasting on my ship. Be happy that we share some things, but keep them in their place, between you and me."

Sata was quiet and thoughtful for the remainder of the walk to the slave market.

✷

Ilika and Sata seated themselves in front of the big desk.

The slave master squinted at what appeared to be a slave sitting in one of his good chairs, but remained silent.

Ilika handed him the list.

The large man was well practiced at keeping his feelings hidden from his business associates, but for a moment his glee showed clearly as he gazed at the length of the list. Once he resumed his business-like expression, he copied the names onto another piece of paper, then rang a hand bell. A guard entered.

"Rope these up, except the cripple can just tag along."

To Ilika he said, "Good choices. They will serve you well."

Sata started to open her mouth, but Ilika jabbed her before she could speak.

The slave master began writing up bills of sale. "Instead of digging through all my records, which would take me hours, shall we just call it five for boys, eight for girls?"

Ilika did the math in his head. "That sounds about right. It comes to five great and seven small gold, I believe."

The slave master did the calculation on paper. "You are right! Where did you learn to figure like that?"

Ilika just smiled as he opened his pouch and brought out the coins.

Sata's eyes nearly bulged out of her head at the sight of so much money sitting on the table in front of her.

Ilika inspected each bill of sale as it was written, signed, and sealed with wax and the slave master's ring. When he had received and inspected all nine, he rose and extended his hand.

As they shook, the slave master said, "Come back any time you need more! Want to sell that one? She looks like a hard worker."

"She's not mine to sell," Ilika replied.

Sata clearly had some strong feelings, but this time held her tongue.

* * *

Chapter 18: Ritual

When Ilika and Sata stepped outside, a roped line of eight slaves, and one more leaning on her crutch, awaited them. Rags barely covered their bodies, while arms, legs, and feet were bare to the sun and wind.

A guard leaned against the wall. "Need to hire someone to get 'em to where you're going?"

"No, I think we can handle it from here."

"Suit yourself," he said, and went back inside, leaving Ilika and Sata to deal with their nine slaves. But unlike any other group of slaves in the entire history of the slave market, these nine slaves were all smiling.

Ilika took a moment to look them over, and they all met his gaze with sparkling eyes. Shaggy-haired Kibi, the oldest girl at about sixteen, grinned from ear to ear. Slender, freckled Rini, thirteen, appeared content with the situation, while little Kodi, the youngest boy at twelve, was ready to do handsprings.

Toli, the oldest at nineteen years and taller than the rest by a head, voiced a concern. "Sir, I thought you only needed five. There are nine of us, ten with Sata."

He gave them the same explanation he had already given Sata and her parents. When they heard about the three great gold pieces, their mouths opened with amazement.

"Is that enough to buy a cart?" Buna, about fourteen, asked with her squirrelly facial expression. "I've always wanted to have my own little cart, and maybe a donkey to pull it."

Ilika laughed. "Buna, three great gold is enough to buy three carts, three donkeys, and an entire farm." While he was speaking, he noticed Sata move over beside thirteen-year-old Mati and her crutch. "When's the last time you guys had a warm bath?" he asked the group.

"Warm bath?" handsome sixteen-year-old Miko said, looking at Ilika with his penetrating eyes. "What's that? Masters don't waste warm water on slaves."

"Sometimes we don't even get water!" fifteen-year-old Neti, pretty even in rags, said with frustration.

"Follow me!" Ilika said, and headed for Market Way at a slow pace.

With no one pulling, the eight on the rope stood in confusion for a moment. Boro, the large fourteen-year-old at the front of the line, found the courage to pick up the end of the rope and follow Ilika. The others moved with him, while Mati and Sata came behind.

Ilika stopped at the entrance to the bath house where Doti awaited. The slaves arrived a moment later, smiling when they recognized the healer.

Ilika spoke with the twisted man, then led his charges into the yard. He motioned for them to sit down on the cobblestones around the pool. Mati carefully lowered herself and her crutch onto an old crate.

"This is a very important moment for us," Ilika began. "Here, in this bath house, the rope comes off and never binds you again." He moved from person to person, untying the rope from their sore wrists. Some of the ex-slaves couldn't stop tears from coming, both girls and boys.

When Ilika finished, he coiled the rope and stood before them. "I'm going to start a pile right here," he said, dropping the rope onto the stones. "The bath house man will burn it with his other trash. This is where your rags go when you take them off, because . . ." He opened his bag and pulled out a tunic. "You all get new clothes as soon as you're clean."

They cheered and clapped with their newly-freed hands.

"Doti is here to treat your head lice."

"That will be so wonderful!" Neti said. "It's really hard to sleep with them walking around on your head."

The healer stepped to the front of the group, her potion bag over her shoulder. "When you get in the tub, I want you to wet your hair. The potion will burn a little, but leave it on while you're doing the rest of your bathing."

Ilika returned to the front. "I realize we don't have complete privacy. You're welcome to keep your underwear on while you bathe."

The tub was soon filling with bouncing, splashing youth, the water quickly turned gray, and the pile of rags to be burned grew rapidly.

Doti sat on the edge, applying the potion to wet heads as they presented themselves, one at a time.

Kibi helped Mati into the tub, then stood with an uncomfortable expression, still wearing her rags. The healer noticed, set down her potion bottle, and approached the sixteen-year-old. "Sister, you deserve this as much as anyone else. You are now part of a new family, and all the people having fun in that tub are your friends."

"I know. It's just . . . scary. It's been so long since I wore anything but . . . rags."

"Now you are free to choose. You can even go back to the slave compound if you want. But if you're going to stay at the inn with everyone else, and get that education, you have to be clean, free of lice, and nicely dressed." Doti turned to Ilika. "Can you take someone to the inn who hasn't bathed?"

"Nope. I could only do it that one day because I had rented the whole common room."

Kibi looked into the healer's eyes for a long moment. Then she slowly took off her rags and dropped them into the pile, one by one, painfully, as if they were living organs of her own body.

Doti stood by for moral support.

Kibi looked at the tub, and her friends made a space for her. Suddenly she started crying, but somehow, through her tears, found the edge of the tub. As her friends splashed her, the tears were soon washed away and she began laughing and playing along with everyone else.

Doti smiled and went back to applying her potion. She did an especially good job on Kibi's head.

*

Everyone dunked underwater several times to rinse off the lice potion, except Buna who preferred to splash water onto her head. By that time, the water in the tub was nearly black. Doti handed a towel to each as they climbed out, and saw their sheer joy at the simple pleasure of using clean cloth.

After a few minutes of trial and error, and some embarrassed laughter, everyone finally received the right size tunic.

"We're all blue, same as you!" little Kodi said with pride.

Ilika smiled. "In the coming days you'll get pants, extra tunics, cloaks, and boots."

"Big warm cloaks you can curl up and sleep in?" Buna asked with amazement.

"Yes, with hoods."

The fourteen-year-old girl danced a little jig of joy right there on the cobblestones.

* * *

Chapter 19: Ground Rules

Outside the bath house, all the ex-slaves lined up, ready to be tied to a rope. Soon, with no rope in sight, they started milling about, each one looking for someone else to follow.

Ilika chuckled to himself. “Okay, let’s talk about getting from here to the inn. We don’t walk in a line — that’s how slaves walk. If we walk as one big group, people will think an army is coming. Let’s walk in pairs or threes, a little space between each. We take our time, because people who hurry give the impression they’re fleeing the scene of their latest crime. We walk straight and tall, with the attitude that this is *our* city.”

Miko and Neti easily formed a walking pair, then Sata and Mati. Doti hooked up with Kibi, and Ilika fell in between Rini and Kodi. Boro and Toli both offered their hands to Buna, who blushed and took both.

The newly-freed slaves were curious about everything around them, often slack-jawed and turning circles as they walked.

“Next lesson,” Ilika began before they had gone far. “If you look like you’re lost, or brainless, people will treat you that way.”

Most of them succeeded at observing their surroundings with a little less drama. Ilika listened to the chatter, and discovered they had all been in the city many times, but had always been rushed from compound to work site, or kept behind locked doors. Walking slowly, with time to talk and look, was a new pleasure.

At the entrance to the plaza, Doti said good-bye and promised to be back that evening. Smiles and waves were exchanged until she disappeared around a corner.

“I wish she was my mother,” little Kodi said longingly.

“I think we’ll be seeing her often,” Ilika said, gently putting an arm around the lad’s shoulders.

*

Lunchtime was long past and the common room nearly empty. Ilika directed his troop to a large table.

"With our room rental, we get basic board. That means whatever's cooking, no dessert or wine or fruit juice or anything else special without paying extra. Sometimes we can get extra goodies here, and sometimes we'll be out and about for dessert or a special meal."

"Well, well!" the innkeeper boomed, approaching the table wearing his apron. "My name is Doko. I know Ilika, and I *think* I know someone else here," he said, winking at Sata.

"That's my father," Sata said, rolling her eyes. "He's being silly."

"I'm Kodi!" the smallest boy said excitedly.

"I'm Neti," the prettiest girl shared with a calm smile.

"My name is Toli," the lanky boy announced proudly.

"Doko," Ilika began after the rest had shared their names, "what would you like these young people to know about staying at an inn?"

"Hmm." The innkeeper looked at the ceiling thoughtfully. "Don't bug the other guests. No running in the corridors or stairs. And upstairs is quiet from midnight to sunrise."

Ilika nodded. "Thanks, Doko. What's cooking?"

"A good stew, even had some myself, and there's a little meat left, I think. Ale?"

Ilika cringed. "Maybe a little with dinner, but I have a million things to teach these guys today."

"What's a million?" Sata asked.

Ilika laughed. "You'll have to wait for math lessons."

Doko laughed too, then shrugged as he turned and headed for the kitchen.

When bread and cheese were placed on the table, it quickly disappeared into nine hungry mouths.

Ilika frowned. "You guys act like you didn't have any breakfast."

"We didn't," Toli said around the bread he was chewing.

Ilika was silent for a moment. "I am so sorry. I would have gotten you something before the bath if I had known."

"Don't worry about it," Miko said after swallowing a bite. "Most days we didn't get breakfast, or if we did, that was it."

Bowls of stew arrived next, then a plate of sliced meat. All nine ex-slaves moved toward it like vultures ready to swoop. Sata started to roll her eyes, but caught herself.

"When we have a common dish like this," Ilika explained, "we have to be careful to only take our share."

They were so careful, with constant glances at Ilika as they served themselves, that some meat remained unclaimed.

Ilika smiled. "You all know where the toilet room is. There's another upstairs. No guards now — can everyone handle that?"

They all nodded as they licked their bowls and fingers, then followed Ilika up the stairs to the inn's largest sleeping room.

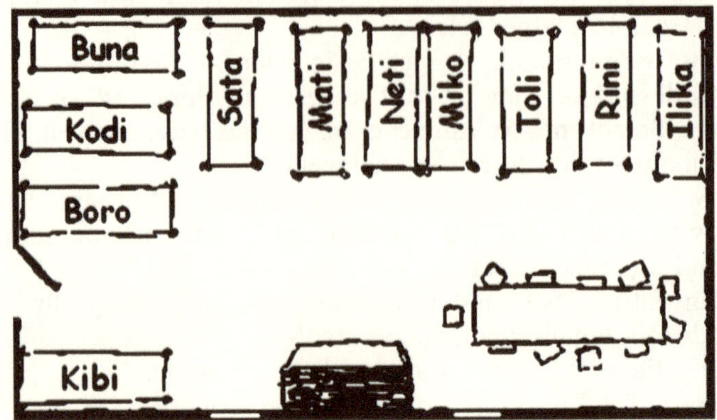

Ilika sat on the raised hearth in front of the small fireplace and scanned his new charges, all sitting proudly on the beds they had chosen.

"Let's talk about how to get along and stay out of trouble. I've thought of a few things, and you guys can help me think of others." He fell silent and looked at his notes.

"Are we free now?" Toli asked.

"Very good question. As far as I'm concerned, yes. You could walk out of here right now and I'd do nothing to stop you. But legally, no. I will see a scribe tomorrow, and it takes him a couple of days to get the bills of freedom prepared. I'll receive a copy, and give it to you if you ever choose to leave.

"That reminds me," he continued, "For the next few days, I want you to only go outside the inn with me. You'll soon get a complete set of clothes, and can go out in small groups."

"Are we going to learn everything here at this inn?" Mati asked.

"No, we'll just be here long enough to get supplies and horses, then we'll wander all over the kingdom, staying at inns, or camping and doing lessons outside in good weather."

Noises of excitement filled the room.

"I've never ridden a horse!" shaggy Kibi declared with a big grin.

Ilika smiled back at her. "To tell you the truth, I haven't either, so we'll all learn together."

"You've never ridden a horse?" young Kodi accused with a frown. "Why not?"

"My country has creatures of about the same size and shape, but they're very smart and don't let people climb onto their backs."

Kodi rolled his eyes and shrugged.

"You don't mind if Neti and me snuggle, do you?" Miko asked.

"That's . . . on my list. Snuggling, and other shared affection, is fine with me, except having . . . what do you call it? Oh, yes – carnal knowledge."

Several people giggled at his choice of words.

"You mean sex?" Sata asked without hesitation.

Ilika nodded, and tried to keep his surprise from showing. "We won't have much privacy, and forming long-term commitments takes a lot of time and energy. I can't educate you if you're busy doing other things."

"How long will that rule last?" Neti asked.

"Just for this learning time."

Neti smiled shyly, then she and Miko looked at each other.

"I think we can handle that," Miko said softly.

They leaned toward each other and kissed, and everyone else smiled or made taunting sounds.

When the room had settled, Boro raised his hand.

"This is a discussion time, so you don't have to raise your hand, Boro."

"Okay. Um . . . can we, like, you know . . . um . . . just sort of like flirt and stuff, as long as we don't . . . you know?"

Ilika smiled at his embarrassment. "Yes. The only rules I'll make are those necessary to get done what we're here to do."

"Thanks," he said.

"Do we have *any* work to do?" Sata asked with concern.

"We have to keep our room clean, care for the horses, stuff like that. But mostly your work will be learning, and I assure you, I will keep you very busy with that. You will be learning in half a year what most people take five or ten years to learn. If you stick with it, by next fall you will be some of the most highly educated people in this kingdom. You will read and write better than most scribes. You will know more mathematics than accountants. You will be better at logic and ethics than most philosophers."

"Wow!" many voices said at once.

*

When no one had further questions, to their surprise, Ilika began to talk about his life.

"My father was drunk half the time, my mother was afraid of everything and everybody, and my older sister tormented me constantly. I had no friends — all the boys wanted to be big, strong factory workers like their fathers, and all the girls wanted to get married and have babies. I spent all my free time on a little flat roof I could get to by crawling out a window. I could see the factories all around me, and the smoke stacks belching fumes day and night.

"But the real reason I went up there was to look at the stars. I couldn't see very many, but every night I would send a wish up to a different star, until my sister started yelling for me to do chores.

"I was eight years old when I was offered a chance to leave. I was on a long walk alone in the barren hills overlooking the town, and the only thing I had with me was a toy animal I would talk to. I was afraid that if I went back home for anything, I'd lose my chance, so I just held my toy and didn't look back.

"For the next two years, I had to learn countless things about my new home. I didn't even speak the language at first. One class I took showed me all the different professions I could follow. I had always liked ships, so when I was ten, I chose the Transport Service.

"For the next nine years I studied and worked on ships, eventually learning every job that most ships have. Then I applied for a command, and after two more years of study, I was given a little ship and my final exam, to find and train my own crew. So here I am."

"What's a . . . factory?" Boro asked.

"A big workshop with hundreds of workers and lots of machines or furnaces. They're usually too hot or too cold, and always dirty, ugly, and smelly. Poor people work in them so rich people can buy things."

"Sounds as bad as slavery to me," Miko said with a frown.

All the other ex-slaves nodded.

* * *

Chapter 20: Witch

The ten students were much more relaxed at dinner, and Ilika let the innkeeper serve small cups of ale for their beverage. The healer arrived just as they were finishing, two large bags over her shoulders. She shared hugs with Kibi, Kodi, and several others before they all returned to the sleeping room.

"This evening is about taking care of yourselves . . . and each other," Doti began as they settled onto their beds. "I brought a number of remedies, some of which I will leave with you."

She scanned the room. "I believe you had the worst rope burns," she said, looking at Miko and going to his bed with a jar of ointment. "That's probably because you fight against whatever is wrong in your world."

"Yep! That's me!" Miko said with pride and a hint of defiance.

"That's a good thing if you fight what you can change, and a bad thing if you only hurt yourself."

"Usually he knows the difference," Neti revealed. "Not always."

Miko looked thoughtful. The others gathered around to listen, while Ilika sat on the hearth building a fire.

"You two are committed to each other, are you not?" Doti asked.

They nodded proudly and happily.

"I think I see . . ." the healer began, but then a slight shadow passed over her face. "I see that you are going to comfort and strengthen each other for your entire lives together."

They both smiled.

"Come, Neti. This is a very soft ointment made from the herbs goldenseal, comfrey, and calendula. It will help his wrists to heal. Take some and warm it up in your hands, then very gently, without rubbing or pressure, coat his wrists."

Miko closed his eyes and smiled as the love of his life cared for him.

The healer looked around. "Let me see. Your name is Buna, is it not?"

"Yes, Madame."

"Let me see your wrists. Yes, you also have some rope burns, but these other sores are a little different." She gently pulled up Buna's tunic sleeves. "They're from something poisonous."

"I was weeding a garden a few days ago, and they appeared that night."

"I bet they itch."

Buna nodded.

"I have something a little different, made from comfrey, white willow, and cloves. This ointment is a little firmer." Then she looked around. "Toli is your name?"

"Me?" he questioned nervously.

"Please come and care for your new sister."

Red-faced and stumbling over his own feet, Toli managed to come forward.

"Use small amounts on a fingertip, gently covering each irritation. But when you're ready to do her wrists, use the soft ointment in the green jar."

Buna had a smirk on her face, clearly enjoying herself.

The healer looked at the two of them intently for a moment, then glanced at Miko and Neti. She frowned, but concealed it by turning her head and speaking. "Oh, yes, Mati!" she said, going to the girl's bed. "You know, Mati, I'm sure you're going to walk someday."

"Really? How?" Mati asked with wide eyes.

"I don't know. I cannot see everything."

Ilika, observing from the hearth while tending the fire, became very interested and wandered close to listen.

"And because of that," Doti continued, "you need to keep this knee of yours as healthy as you can. I have a special oil here, made with the herbs cayenne and elecampane, that will make it warm and happy."

"I'll put it on," Sata offered.

The healer looked at her for a moment. "No, Sata, I have a more important job for you." Then she looked around, and quickly spotted the right person. "Rini is your name?" she asked the very quiet freckled boy.

He nodded.

"Will you care for Mati?"

He nodded again.

"About a spoonful in your hands, then rub them together to warm it. Now here's the tricky part that will require good communication. Start massaging very gently, and slowly become firmer and firmer until Mati says it's starting to hurt. Back off a little, and massage it for a few minutes."

With a thoughtful expression, Ilika returned to the hearth.

"Sata, I need your help with something very important," the healer said.

"Sure, anything."

"Boro?"

"Oh, no . . . not my back," he mumbled under his breath.

"Yes, Boro, your back. You may remember, Sata, that Boro was taking great pains at the bath house to keep people from seeing his back. He has a wound there that isn't healing well because it has some dirt trapped inside. How did it happen, Boro?"

The silence stretched for nearly a minute and a dark shadow came over Boro. His eyes looked far away as he began to tell his story.

"My earliest memory is living on a cattle ranch, maybe four years old, but I can't see it clearly. I think I was happy. Then I remember a day when someone said there was a stampede, and I never saw my mother and father again.

"After that I lived with aunts and uncles, but they were always saying I was too gentle for man's work, too clumsy for woman's work. They would make me take a cow on a lead rope from one ranch to another, which was way too dangerous for a little kid. Twice I lost the cow and got whipped for it.

"One day I was walking a cow and a soldier came by. He didn't believe me when I told him where I lived, said that if someone cared about me, they'd come to the guard house to pay my fine and get me out. No one showed, so I became a slave.

"I guess I'm still too gentle and too clumsy. The last master I had made me wash dishes. I broke one and he jabbed me with the broken piece."

After a moment of silence, Doti nodded and said, "Thank you, Boro. Wrap this blanket around your middle, then take off your tunic, please. Sata is your sister now, you are members of a team and have to take care of each other. Am I not right, Ilika?"

"Completely right. We will be traveling together, even just in the learning period, and travel is dangerous without others to look after you. That's why few people travel alone."

"Boro is a very sweet boy," the healer continued, coaxing him to lie down on his stomach, "and he sees and feels many things, but has trouble sharing them with others. Now he will have to let someone help him, or this wound will get worse and possibly kill him."

Sata swallowed.

"What we're going to do, Sata, is put a few drops of this cleansing potion on the wound. Now we work it in, and in a moment Boro will start screaming."

"I will?" he questioned, his voice muffled by the mattress.

"Yes, and when you do, you will stay right where you are and let Sata do what needs to be done."

All the others held their breath. It wasn't long before Boro started moaning and shaking from the pain.

"See how it's opening up the wound where the dirt is trapped? Now we wipe it with a clean cloth . . . you still with me, Sata?"

"Yeah, I'm okay. I had to help my brother when he stabbed his hand with a kitchen knife. It took weeks to heal."

Boro's moans became louder.

"Okay, we've got out all we can, so now we use a bit of this healing oil and rub it in."

The patient quickly relaxed and fell silent.

"Can you trust Sata to do that once a day for the next week?" she asked the boy, still lying face-down.

"It's embarrassing."

"Dying is worse," Doti pointed out.

"Yeah, okay, I get the message."

"Sata, you have strong hands, and I bet a little shoulder massage would feel good to Boro right now, and help him to trust you."

Sata had a slight smile on her face as Boro began to make contented sounds.

Doti looked around the room, and was happy to see Kibi treating Kodi's wrists. The healer brought out a few more ointments and oils and explained their uses to everyone. Then she remembered what else needed to be done, and who needed to do it.

"Ilika, I have a task for you that will require extreme gentleness."

"What can I do?"

The healer spread out a cloth on the floor. "Kibi?"

"Yes, Madame?"

"You had one of the worst cases of lice I've ever seen."

The sixteen-year-old grinned sheepishly.

"Sit here, please. You trust Ilika already, don't you?"

Kibi nodded vigorously.

The healer brought out a fine-toothed comb and handed it to Ilika. "I had to have this specially made."

For the next hour, Ilika carefully worked through Kibi's tangles. She drifted into a sleepy trance, swaying slightly as he worked on her thick, shaggy black hair. Thousands of tiny dead bugs collected on the cloth below.

Ilika had no idea how the healer could sense which students would become most closely bonded. But, he admitted to himself, as far as he could tell . . . as far as he could guess from their personalities . . . and, in his own case, as far as his heart was making its wishes known . . . she was right.

* * *

Chapter 21: The Puzzle

When the ten students began to wake the following morning, Ilika was already gone. As each went to use the toilet room, they looked around for someone to tell them it was their turn – and found no one to ask. When they finished their business, they expected someone to see if they had left a mess – but no one was checking. On the way back to the sleeping room, they looked up and down the corridor to see who was watching where they went – and found no one paying any attention.

Although they were all quite hungry and could smell food cooking, they couldn't help but steal glances at the mysterious unopened wooden box on the table. Ilika had said that after breakfast and before lunch, they should "do the puzzle." He had refused to say any more.

So they took turns, every few minutes, creeping to the stairs to see if a large table was free. Finally, Kodi ran back smiling and bouncing up and down.

"Remember what the innkeeper said about running!" Neti scolded gently.

"Oh, yeah," he said with an impish grin.

With some anxiety, they made their way down to the common room. Kodi was careful to walk very, very slowly.

Their anxiety faded when they were served sweet tea and porridge, just as if Ilika was with them. Bowls of honey, cream, and berries were set in the middle.

Buna put one of the berries directly into her mouth and shuddered at its delicious sour taste.

*

Back at the large table in the sleeping room, they all gazed longingly at the ornate wooden box.

"I think we need a leader," Rini said confidently, "and I think it should be Miko. But only if we all agree."

Nods and thumbs-up circled the table.

"But just for this puzzle thing, right?" Toli asked, slightly worried. "I mean, other people might be good at leading other things."

More nods and sounds of agreement made Toli smile.

"Well . . . I've always wanted to be a leader," Miko said, "but when you're a slave . . ."

Everyone laughed.

"I will try to be a good leader. I guess . . . we should open the box!" He lifted the lid and they all peered in and beheld hundreds of strangely shaped pieces of thin wood. No two seemed to have the same shape. He took a few out and laid them on the table.

"I think we should be careful not to break them," Mati said, almost holding her breath.

"Yeah," Miko agreed. "They all have a bit of painting on them."

"Slaves aren't allowed to touch paintings," Rini said with a serious voice.

"But we have to touch them to put it together!" Toli burst out.

Rini smiled and picked up a piece.

"This is a test, isn't it?" Neti asked.

"Everything's a test," Boro replied. "Remember, there are twice as many of us as he needs."

"I have a suggestion," Sata said. "I think we should all wash our hands before we touch the pieces anymore."

Miko looked around the table. "Yeah!"

They all filed downstairs and out to the trough in front of the inn. After being dried on their tunics, the twenty cleanest hands in the city returned to the sleeping room.

Miko took a deep breath. "I'll put the pieces on the table, painting side up, and then we can see what it looks like." He worked for the next ten minutes as everyone watched intently.

Most of the students frowned with confusion as they gazed at the hundred or more pieces on the table.

"What the heck is it?" Boro wondered aloud.

Sata shrugged. "No idea."

Several others had similar comments.

"I can see it," Kibi said, barely louder than a mouse.

Buna's mouth twisted into a little smile. "Me too."

The others tried again to see something in the fragmented, disorganized bits of painting, but could not.

"We give up," Miko said. "Please tell us."

"It's a bunch of blue flowers in a green jar," Kibi said.

Buna flashed her a grin.

"Some of the pieces have a straight side," Toli observed.

"So?" Kodi challenged with frustration, chin in his hands.

Boro and Sata looked at each other with raised eyebrows. "Those are the sides, I bet," Sata said.

"Will you two work on the sides, see if you can put it together?" Miko asked.

"Hey! It was my idea!" Toli whined.

"I guess . . . you can work on the sides too, Toli. How about . . . Kibi and Buna start on the flowers. They look like the hardest part, and you guys can see them best."

"Now that they told us what to look for, I can see it too," Mati said. "Can I help?"

Kibi and Buna nodded.

Miko looked around. "That leaves the jar for me, Neti, Rini, and . . ."

"There's nothing for me to do!" Kodi said in a hurt tone.

"I was just about to ask you to work on the jar with us."

"I don't want to!" the youngest boy said with a pout as he went to the hearth to play with sticks.

"Okay, fine. Me, Neti, and Rini are doing the jar."

"Flowers are being made at this end of the table!" Kibi announced, and Buna moved over.

"Let's save the middle of the table for the sides of the painting . . ."

*

Ilika returned about an hour after noon.

The completed puzzle lay on the table, a variety of blue flowers in a green blown-glass jar, with bits of clouds and sky in the background. Most of the students had smirks on their faces.

"You guys are good!" Ilika said, looking at the masterpiece. "There's a free table. Anyone hungry?"

"I am!" they chorused.

Down in the common room, when everyone was supplied with stew and bread, cheese and a few fresh greens, Ilika spoke. "The documents I mentioned have been started, and should be done tomorrow. We have a tailor coming later this afternoon to outfit all of you. The bootmaker is coming tomorrow."

As Ilika ate, he began to notice the tension in the group. It was difficult to pinpoint the source, as several people talked happily among themselves, laughing about the difficulty of matching and fitting some of the puzzle pieces. Miko was unusually quiet.

Once back in the sleeping room, Ilika took up his perch on the hearth.

"You guys are a team. You're a learning team right now. Someday, five of you will be the crew of a ship, and the other five might choose to be a team also. The most important thing about being a team is trusting one another. Because of that, I will never ask you to tell on each other. That only destroys trust."

"Our masters always wanted us to do that," Kibi said, "but we wouldn't."

"Good. I noticed on the test day that confidence was a strong value with all of you. It's also important to share your thoughts, feelings, ideas, and experiences, so I'll teach you how to do that in ways that build trust.

"The main rule is to only talk about yourself. You are the only person whose thoughts and feelings you really know. We can only guess why someone else does, or doesn't do, something."

He paused to see if they were with him. Most were nodding.

"This morning you had your first experience together without me controlling everything like a . . . well, like a ship's captain. I can sense there were some challenges. Anyone who wants to work on a ship – or do anything else that takes teamwork – has to be willing to report everything he sees or thinks that might be important to the team.

"But, like I said, you are only talking about yourself. If someone else made you feel something, that is your feeling. Say, 'I was angry,' not 'Sata made me angry.'"

Sata grinned without concern.

"See the difference?" Ilika asked.

Some nodded understanding. Most looked thoughtful.

"Sata, what can you report about your experience in the puzzle project, from your point of view, without using anyone else's name?"

"Um . . . I had fun. I was finding the sides with . . . one other person. It was easy to pick out those pieces, but hard to put them together. I loved it when the other parts were moved into the frame."

"Miko, what can you report?"

"Well, um . . . someone suggested I be the leader of the project, and I tried, but I don't think I did a very good job." He fell silent.

"Why do you think that?"

"I think if a leader is good, everyone in the project would be happy, but . . . not everyone was." He looked at his blanket.

"Do you think a leader is responsible for everyone's happiness?"

"Um . . . I don't know. Now that you say it like that, it sounds a little strange."

"I hope it sounds a little strange," Ilika asserted. "We'll talk about that idea more later, but I want to get everyone's report first. Kibi, how about you?"

"I had lots of fun, and me and . . . someone . . . were able to see the picture before it was put together, and it made me feel closer to . . . that person. Then three of us put the flowers together. I think . . . the leader was really good, and I think everyone is responsible for their own happiness."

"I agree with you. Kodi?"

"The leader was really good and the picture was really pretty," he said in one breath, barely louder than a whisper.

Even though Kodi hadn't said much, the looks on others' faces at that moment told Ilika a great deal. "How about you, Rini?"

*

From everyone else, Ilika received reports of happiness with the project, some minor frustration with the puzzle pieces, and pride in the completed product.

"So, Miko, I've heard nothing but glowing praise about your leadership. What do you think of that?"

"Gosh. I'm . . . surprised. I guess I'm not really sure what a leader is, even though I've always wanted to be one, ever since I ran away from home."

"Is that how you became a slave?" Buna asked.

"Yeah. I was about nine. I hated my mother, 'cause everything had to be done exactly her way. Even if me or my brother knew a better way, she'd beat us if she caught us. If we asked why we had to do it her stupid way, she'd just say, 'Because I said so!' and then she'd beat us for asking.

"My father would never lift a finger to her. She even told *him* exactly how to do things, and he'd say, 'Yes, Honey,' and then do it the way he knew was best.

"I don't regret leaving home, but I should have waited a little longer. I just left one day when she made me really mad, and I didn't have anything but the clothes I was wearing. I wish I'd waited another year or two, saved up some coppers and stuff. I lasted about a week, stealing food from gardens and cellars. Then I got caught and I've been a slave ever since."

After a long silence, Ilika nodded. "Thanks, Miko."

"I've been working up my courage ever since Boro told his story," Miko added.

Ilika continued. "Kibi already mentioned that a leader is not responsible for others' happiness. There are people who can be happy even in the worst situations in the world, like being a runaway or a slave . . ."

They all smiled or chuckled.

". . . and there are people who are rich and famous and are unhappy. Happiness has very little to do with anything outside of you, including who is leading."

He let his words linger in the air for the ten to think about. Just then a knock rattled their door.

"Kibi, would you answer that, please?"

She sprang from her bed and opened the door. The innkeeper and the tailor, with a load of samples over his arm, filled the doorway. Little waves were exchanged between Sata and her father. The tailor entered.

"There are many other things about leadership we will learn in future lessons. Thank you all for your excellent work on the puzzle, and your thoughtful reports."

They all glowed with pride at his kind words — all but one.

* * *

Chapter 22: Learning to Learn

Their first baby step into the world of fashion consisted of four color options — dark blue, dull green, brown, and gray. Those few choices made all of them, even Sata, nearly giddy with happiness.

When the tailor had taken all their orders, and dealt with several changes of mind, Ilika added plenty of shorts and socks to the order.

The man departed, promising their clothes in two days.

"Okay, let's do some math," Ilika said, getting out sheets of paper. "But before we start, I want you to understand this is not testing anymore. Everyone has to learn every bit of this, and we don't move on until you can all do it in your sleep. See the difference?"

Thoughtful nods filled the room.

"Our digits range from zero to one less than our base. What is our base?"

"Five!" Kodi answered confidently.

"Nope. That was a pretend situation for the test."

Kodi squirmed, but seemed to recover.

"We have two hands, and in this kingdom we use base ten. So our highest digit is nine. Let's count." He held up a sheet with nine dots in a row and they counted the dots together, some students leading, some echoing a fraction of a second later.

"Now, as I hold up sheets with dots and say someone's name, that person will count the dots aloud. Everyone else will follow silently. Mati?"

"One, two, um . . . um . . ." She stopped and turned red.

"Three!" Toli blurted out.

"It wasn't your turn, Toli," Ilika said firmly. "That's showing off. We're not doing that. We're doing math, teamwork style, trust-building style. Okay?"

"Okay," Toli said in a flat voice.

"Mati?" Ilika prompted again.

"But . . . someone already said the answer," she whimpered in a voice close to tears. "Someone else always gets to do things instead of me, it's always been like that, all my life."

Sata put her arm around the trembling girl, and Ilika came close to listen to what she had to say.

"I guess I had parents once, but they just passed me around from one relative to another. The other kids had copper pieces to spend, but not me. The other kids got to learn how to cook, or garden, or keep animals, but not me. I think my parents eventually forgot who I was staying with, and the relatives forgot I was a relative.

"For a while I slept in a shed with the slave, a big, simple boy who was kind and kept me warm. I helped him weed the garden sometimes, and that made me so happy. But then the relative got sick, his farm was sold, and I went with the slave.

"I've been sold and resold many times since then. I'm worth a little silver piece at the most, sometimes just a few coppers . . ." Her words broke into deep sobs as Sata and Neti surrounded her with their arms.

Ilika's eyes glistened. "That's all in the past now," he assured. "Are you ready to continue your education?"

Mati managed a tiny nod as her teacher held up the sheet of paper. "Um . . . one, two, um . . . three," she whispered with her feelings barely under control.

"Everyone see how easy it is to hurt someone, destroy trust, and ruin a lesson?" Ilika said to the entire group.

"I'm sorry," Toli said as others nodded thoughtfully.

Ilika held up another sheet. "Rini?"

"One, two, three, four, five."

"Toli?"

"Four!"

"Count them aloud please, Toli. We'll get to recognition soon."

"One, two, three, four," he said with a huff.

"Buna?"

"One, two, three, four, five, um . . ."

Everyone kept their lips tightly sealed as Buna struggled to remember.

"Six!"

"Kibi?"

"Um . . . um . . . what was that called?" she said as she stared at the blank piece of paper. "Zero!"

Ilika smiled. He continued to make them count dots until he was sure they were masters of the art.

"Neti, the number of legs on the table?"

"One, two, three, four!"

"Miko, the number of pieces of firewood on the hearth?"

"One, two, three, four, five, six . . . seven . . . eight, and . . . um . . . nine?"

"You guys are good! That's why I picked you. Now to what Toli tried, recognition. Count silently if you must, but try to just *know* how many dots there are. Kibi?"

"Um . . . three?"

"Toli?

"Wow. Five?"

"Kodi?"

"Two!"

The recognition drills continued, first with the dots in nice, neat lines or squares. Ilika worked with them on the ones that gave them trouble.

Then he started flashing small numbers of disorganized dots. They did well through four, but five and above forced them to count.

"Try this hard one, Sata."

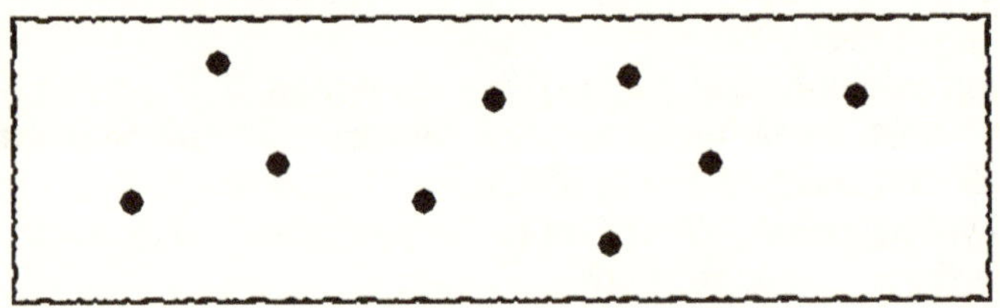

There was a long silence. "Eleven, I think."

"Other opinions?"

"I got ten," Mati said, glancing at Toli with a gleam of warning in her eyes.

"There are only nine dots here," Ilika said, "but the fact that they're disorganized, and you aren't close enough to mark them as you count, makes it easy to count some dots twice." Then he counted them aloud, making a mark through each dot as he went.

He held up another sheet with disorganized dots. "Kodi?"

The lad hopped off his bed, grabbed a pencil from the table, and counted the dots to himself, marking them as he went. "Seven!"

"Congratulations! On that note of success, let's go see what's cooking, shall we?"

* * *

Chapter 23: A Real Test

A tasty dinner of seafood stew, fresh bread, and soft cheese greeted them in the common room. The tension Ilika had noticed at lunch seemed to have disappeared. The students chatted about the clothes they were getting, and some of them described finer clothes they had seen and dreamed of wearing.

"With our new clothes, can we go into Cobble Town?" Neti asked, a huge smile on her face. "I used to live there."

Many eyes turned in her direction with a mixture of shock and wonder.

"Tell us all about it!" Buna said from across the table after quickly swallowing a bite.

"You can wait for the privacy of our room if you want," Ilika said.

"I don't care. Miko knows. I've had three different masters who bought me for . . . you know . . . affection. Two of them lived in Cobble Town. But even though I've lived there, I could never go out and see anything."

"How did you become a slave?" Kibi asked.

"I think my parents couldn't pay their taxes or something like that. I was about six. I saw my mother in a slave compound about two years ago. She was dying."

Everyone was quiet for a moment.

"I'm sorry to hear that," Ilika said softly. "I think we should wait on going into Cobble Town until you have boots and have practiced carrying yourselves with confidence. We'll start in the marketplace. That reminds me – when I go out tomorrow, I need to reserve the bathing pool."

"We get to take *another* bath?" Buna asked with wide eyes.

Ilika only smiled.

"I think I hear some music out in the plaza," Sata said with her head cocked.

They could faintly hear pipes and a drum. Smiles slowly grew as they listened.

"Shall we go over to the bakery and see if Tori has any tarts, then go listen to the music?" Ilika proposed.

Everyone nodded excitedly.

"Some things to remember. We walk, in twos or threes, calmly and confidently. We respect all people we pass, even if they were hated masters once. Everyone okay with that?"

Some had to think about it, but eventually they all agreed.

*

After finishing dinner, they stepped out into the twilight and crossed the plaza toward the bakery.

"Well, well! This is quite a following, you have," the baker said while looking them over.

"These are my students. Everybody, this is Tori, the best baker in the city."

They all greeted him, most sharing their names.

"If it wasn't for Tori's knowledge of the city," Ilika explained, "I never would have found you guys. He suggested I look in the slave market."

The baker looked puzzled. "These are slaves? I mean . . . other than Sata?"

"Not anymore," Ilika said with a faint smile.

"They seem as well behaved as any apprentices."

"They are. I wouldn't have picked them otherwise. We were wondering how you're stocked on those delicious tarts."

"Hmm . . ." He went to the back and opened the oven. "Ahh! Can you smell that?" The aroma of sweet dough and berries filled the air. "These look done." He grabbed a large shingle. "They're hot!"

"We'll be careful," Kibi said with her dark eyes gleaming in the lantern light.

The baker took a long look at Kibi, who was standing close to Ilika, and smiled.

Ilika dug into his pouch and brought out five copper pieces. "Some for the children, of course."

"I know some who will be by any minute now with hungry looks on their faces."

"Thank you, Tori," Neti said with almost an air of nobility in her speech.

"Thanks!" several others echoed.

"Good-bye, all!" the baker called as he turned to another customer.

The group followed the sound of the music to the stage between the market and the palace. Torches flickered, giving the musicians some light and casting a mysterious glow over the crowd. Hundreds of people sat on benches or the ground, or stood at the back.

Ilika spotted a free patch of ground off to one side, and gestured for everyone to squeeze in and sit close together. Most of the students plopped onto the ground without hesitation. Sata helped Mati down, then sat beside her. Ilika passed out the tarts as soon as everyone was settled.

Two pipers created the melody, a drummer set the rhythm, and a four-stringed instrument added harmony. The simple tunes somehow captured the feel and rhythm of life in the medieval walled city. Ilika noticed that most of the audience appeared, by their clothing and manners, to be from Rumble Town.

The song ended and all the people clapped, cheered, or stomped to show their appreciation. The musicians began a new song, a slow ballad about a wanderer who endlessly sought his lady love.

Unknown to Ilika and the students, a merchant and his slave wandered through the area. The well-dressed man stopped to talk with someone and the slave sat down in the dirt to listen to the music.

Suddenly the gruff voice of a guard shouted, “Hey! No slaves allowed!”

Most of Ilika’s students were immediately on their feet, looking very frightened and ready to bolt.

“Kibi, Rini, sit down!” he said as loudly as he dared. “Buna, sit!” He pulled Kodi down beside him. Sata tried to comfort Mati and Boro. Miko and Neti were holding onto each other and staring with wide eyes.

Soon they were all back on the ground, but still looking around like scared rabbits without a rabbit hole.

“Relax! Focus on the music!” Ilika coaxed.

“They acted like the guard was talking to *them!*” a man sitting near said in a suspicious tone.

“They’re new students of mine, not used to all the noise in the city,” Ilika explained.

The man chuckled, and other people nearby seemed to also accept the explanation. The merchant and slave were gone and the guard had moved on. Soon, no one seemed to be looking at them. Ilika allowed himself to breathe again.

The next musical piece featured only the drummer while the other musicians danced wildly around him. Most of the people began clapping to the beat, and Ilika joined, hoping his students could put the incident behind them. Kibi was smiling and clapping, and Neti and Miko clapped each other’s hands. Kodi and a few others still looked nervous.

All the musicians returned for a lively piece, perfect for any victory celebration. The people were so moved, they stood and clapped at the end, and Ilika and his students did the same. As the musicians put away their instruments, the crowd slowly filtered away into the streets of the city.

Once the group was alone, several students started to speak, guilty looks on their faces, but Ilika put a finger to his lips. He ambled to one of the water troughs to rinse his hands, and they joined him.

Sata and Mati started back toward the inn, and the rest paired up and followed. In the sleeping room, a tall candle glowed from the table to welcome them.

“That was a close call,” Ilika said as soon as they were settled on their beds. “Did everyone learn from it?”

All nine former slaves nodded. Sata remained still.

"Miko, that was an example of poor leadership," Ilika continued. "One of the duties of a leader is to prepare his charges for what might happen. I'm sorry I didn't think of that."

"We're sorry too," Rini said with feeling.

"No apologies necessary. The important thing is that you are not slaves, and your best strategy for staying free is to never act like slaves."

A long silence lingered.

"Okay. I believe most of you need ointment on your wrists, Buna gets the other ointment for her rashes, and Boro needs his wound cleaned."

The large boy moaned.

"Other than that, we'll just have a relaxed evening, share some massages or hair combing or quiet conversation, and people can go to bed whenever they want. I've had a long day, and I'm not good for much more."

After glancing at Boro's back and the other sores and rashes, Ilika took a moment to look at his notes. Before long he felt gentle hands on his shoulders, then a comb carefully working the tangles out of his hair.

"Hi, Kibi."

"Hi, Ilika."

"Thanks."

"You're welcome."

* * *

Chapter 24: Consonant Stops and Nursery Rhymes

The day after the public musical performance was bright and sunny, and everyone was in good spirits. A bowl brimming with berries came with their porridge, and Ilika bought fruit juice for everyone.

Back in their room, Sata stood in the middle of the floor and took several deep breaths. The others could tell she had something to say.

"I used to think my life was rough, but now I know I was wrong. You guys have been through a lot more than I have, and I'm really glad you're my friends now."

"You've worked hard and had few choices too," Kibi said with sympathy. "We're glad you're our friend."

"I've probably had some choices . . . I don't know . . . but the first time I ever opened my mouth and said I wanted something was to be tested by Ilika. And I'm sure glad I did. I've always wanted to learn things, but there was never anyone to ask, except . . . you know, my mother about cooking and sewing and stuff. Even though we've just started, already the things I'm learning are swirling around in my head. I think I counted dots in my dreams last night . . ."

The room erupted with laughter.

"The truth is . . . my parents are going to give the inn to my brother, and I'm sure he'd let me work here, but someday he'll probably get married, and then there would be two women running the inn . . ."

"Bad idea," Buna said with a scrunched face.

"Yeah. And . . . there's something out there I want to find, something I don't know anything about yet, but I want to keep looking until I find it."

She sat down on her bed and Mati reached across to touch her on the shoulder.

"Thanks, Sata," Ilika said. "Speaking of learning, how many of you can read?"

Sata's hand came up about a quarter of the way. Everyone else was motionless.

"Your written language uses letters that stand for sounds," Ilika began. "But there aren't enough letters in your alphabet, so some letters make two or three different sounds, depending on the word. Other times, two letters are used together to represent a single sound. As a final difficulty, some letters are completely silent, but they may change the sound of other letters."

"Who made it so complicated?" Toli asked with a disgusted look.

Ilika smiled. "It's so complicated because no one made it — it evolved over a long period of time, and has roots in four or more different languages. We'll start with vowels, continuous sounds made with an open mouth. I will write and speak, then you speak."

He wrote A. "Ahhhhhhhhh like in bar."

"Ahhhhhhhhh," they echoed, some a little more shyly than others.

He wrote A again. "Aaaaaaaaaa like in cat."

"Aaaaaaaaaa," they repeated, some looking confused.

He wrote E. "Ehhhhhhhhh like in pet."

"Ehhhhhhhhh."

He wrote E again. "Eeeeeeeeee like in keep."

"Eeeeeeeeee," they repeated.

When finished with vowels, they had six letters making nine sounds, and most of the students looked very frustrated.

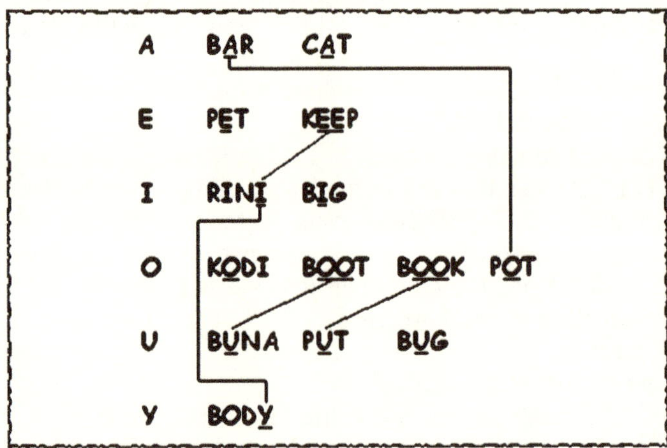

"I know some of you are ready to throw things at me, but it will all make sense as soon as we learn the consonant stops, sounds that are just a little burst to put before or after a vowel." He wrote P, T, and K, then pronounced them.

They repeated.

"Can you feel the three places in your mouth? Lips, gums behind the teeth, and the roof of the mouth?"

Most of them nodded.

"Those were unvoiced — no vocal cords making sound. When we add voice, we get three more letters." He wrote B, D, and G, and added, "This is your hard G." Then he pronounced them, and they echoed.

He wrote P, B, T, D, K, and G, and spoke aloud the series of sounds. The students were quite tongue-tied until they saw the pattern, Kibi and Sata leading the way, most of the others not far behind.

"Now we can make many words." Ilika went to the table and spread out a piece of large paper with dozens of two and three letter words. His students gathered around and were kept busy for the next hour, practicing the words until they were making few mistakes.

UP AT IT PA PEP POP PUP PAT PET PIT
POT PUT PEG PIG TO TAP TIP TOP TAT
TIT TOT TAB TUB TAD TAG TUG KIT
KID KEG BE BOP BAT BET BIT BUT BIB
BOB BAD BED BID BUD BAG BEG BIG BOG
BUG DO DOT DAB DAD DID DUD DIG
DOG DUG GO GAP GET GOT GUT GAB
GOB GOD GAG GIG

The sound of knocking came from the door.

Kibi opened it to find the innkeeper and a wrinkled man with boots on his feet, boots tied over both shoulders, and the outline of a boot on his tunic. "Ilika, I think the bootmaker is here."

"Good time for a break from reading."

"Yeah!" many agreed.

For the next hour the jolly bootmaker traced each student's feet onto a piece of paper, telling little nursery rhymes as he worked.

"The dragon of the east *always* knows when apprentices have avoided their chores. You could line up five apprentices in front of his dark, mysterious cave, just like five toes on a foot, and he would skip over the first three," he said, touching the first three toes of Buna's foot, "because they were the good apprentices, and go right to the fourth one!" he said, pinching that toe and making her squeal and laugh.

The boys received more serious jests.

"There was this one bootmaker who wasn't very good and always left a nail sticking up somewhere inside the boot."

Boro tried to keep a straight face as the man traced his feet.

"Funny thing was, the nail always hit somewhere soft and tender," he said, and continued tracing as he hummed. Suddenly, when Boro least expected it, the man's pencil made contact with soft flesh. "Right about there!"

Boro burst out laughing when he saw the bootmaker's cheesy grin.

"I bet you haven't heard about the snake that likes to lick toes, have you?"

Neti drew her feet back under the stool, but she was smiling.

"It's okay. Those tender, juicy toes can come out because the snake only likes to lick them . . ."

She slowly brought her feet back out to be traced.

"You know, snakes are very picky about what they eat. If it doesn't smell like a mouse and taste like a mouse, they just aren't interested. And you know how snakes hold onto a mouse with irresistible strength and slowly swallow it?"

"Yeah," Neti said, looking into his wrinkled, smiling eyes.

"Well, same thing happens when they find toes they like!"

She tried to pull her feet back, but it was too late. His strong fingers held both of her big toes tightly. He grinned up at her, and she couldn't stop herself from howling with laughter.

The man, however, was very careful when he came to Mati. He listened to her describe her physical challenge, made the tracings, and added some symbols to the sheet.

"I can have your boots done in six days!" the bootmaker announced after the last tracing.

Ilika squinted thoughtfully for a moment. "What if an extra silver piece came with each pair?"

"Ahhh! With my son helping, three days!"

"Good. Three days. Thank you!"

*

After the bootmaker departed, the students gathered back at the table.

"It wasn't easy," Ilika began, "but I managed to make some sentences from the words we've studied so far. Try to figure them out silently." He took a blank sheet and wrote. After a minute, several of the students were laughing.

"If you think that was bad, try this!" Ilika wrote again.

This one took longer, but Kibi was soon chuckling.

"Okay, last one."

This time Sata was the first to break into giggles, but she soon had company.

BIG BAD DOG DUG PIT.

PIG GOT BIG BUG AT BOG.

PAPA GOT KEG. PUT PET PUP AT TOP.

Ilika quickly learned that Boro, Buna, and Kodi were his slowest readers, and he took the remainder of the morning getting them comfortable sounding out all the words. Finally, they received the honor of reading the three silly sentences aloud.

* * *

Chapter 25: Freedom is Worth a Million

"I've always felt I was in the wrong place," Kibi said from her heart when they returned from lunch. The others all gathered to listen.

"I've always loved words, especially important words that say a lot. I learned quickly that I couldn't ask my parents about words. The list Ilika gave us this morning would have been enough for them. So I talked to every traveler who came by. When my father found out, he started beating me and telling me strangers were dangerous."

Everyone could see she was holding in tears.

"By the time I was eight, everyone around knew I was smarter than my parents. When another farmer came by to trade something, he'd talk to me first. So my parents told me that if I was so smart . . ." She stopped to deal with her deep feelings. "If I was so smart, I should go off on my own.

"They were wrong," she continued with mixed sadness and anger. "I needed them. But I went, because I was really tired of the beatings. I didn't last long, of course. Once I was a slave, most of the masters liked me because I could figure out how to do complicated things. But their wives hated me. I knew words they didn't know. I knew how to do things they couldn't. So they had me beaten and whipped when their husbands weren't around. I learned to keep my mouth shut."

As Kibi finished her story, she looked for acceptance in Ilika's eyes.

He looked back and smiled. "I, on the other hand, picked you *because* you are smart, and *because* you have good language skills. And I want you to tell me any time you think I'm wrong.

"In fact," he continued, speaking to the entire group, "I've decided to make leadership a regular part of your lessons. Each of you will lead lessons or activities, and then we'll talk about what worked and what didn't, for both the leader and the group."

"Girls too?" Kibi asked with slightly narrowed eyes.

"Of course girls too!" Ilika replied firmly. "Where I come from, there are no differences between boys and girls in anything, except . . . you know . . ."

Several students giggled, mostly girls, and several blushed, mostly boys.

"Today I have to do something for about an hour. So I am putting . . . Mati . . . in charge of doing a good review of the digits zero to nine, both counting and recognition."

Kibi smiled.

✷

Ilika's first stop was the hat maker on Market Way. He selected a cloth sun hat with a neck strap, and arranged for the hatter to come to the inn the following morning.

After reserving the bathing pool, Ilika went by the scribe's shop where his nine bills of freedom were ready. The scribe assured him the official copy had been filed that morning. Ilika paid for the work, and slipped the copies into his shoulder bag.

Just for peace of mind, he went by the city clerk's office near the plaza to see if they had indeed been filed. They were in a pile of things to be done someday, when nothing important was waiting. A large silver piece got them moved to the pile of things that were important.

✷

When Ilika returned to the inn, Buna was counting the toes on Toli's feet, and everyone was laughing.

"Five!" she announced dramatically.

Many of them looked at Ilika to see if he was upset with them.

"Buna, you'd better check the other foot," Ilika said, "see how many toes are over there."

"Five there too!"

Everyone laughed again.

"So," he said when the laughter died down, "what sort of leader was Mati?"

"Funny!" Kodi said.

"She was great," Kibi added. "We really did review, we were just running out of things to count."

"Did you have any trouble with your students?" Ilika asked Mati.

"Yeah! They were in a goofy mood. I sure am glad I didn't have to teach them anything new."

"Uh oh. I'm in trouble, because now I have to teach them something new. But first, I want you all to know that you are officially NOT slaves anymore."

The room broke into cheers and whistles.

"I have copies of your bills of freedom, they look like this," he said, holding one up. "This is my signature, and this is the scribe's seal. I'll read one, and as soon as you know the rest of the alphabet, I'll teach you to read them yourselves."

All ten students became very quiet.

Let all Men know by this Record:

RINI

who was a slave,

as of this date has completed his

Service and has been granted his

FREEDOM

from all previous Servitude.

Witnesseth the granting Master:

Witnesseth this Scribe for

His Majesty

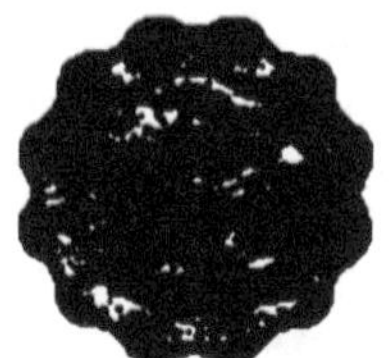

"Wow . . ." Rini said with amazement. "Thank you!"

Ilika nodded. "Is it okay that I keep these safe for you in my shoulder bag?"

"I want to see mine first, please," Neti said.

"Me too!"

"Me too!"

"I should have guessed." Ilika passed them out, and they all sat on their beds gazing at their bills of freedom as if in a trance, smiles frozen on their faces. Sata kept silent, very happy for her new friends.

After a suitable time, Ilika broke the spell. "Are you all ready to learn some numbers now?"

They slowly came out of their trances and placed their precious pieces of paper back into his hands for safekeeping.

*

"Numbers wouldn't be very useful if we couldn't count anything greater than nine," Ilika began.

"We couldn't even use both hands or both feet," Mati admitted, "without getting to ten, and only Sata knows how to write a ten."

"Yes, to make numbers that can express very large values, we have to break them into several different places. Each place has a digit in it, but the digit means something different in each place."

He drew seven boxes side by side on a sheet of paper. "The place on the far right is always the ones place, no matter what base you're using. The digit in that place means just what it says. If there's a three in it, it means three.

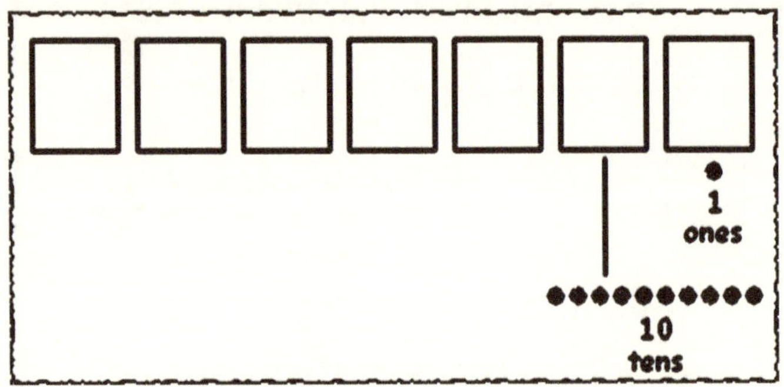

"The next place to the left is the number of bases in our value. Our base is ten, the number of fingers we have, so the digit we put in this box doesn't mean the digit itself, it means that many tens. Let's try it."

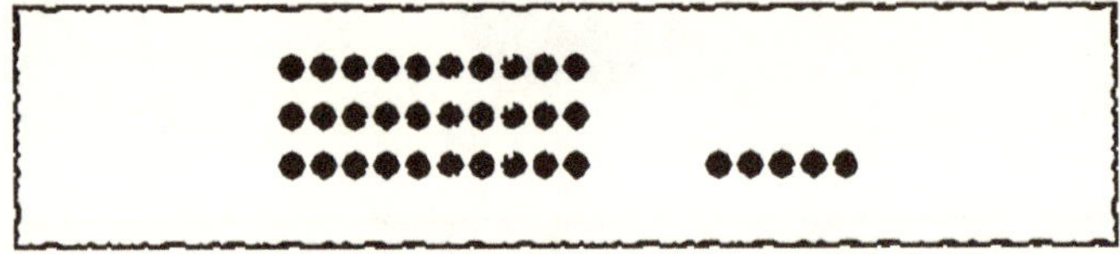

"First I look for whole groups of ten, and there are three of them. Then I look for left-over ones. The answer is thirty-five."

Some students glowed with understanding, while others were unsure. Ilika worked through several more examples, then had each student try one. When he felt they had mastered two digit numbers, he introduced the hundreds place using squares of dots, and the thousands place with cubes of dots sketched as best he could.

"Above the thousands place, there's no easy way to draw them. Just remember that each place, going from right to left, is ten times more than the one before it. Now let's review all the places, including the larger ones we haven't studied yet . . ."

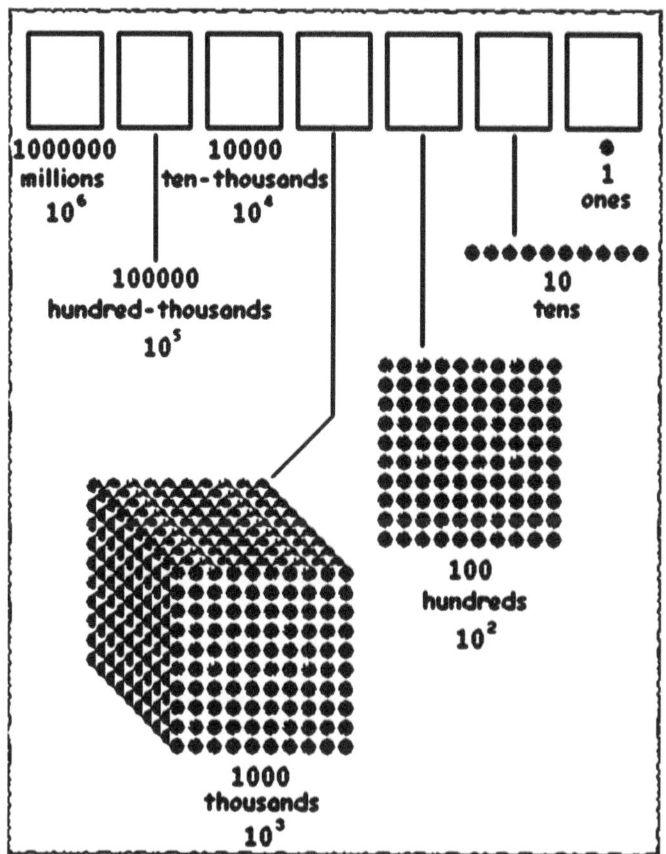

Toli's eyes lit up as his teacher moved from ten, to hundred, to thousand. "Ten thousand, or ten to the fourth power," sounded like a magic spell, and Toli craved to learn all about it. When he heard, "One hundred thousand," his eyes opened wide with wonder.

"One million has six zeros," Ilika explained, "and it is ten to the sixth power. Sata, you once asked me about it, but at the time, I was exaggerating. People often say a very large number when they just mean *way too many*. A real million is a thousand thousands."

Sata wore a very uncomfortable expression, almost a frown, as she struggled to comprehend the huge numbers she was learning.

* * *

Chapter 26: The Gold Piece

After a break, Ilika smiled with an idea. "Let's look at the place values using money. I need to teach you about it anyway. Gather around the table, everyone." He laid the sheet with seven boxes flat on the table.

Everyone got a stool and scooted in close.

Ilika opened his coin pouch. "Luckily for us, your money is also in base ten. Here's a copper piece. Since it's your smallest coin, I'll put it in the ones place."

"I had one of those once," Toli said softly, lost in a memory, "but my master saw it and took it away."

"Slaves aren't allowed to use money," Kibi explained.

"Pass this around so everyone can see it," Ilika said. "A copper piece will buy you a meal or a bath."

The copper piece soon returned to the ones place box.

"This is a small silver piece. It's worth ten copper pieces. When it comes back around, it goes in the tens place box."

Buna's eyes became big and round as she received it. "I've never even touched one before!"

Ilika smiled. "Next comes the great silver piece, worth ten small silvers, or a hundred copper pieces."

All ten students handled the large silver coin with great respect.

"Then we have the small gold piece, worth ten great silvers, and it will go in the thousands place box."

Sata suddenly remembered something about a gold piece she was hoping to earn, and opened her mouth to speak, but shut it without saying a word.

"And finally, the largest coin this kingdom uses, the great gold piece, worth ten small gold pieces, or ten thousand copper pieces."

"Is that the one we get if we finish the lessons but you don't pick us?" Miko asked.

"Yes. Three of them."

The great gold piece went around the table slowly with many comments of amazement at its weight and value. Finally it was placed in its square on the paper.

Ilika immediately saw a problem. "Who still has the small gold piece?"

No one said a word.

"I would like the small gold so I can finish showing you how the coins relate to the places," Ilika said, more firmly.

"I saw it, but don't have it anymore," Kibi said, seated about half-way around the table.

Ilika looked at Boro, seated after Kibi. "Boro, have you seen it?"

"Yes. And passed it on."

Next was Kodi, trying very hard to look innocent. Ilika skipped him.

"Mati, have you seen the small gold?"

"No."

"Rini?"

"No. After the big silver came the big gold."

Ilika took two deep breaths.

"Kodi, it seems the small gold piece disappeared somewhere around you."

Kodi was silent for a moment, but his face revealed the battle raging inside. "Ohhhh . . . here it is!" he yelled and slammed the coin onto the table. Then he knocked over his stool, dashed to his bed, and quickly hid under the blankets.

No one else made a sound.

Ilika took several more slow, deep breaths. All eyes were on him, except Kodi's. He slowly picked up the small gold piece from the table, then sat down on the hearth. A long minute passed before he spoke.

"Kodi . . . I have a gift for you."

Kodi was so surprised at those words that he peeked out from under the covers. He saw Ilika just sitting on the hearth. "You're not going to beat me?"

"No, I'm not. I would never beat anyone for anything. But I need you to come and face me and receive what I have decided to give you, so that we can both get on with our lives."

Kodi slowly crept out from under his blankets, keeping his eyes on Ilika the entire time. He carefully crossed the space between his bed and the hearth, stopping far enough away to dodge a blow.

"Actually, I have two gifts for you," Ilika said in a soft, sad voice. He pulled the bills of freedom out of his shoulder bag, found Kodi's, and put the others back. "I paid five small gold to get you out of slavery. I have given you your freedom, and this bill is yours to keep."

Kodi took the document with a trembling hand.

"This small gold piece must have been very important to you. I give it to you, to do with as you please."

Kodi could barely make his fingers work well enough to take the coin.

Ilika continued. "I do not know what your path in life will be, but I know it is not upon my ship. Since a great deal of trust will be necessary for this group to learn all the things I must teach them, I cannot allow people who destroy trust to stay in the group. Tomorrow we will learn to use the money changer. You may stay until then, and that will give you time to say good-bye to the others."

Kodi was on the verge of tears, but would not let himself cry. He stood a moment longer, then suddenly turned and ran for the door, jerked it open, and bounded down the stairs and out of the inn as fast as his legs would carry him.

*

After the echo of Kodi's footsteps faded, the silence that filled the room was deafening. Ilika closed his eyes tightly, forcing tears to run down his cheeks. Soon he heard faint whispering, and a few moments later, the door closed.

With great hesitation, Ilika opened his eyes. His students were all gone, even Sata. Ten beds for his ten students, and now they were gone.

After several minutes of sitting with his feelings, he made himself stand up. His shoulders remained slumped and his head bowed as he wandered to one of the windows. He could see part of the plaza, even the bakery, but none of his charges . . . his former charges . . . were anywhere in sight.

Suddenly the door opened.

Kibi strode in carrying a tray stacked with bowls and rattling with spoons. Boro came next bearing a lidded cooking pot. Miko and Neti had trays of bread and cheese. Rini had a bowl of fresh greens. Buna carried a tray of cups and Toli had a pitcher of ale. Mati just brought herself and her crutch. At the very end, Sata entered with a wooden shingle stacked with tarts from the bakery.

Ilika appeared completely confused. "Um . . . what's going on?"

"We're celebrating!" Kibi announced with a tone that meant it should have been obvious to anyone with half a brain.

Rini spoke with sympathy. "We could see you needed some time alone."

"We all went downstairs and agreed it would be a really good day to eat in our room," Mati reported.

Sata grinned. "And celebrations require desserts!"

"And ale!" Toli added.

Ilika's eyes remained red and his cheeks were still wet, but he smiled. "I thought . . . I thought you guys were mad at me and had left."

"Mad at you?" Kibi said with disbelief. "We all want to kiss you and hug you and thank you! Why would we be mad at you?"

"Because . . . what I had to do with Kodi . . . maybe was too much like a master-slave thing?"

"That was *nothing* like what a master would have done," Neti informed him. "You are *so* obviously from far away where they don't have slaves."

"You see," Rini began, "we know a lot more about Kodi than you do."

"Kodi's been a thief all his life," Buna blurted out. "Always stealing from his masters."

"We don't much care about that . . ." Kibi began.

"But he's a snitch, too," Miko spat out. "Always ratting on other slaves. If a master offered an extra potato to find out who'd been goofing off, Kodi was always right there, naming names and pointing fingers."

"The really funny part," Neti said, shaking her head, "is that he always goofed off as much as anyone else."

"Wow . . . I'm . . . surprised no one . . . told me sooner," Ilika said hesitantly.

"We don't like snitches, and you don't like snitches," Boro explained, "so we had to let you find out for yourself."

Ilika sighed. "I . . . guess I found out . . . the hard way!"

"Yeah, and we are *so* happy about it," Mati assured.

"You mean . . . you're glad it happened?"

"That's what we're trying to tell you!" Kibi said, waving her arms. "If you had picked Kodi for your crew, your ship would be on the rocks somewhere in no time."

"And all of us would have taken the three gold instead," Miko said with a serious look.

"Wow. I sure am glad I found out about him now, instead of later. Okay . . . well . . . shall we eat?"

"As soon as you put away all this *money* you left sitting on the table," Sata teased.

✷

Kodi ran.

Mosa saw him bound out the front door, but only shook her head.

Kodi clutched his crumpled bill of freedom in one hand, his small gold piece in the other. He bolted across the plaza toward Rumble Town.

The baker saw him dash and bump into several people. They cursed at him, but he was soon out of sight into one of the alleyways.

When the twelve-year-old was finally alone in a narrow street, he began to feel safe and slowed to a walk. His heart pounded in his chest.

At that moment a large man came striding around a corner with a hundred pound sack on his shoulders, not in the mood to give way to some scrawny kid.

Kodi went flying into a pile of old rotten hay. He lost his hold on the bill of freedom, and the breeze took it.

He sprang up and tried to chase it, grabbed several scraps of paper and cloth he found as tears began to fill his eyes, but none of them were his precious paper.

Wandering in the direction of the wind, he looked for the piece of paper that said he was free, and when he could no longer follow the wind, he wandered aimlessly, still looking. He didn't bother to hold back the tears anymore as shadows, then darkness, filled the streets.

*

"This is a celebration for getting your bills of freedom!" Ilika said, raising a cup of ale.

"Yeah!" Toli joined him, "and that includes the freedom to be a thief and a snitch, like Kodi."

"I'd rather be a navigator, or something like that," Mati said with a thoughtful expression.

"Yeah!" the others agreed.

"Mmmm. Good stew," Kibi commented after taking a bite.

"My mother loves cooking for us because she doesn't have to use much meat," Sata said. "She's good with spices."

"Our masters ate meat all the time," Miko said, balancing a chunk of potato on his spoon. "You've got plenty of money, Ilika. Why don't you eat meat?"

Ilika smiled. "Nobody eats red meat where I come from, and I've heard it can cause all kinds of health problems unless you live in a cold place and do lots of hard work."

"Will there be hard work on your ship?" Rini asked.

"Very little."

"Strange ship!" Miko said with a tone of disbelief.

Ilika just smiled.

*

Kodi eventually dried his tears as he stumbled through the dirt streets of Rumble Town. He still clutched the small gold piece in one hand. It was way past dinner time and he was getting hungry, so he wandered on until he came to an eatery. With some fear, he went inside.

"Wha'dya need, lad?"

"Can I get dinner?"

"Show me your money."

Kodi held out the little gold piece.

"That'll buy you all the dinner you want!" the man said with a huge smile, taking the coin.

Kodi felt funny about what he had just done, but his stomach was yelling at him, and he could smell the cooked meat and fresh bread. Soon he was seated at a table and had a large plate of sliced red meat, bread, cheese, a big tankard of ale, and two dishes of custard.

"If you want more, just yell!" the man assured, returning to the kitchen.

By the time he had eaten half his food, Kodi couldn't take another bite.

"What'sa matter kid?" the man asked when he came through collecting dishes.

"I can't eat all this. I gave you way too much money for half a meal," Kodi said, his voice beginning to shake.

"I ain't no money changer," the man said sternly. "If you needed to change money, you should have gone to a money changer."

Kodi began to realize what he had done. Tears were threatening to come back, but he wouldn't let them, not again. He wanted to be strong. He wanted to be smart. He had seen other people pay a copper piece for dinner. He remembered the copper piece in the ones place. He remembered the small gold piece was supposed to go in the . . . the thousands place.

He ran out of the eatery and didn't stop running for a long time.

✷

"Do I owe the baker for these tarts?" Ilika asked as he licked the tasty purple filling.

"Nope. They're paid for," Sata said with a smile of pride.

"We couldn't have gotten them without Sata," Kibi explained. "She's the only one with money."

"Would you like me to pay you back?" Ilika asked the innkeeper's daughter.

"No, my treat! You've done lots of wonderful things for us."

"You all need coin pouches," Ilika said thoughtfully, "so you can get used to handling money and doing some of the buying."

"Wow!" Boro said with amazement. "You'll let us go out and buy stuff? But where will we get the money?"

"I'll give it to you, as long as you spend it wisely."

They all looked amazed but happy.

"We'll do more money lessons tomorrow. Let me think . . . we have clothes coming, and a bath in the afternoon. Oh, yeah, the hatter is coming in the morning. We can squeeze in some lessons."

"What will Kodi be able to do with that coin you gave him?" Rini asked with concern.

"Well, if he uses it wisely, he can eat at inns for almost a year, or buy food in the marketplace for about two years. Or he could buy a cart and an old horse or a donkey."

"I'm glad," Rini said, relieved. "I wouldn't want him to be out there with nothing."

"That's why I gave it to him."

"I'd *never* trade all the stuff you're going to teach us for one measly gold piece," Buna said.

"Me neither," Sata agreed. "There's no way to get an education unless you're noble-born."

"I've been in the College of Nobles," Ilika said. "I don't think they learn very much there. Not nearly as much as you guys are going to learn."

"Do you think they learn what a million is?" Sata asked.

"I doubt it."

"I know what it is now!" she said proudly. "Um . . . I think . . ."

Everyone chuckled.

✷

A light rain fell that night, then toward morning the air became quite cold. Kodi found old hay behind some barrels, but was shivering and tossing and turning to stay warm. A city guard heard him rustling.

"Hey, lad. Don't you have somewhere to go?"

"No. Not anymore," Kodi said with a shaking voice.

"Do you have any family?"

"No . . ."

"Do you have money for an inn? A copper will get you bed and mush a few blocks from here."

"All gone."

"Come on. I can't let you stay there. I'll take you somewhere they'll give you something to eat, a place to sleep, and work to do."

"Okay." He knew what the guard meant. He was ready to go back. This freedom stuff was just too strange.

* * *

Chapter 27: Walking Tall

Lively conversation and funny jokes bounced around the breakfast table, with hardly a comment about the incident the previous day. While they ate, the innkeeper removed the extra bed.

"Okay," Ilika began as they scraped their porridge bowls, "I'd like . . . Miko and Neti to do a little shopping for us."

The young couple's eyes lit up.

"A big wagon of leather goods comes to market every day. See if they have money pouches. Sata already has one, so we need eight."

"Can we go into a shop?" Neti asked with barely-controlled excitement.

"Yes, but only on Market Way. One of you should deal with the money while the other handles the goods. Keep an eye out for each other. Remember what you are not."

They both grinned.

Ilika untied his own pouch from his belt and handed it to Neti. "Two silvers and eight coppers inside. It's okay to use a silver if the bill comes close, as we have to pay a fee any time we change money, and everyone loves a tip."

The hatter showed up just as the group was finishing breakfast. Ilika had him measure Miko and Neti, then the pair headed out into the marketplace for their first adventure together as a free couple.

*

The hatter took his measurements with a straight face and departed, promising the hats in two days.

Ilika then asked Boro and Sata to go shopping for belts. Sata carefully emptied her own copper pieces onto her pillow and counted them before receiving the shopping money from Ilika.

Not long after those two departed, the tailor arrived with a huge sack over his shoulder. Ilika paid for the lot, and the remaining five students sorted tunics, pants, shorts, and socks, making a stack on each person's bed.

Soon Miko and Neti were back with eight money pouches, all of different colors or designs. Everyone gathered around and listened to their report.

"We found the leather wagon right next to a sweet biscuit cart," Miko began. "It smelled so good! We bought one pouch at the wagon, but they were all the same."

"So we went to look for a shop," Neti continued. "That's where it got a little scary."

"I was just carrying the pouch from the wagon . . ."

"And the shop clerk thought it was one of his."

"But Neti was smart. She pointed out that it was different from the ones he sold . . ."

"And I said I'd go get the leather man from the wagon if he still didn't believe us."

"He backed off, and it's a good thing," Miko said.

"Because then we bought seven pouches from him!"

"Very well handled, both of you," Ilika said, nodding. "What lesson should we learn from your experience?"

"Don't take stuff you buy at one place into another," Miko said with a serious voice.

"Everyone see the sense in that?" Ilika asked, looking around the group. "I am only displeased with one thing in your report."

Neti's face lost its smile.

"You smelled sweet biscuits and didn't bring any back."

Everyone started snickering, and soon Neti was smiling again.

"Go finish your shopping!" Ilika commanded with a grin.

Miko and Neti laughed all the way out the door.

*

Boro and Sata soon returned with nine belts, and not much later ten sweet biscuits came in the door. Before they sat down to a mid-morning snack, everyone wore a belt and a money pouch.

"There's a lesson in what happened to Miko and Neti that I want you to understand," Ilika began after eating part of his biscuit. "I did not choose you because you are mindless slaves. I chose you because you are smart and have strong spirits. Some of you will be the crew of my ship someday. Some of you will, I hope, begin honorable professions here in this kingdom. In either case, you will have to make decisions, sometimes hard ones, sometimes on the spot. You should begin practicing now. When I send you on an errand, I want you . . . no, I *need* you . . . to make all the decisions that life will call upon you to make. Sometimes it will be little things, like sweet biscuits. Sometimes the issues will be bigger, maybe even life or death."

He looked around the table. They all seemed to take in his words.

"I think this shows you the difference between the master of a slave and the captain of a ship. The master just wants you to work, not think. As a ship's captain, I will be overjoyed whenever I do *not* have to tell my crew what to do."

"Damn!" Boro said. "Me and Sata saw some candy."

Everyone else pointed at the door until he and Sata got the message and scurried out.

*

When everyone was back in the room, Toli stood up clumsily and cleared his throat until everyone was listening.

"I was very young, so I'm not sure if I remember it right. I know my mother died. Then it seemed like my father had a new wife right away. For a while I was really confused, 'cause my father wanted me to think she was my mother.

"The only problem was, she hated me — at least that's what it felt like. I think she wanted a slave, but my father wouldn't get one. So she used me for one."

"So you were a slave before you were a slave," Buna said with understanding.

"Yeah. Then my father died, so there was nothing to stop her from treating me like a slave. I slept in the shed, worked all day . . . you know. But it made me mad, so I didn't do things very well. By that time I was about ten.

"Eventually she started running out of money, so she sold most of the land, and then she sold me. I yelled and screamed that I was her step-son and she couldn't sell me, but no one listened."

Toli paused to deal with the painful memory. After swallowing several times, he continued. "I think my father was smart, and would have taught me many things, but we just didn't have time . . ."

Toli's story faded into silence as he looked at the floor. Buna stood up and gently put her arms around him.

*

The feelings that lingered from Toli's story made the group very quiet during lunch and the afternoon hours that followed. Ilika talked about money changers, and explained the one-tenth fee that was charged.

When he judged they were ready, he gave each a great silver piece and they walked to the nearest money changer. The guard let in one person at a time, who emerged wearing a smile of pride and a jingling money pouch.

* * *

Chapter 28: Pastries and Ethics

As soon as the group settled into their room after getting a late lunch, Ilika jumped right into language studies, first reviewing the consonant stops, then adding the fricative and the nasal sounds. Toli grumbled that TH could be two different sounds. Mati felt it unfair that one of the voiced fricatives didn't have a letter. Every sound deserved a letter, she asserted.

	lips	teeth	gums	roof
stops				
unvoiced	PAT		TAB	KEG
voiced	BAT		DAB	GET
fricatives				
unvoiced	FAT	THIN	SINK	SHOP
voiced	VAT	THIS	ZERO	VISION
nasals	MAT		NUT	SING

After they all practiced the sounds, Ilika brought out a large sheet of paper with many words on it, all made from the letters they had studied. It kept them busy for the next two hours.

*

"Can I tell my story now?" Buna asked as they splashed and frolicked in the bathing pool later that afternoon.

"Sure," Ilika said, "unless you want the privacy of our room."

"No, I want to do it while I'm in a good mood. If I let myself get gloomy about it, I might throw things or kill someone."

Ilika and the other students sensed she was at least half-serious, so they gave her their complete attention.

The story began with a very poor family who lived in one small room somewhere in Rumble Town. Buna remembered clearly the day, sometime during the winter of her seventh year, when her mother, tears streaming down her face, explained that her father was dead, and there was only one way they could both survive the winter. A strange man handed her mother a coin and took Buna, kicking and screaming, to the slave compound.

As the years passed, Buna saw how the pretty girls were used by men, so she hardened herself and did everything possible to make herself ugly and crude.

"I guess it worked. I know it made me kind of . . . rough. It was just what I had to do. I don't blame Neti for doing it differently. And if I'm ever rough with any of you . . . it's not because I want to be . . . it's just a habit."

Many voices assured her they understood, and soon everyone was splashing and laughing again.

Ilika looked at his nine charges. Kibi was combing Neti's wet hair, while Rini blew bubbles underwater. Sata and Mati were busy splashing each other. As comfortable as they were bathing together, they were also very respectful of each other. He never saw any of the boys, other than Miko, touch or bump into Neti, and it appeared that Toli and Buna might be developing the same status.

Soon the students began climbing out of the pool, chatting excitedly about their new clothes.

Ilika asked Mati to walk with him. As they moved slowly along, he observed how she gripped the shaft of her crutch tightly.

"Tomorrow, you and I shall visit the woodworker. I think we can get some improvements made to your crutch."

Mati smiled. "Are captains always as nice as you?"

Ilika cleared his throat and spoke in a stern voice. "I've heard stories of crusty old pirates with peg legs who shoot their crew members if they don't work hard enough."

Mati looked at him with a grin. "If you were like that, you wouldn't have picked me."

Ilika smiled, then called ahead to the lead couple. "Buna and Toli! Would you poke around the marketplace and find some dessert for us?"

"Sure!"

*

When Buna and Toli returned, they proudly set a wooden plate in the middle of the table that bore ten little pastries.

Ilika, however, took the next hour teaching them the difference between addition and multiplication. Most of the students were sorely tested by the need to keep their attention on their teacher's words and the sheet of paper, instead of the pastries.

But slowly, student by student, they all came to a clear understanding of the difference between ten plus ten, and ten times ten. Toli and Sata led the way, and Boro brought up the rear.

*

After dinner, they all gathered around the plate of pastries once again.

"There are many ways to divide up something valuable. I'll propose a method, you tell me what you think."

"This is a lesson, isn't it?" Buna asked.

"Yes, an ethics lesson about right and wrong ways to treat each other."

Many serious looks surrounded the table. Rini wore his usual contented smile.

"First method," Ilika began. "I get them all because I'm the captain."

Ilika could feel the anger in the looks that flashed his direction from nearly everyone. "Kibi?"

"That would make you like most of the masters we've had."

"Ouch. Toli?"

"Me and Buna bought them for everybody!"

"Good point. Sata?"

"I wouldn't want to be on a crew with a captain like that."

"Me neither. Do we all agree that method stinks?"

Everyone nodded.

"Good, because where I come from, a captain doesn't get any special privileges. Method two. We fight, and the winner gets all the pastries, maybe sharing them with friends."

Mati pouted. "I'll *never* get any."

"I wouldn't want any," Rini said flatly.

Miko spread his arms. "Nobody here is a fighter!"

"True. But we must remember," Ilika said, "that's how it's done in most places, even though the fighting may be with money or words instead of fists.

"Method three. Since it's food, bigger people get more. Slender people like Mati and Rini only get half a piece."

Many thoughtful faces struggled with the notion. Boro's hand crept up.

"Boro?"

"Well, I'm the biggest, but I don't like the idea. If it was regular food, and I was working more than the others, I could almost see it. But this is dessert!"

Ilika smiled and nodded at Boro. "I noticed that Mati and Rini stayed very quiet."

Kibi raised her eyebrows. "Slaves get a lot of practice at being quiet about things they can't change, which is just about everything."

"Method four. Boys get most of them, girls get the crumbs."

"That's stupid!" Buna blurted out. "Girls are just as good as boys."

Miko raised his hand. "I think it should be the other way around. Girls have to have the babies. That's not easy. Sometimes they die when something goes wrong. I think girls should always get the best of everything."

Neti was glowing.

Ilika nodded. "I made sure, from your test answers, that all of the boys I picked were capable of respecting girls."

Kibi smiled to herself.

"Method five. We are all members of a team, and we share the pastries equally, even if we have to cut them."

"Yes!"

"Hooray!"

"Yeah!"

But since they had ten pieces, no cutting was necessary. Miko proposed, and everyone agreed, that the girls get first choice.

*

Ilika finished the day by talking about the last three letters that made a unique sound. Then he listed several odds and ends that made one or two sounds they had already studied. Toli nearly pulled out his hair with frustration, and proposed they never, ever use those letters. The other students smiled.

HAT	C = S or K
LONG	CH = T+SH
RAT	J = D+VISION
	Q = K
	W = TUBE
	X = Z or K+S

To indicate lessons were over, Ilika blew out one of the candles and stacked the sheets of paper. Without a word, his nine students got out ointments, oils, and combs.

Ilika watched as Sata cleaned Boro's wound. The pain was minimal, and it appeared to be healing.

Next, he glanced at Buna's rashes, now almost completely gone. He also saw the trust she was building with Toli.

Tonight, instead of Rini working on Mati's knee, she massaged his slender shoulders with her little hands, and he wore a blissful smile.

Ilika didn't take too long checking on the others. Someone was sitting on the hearth waiting for him, someone who had never before in her life trusted anyone else to comb her hair.

* * *

Chapter 29: Prized Possessions

Shortly after breakfast, the cloak-maker and his apprentices arrived bearing armloads of thick hooded cloaks, all in the same dark-brown fabric.

Sounds of delight filled the room, and most of the students clearly intended to wear their new cloaks, with the hoods up, all day long, and probably sleep in them as well.

Sata gave a more moderate example. She examined hers with as much joy as the others, tried it on, plunged her hands into the deep outside pockets, then took it off and laid it over the foot of her bed.

Most of the others glanced at the fire in the fireplace, and did the same. Mati, Rini, and Buna were not so easily swayed.

Ilika smiled. "Kibi, would you lead a review of all the letters and words we've studied? Mati and I need to go visit the woodworker and the seamstress."

"Sure!" Kibi said, coming up to the table and picking out the sheets of paper she needed.

*

In the woodworker's shop, after spending a quarter hour experimenting to select just the right place, Mati watched from under her hood as the craftsman made a hole in the shaft of her crutch with a hand drill. Then he carefully pounded a length of smooth, round wood into the hole.

Mati tried it, and could easily transfer most of her weight to the handle. After some finishing touches, Ilika paid the craftsman generously.

In another shop, Mati again watched as the seamstress made a new wool pad for the top of her crutch, and a pad for the handle. The woman used waxed canvas that would keep out the rain, and sealed her stitches with more wax. Both Mati and Ilika were pleased.

On the way back to the inn, Ilika steered Mati toward the bakery.

"Tori, I need to buy a book. Where should I go?"

"There's only one place, deep in Cobble Town. My son can show you. He'll be here soon."

"Okay. I'll take Mati back, then return."

Mati hesitated. "Ilika, I want to make my first purchase. I think we need tarts for after lunch."

"Hmm. I'm not sure 'need' is the right word to use when talking about tarts," he said with a wink.

She grinned. "Okay, want! But . . . you'll have to carry them for me."

"I would be happy to . . . as long as I get one."

Mati nodded, then carefully paid the baker.

Back in the sleeping room, Rini was fascinated by the improvements to Mati's crutch. Everyone else was more interested in the tarts.

"Hands off! They're for after lunch!" Mati asserted.

"How is the review going, Kibi?" Ilika asked.

"Good. We're almost done."

"I need to go out again. I'd like Rini to lead next, and the goal is for everyone to be able to write everyone's name."

Rini swallowed. "Um . . . okay."

*

The baker's son was a mature lad of fifteen, in training to be a scribe. As soon as he finished unloading sacks of flour from a cart, he changed into the set of good clothes he always kept in his bag, and quickly proved to Ilika that he knew Cobble Town well. When they arrived at the bookseller, Ilika gave the lad a coin and wished him well in his studies.

The bell above the door jangled as Ilika entered the tiny shop. Shelves lining most of the walls held many books, some nearly new, others falling apart. A short, hunched, elderly man came out of the back room.

"Greetings to you, young master. What is your pleasure?"

"A good adventure story. Something long and complex, and with a sturdy binding."

The clerk carefully climbed onto a stool, his aged knees shaking. "Hmm. Perhaps . . . no. I think . . . perhaps this." He brought down a thick volume. "Let me see your hands!" he demanded before putting the book within reach.

Ilika presented his hands for inspection.

"Ah! A man who believes in cleanliness. Rare these days. You may examine the book. If you tear a page, you must buy it, or work it off in slavery."

Ilika was very careful. *Bato of Tirenland, Lord of the Isles* appeared to be the type of story he wanted, but was done with intricate, hard-to-read lettering. "I need something that can be read by youth who are just learning . . ."

"Humph. No one appreciates good calligraphy anymore." The clerk took the book and lovingly returned it to its shelf. "Hmm. One of these new story books, I guess."

Ilika opened the cover and found simple lettering with illustrations of battles against dragons, explorations of dark caves by torchlight, and horses rearing up to paw the air while the rider held his sword aloft.

"This is the one I want."

"Ah! Are you aware, lad, what a book like this costs?"

"No . . ."

"A volume like this cannot be had for coppers, you know? Even little silvers pale next to the worth of such a magnificent work of art!"

Ilika nodded.

"I hope you brought your great coins, for a great book can only thus be purchased."

Ilika smiled politely.

"For most people I would not part with this treasure for less than three great silver pieces. But for a lad with clean hands, it will break my heart, but I will allow it to slip out of my grasp for a mere two great silvers. But I'll understand if you've never even seen that much money."

Ilika placed two great silver pieces on the counter.

The clerk smiled.

✷

Ilika strode directly to the seamstress and asked her to make a waterproof cover for the book. She took measurements and promised it that evening.

When he returned to the sleeping room at the inn, nine sheets of paper greeted him, each with ten crudely printed names.

"We couldn't have done it without the lessons you've been teaching us," Rini said with humble pride.

Ilika took the time to look carefully at each sheet of block lettering, and to compliment its author. When Boro came up, he shuffled his feet and held out two more broken pencils. Ilika smiled, and a moment later Boro did the same.

"I am very impressed," Ilika said to the entire group. "Now that you know the letters, I bought you something to read." He opened his shoulder bag and placed the book on the table.

Toli jumped up from his bed. "Wow! A book!"

Mati frowned. "Our masters would never let us in the same room with a book!"

"What's it called?" Miko asked, brimming with excitement.

"You'll have to find out by reading," Ilika replied with a grin.

"Can we start now?" Rini begged, bouncing up and down.

"No! It's lunchtime and I'm hungry."

"And there's dessert!" Mati reminded everyone as they headed for the door.

✷

"Tuh . . . huh . . . eh," Mati said carefully, sounding out the letters of the first word in the title of the book.

"Tuh, huh, eh," Toli confirmed, looking over her shoulder.

They looked at each other. They looked at the others squeezing in around the book as closely as possible. Most everyone shrugged.

Ilika said nothing.

"Tuh, huh, ee," Kibi tried.

Everyone still wore blank looks.

"In this one little word," Ilika explained, "you are experiencing the entire process of learning to read. Remember, you already speak this language. You already know all the words in this book. All you need to do is recognize them."

"Tuh, huh, ee," Mati tried again.

"You are remembering the sounds of the individual letters, but have forgotten that sometimes two letters work together to represent a different sound . . ."

Suddenly Kibi burst out laughing. Everyone looked at her. "Thththeeeee!" she said with a big grin.

"Yea, Kibi!"

"Why didn't I see that?" Toli grumbled with envy.

"Okay, let's look at the process," Ilika said. "You tried the simplest thing, the usual sounds of the letters, and you didn't recognize the word. No need to stop, just try something else."

"Actually, I thought of the unvoiced TH first," Kibi admitted. "But it didn't do any good."

"Eventually, if you keep trying things, you'll find a word you recognize," Ilika continued. "Now you have to memorize the word. If you had to go through this whole process every time you came to that same word, you'd never be able to read anything. Look at the word. Say it aloud. Burn it into your minds."

They stared at the word. They spoke the word. It became their first prized possession in the world of reading.

*

"The Adventures of Godi and Tima," Buna read proudly, putting together what they had just taken an hour to figure out.

"Godi must be the warrior guy in the picture," Miko speculated, a bit more puffed up than usual.

"And Tima's that Elf girl with the bow," Mati said with admiration.

"I know it seems painfully slow right now," Ilika said, "but as you learn more and more words, it'll go faster and you'll be able to read more at a time."

After they gazed at the title page for several more minutes, learning all they could from the title and the illustration, Buna lovingly closed the book.

* * *

Chapter 30: Plans and Preparations

Early the following morning, as Ilika lay in bed thinking about the supplies he wanted to get for his students that day, elsewhere in the city others were awake, preparing to deal with issues that were, to them, much more important.

The high priest stood at the front of the windowless stone room, making eye contact with each of his associates as they entered. Rarely-used secret handshakes were exchanged as the guests settled themselves into the soft, throne-like chairs.

Once all the guests had been checked off the list by the priest at the door, he departed, closing the door behind him.

"Brothers," the high priest began, his arms outstretched. "Events that Almighty God set in motion long ago are coming to pass."

A rumble of curiosity filled the room. The high priest let it run its course.

"The king has proven he is not going to cooperate with the Powers from On High. His most recent mistake was to deny our righteous request to not be taxed like peasants."

The murmur that followed lasted several minutes, but eventually died down and another high priest slowly rose from his seat and spoke.

"The king is standing in the way of the Church, we all know that. But he is very popular with the people, and has the complete loyalty of the city guards and the noblemen. It would be impossible to rise up against such a king."

Agreement rippled through the room as the speaker lowered himself back into his chair.

"Well spoken, my friend. As things are, we cannot make a move. We must first tarnish him in the eyes of the people. I have my ears to the streets, just as you do. Many people are starting to grumble about the king's open policies concerning the port, the roads, and the city gate."

"Surely," the head of another order said as he rose, "there are a few travelers and some strange goods entering the kingdom. They haven't caused any trouble, and I must say, some of those strange goods are quite tasty."

Laughter filled the room for a moment, and the high priest at the front smiled. "We don't need to wait for them to cause any trouble. We just need to make the people *think* they are going to be trouble."

"How do you propose to do that?"

"A young character has appeared in the city recently who pretends to be a captain even with no ship in the harbor. I have interrogated him, and my agents have been tailing him for several days. He is from so far away that his values are completely different from ours. He has purchased a number of slaves, freed them without so much as a day's work, and seems to be *educating* them."

The rumble of anger that ran through the room made the high priest smile.

*

"I need four strong helpers," Ilika announced after breakfast, looking around the room. "Toli, Miko, Boro, and Sata. Neti is going to lead a mathematics lesson for the rest of you."

"Me?" she said with a very unsure voice and a troubled expression.

"Yes, you. A leader doesn't have to know everything. A leader leads. All of you can work together to figure out the answers. Remember when I explained the difference between addition and multiplication?"

"Um . . . addition is one number *and* another," Neti said, searching her memory, "and multiplication is . . . I forget."

"Can you help, Mati?"

"Ummmmmm . . . repeating a number so many times?"

"Right. I've made some little pieces of paper with problems on them. The cross means addition. The X means multiplication. You can use paper and make dots if that will help."

"So . . ." Neti said, looking at a problem, "two X three means two repeated three times?"

"Exactly."

"Okay. This isn't so hard."

*

Ilika set a leisurely pace as he and his four helpers walked up Market Way toward the city gate.

"It's always a little spooky going this way," Toli said with an uncomfortable look.

"Yeah," Boro agreed. "This is the way to the . . . you-know-what."

"The slave market?" Ilika guessed.

Miko frowned. "The one place in the city I *never* want to see again."

Ilika grinned. "But now you could just go in, buy a mug of tea and a biscuit, and sit down and watch the show."

"Yeah, and what if we saw an old friend on the block?" Boro said, his voice full of feelings.

Ilika dropped his fake grin. "I know. I was almost sick the first time I wandered in. That was before I learned I could find people like you in there."

"Where are we going?" Sata asked.

"Saddle shop, up here on the right just before the . . . you-know-what."

The five entered the large shop and looked around. Everything necessary for horses and wagons filled wooden bins or dangled from pegs on the walls – saddles, harnesses, bridles, ropes, and brushes.

"Here's what we want," Ilika said when he found the leather saddlebags. "It looks like they have plenty. Help me check each one, make sure it's in good shape."

The clerk took each set of bags after it was inspected and stacked it on his table. "They're all newly oiled – should last you a lifetime."

"Bedrolls?" Ilika inquired.

The clerk stacked up ten canvas bedroll covers. "Saddles? Bridles?"

"We don't have the horses yet. Besides, this is all we can carry today."

"Okay . . . the bags are a silver, and the rolls are new, so they're a silver too . . . so that's two greats."

Ilika paid and the clerk showed them how to put the saddlebags over their heads, each person carrying two.

"These are heavy!" Toli complained.

Sata rolled her eyes, and made no attempt to hide it.

✷

As soon as they unloaded themselves, placing a pair of saddlebags and a bedroll on each bed, Ilika set his previous helpers to the math problems, and drafted Buna, Neti, Rini, and Kibi. "Sorry you have to sit out these shopping trips, Mati. You are now the leader."

Mati nodded and started organizing the flash cards.

The cart in the marketplace that sold woven wool blankets stocked a variety of colors and patterns, which delighted Kibi and Buna. Neti paid more attention to the quality of the workmanship. Rini was happy just to stand in the sunshine.

Ilika loaded each person with four thick blankets. They staggered back to the inn, barely able to see over their burdens.

✷

"Let's see how the math is going," Ilika said. "Mati, you were here all afternoon. How would you guys do seven plus four?"

Everyone gathered around the table.

"Um . . . we'd make seven dots, then four more, and count them all."

"Okay . . ." Ilika began with a slight smile. "The human mind is capable of doing several things at once. If I start counting up from seven with part of my mind, and count the number of times I've done that with another part of my mind, I can do this problem in my head. I say, 'eight, nine, ten, eleven.' I stop when I've counted up four numbers, and there's the answer, eleven."

"Huh?" Neti said with a confused look.

Ilika went through the process on paper with Neti while everyone watched. He knew from facial expressions that Sata and Toli were ready to jump in with both feet.

"Five plus three," Ilika said to Neti.

"Six, seven, eight, ni . . . no, just eight."

"Yes! You've got it!"

Ilika did one with each student, giving Sata and Toli harder problems. As the numbers got larger, Ilika showed them how to break the number being added into several chunks. Rini tackled the last problem of the lesson, fifteen plus nine, after being reminded that nine was three threes.

"Sixteen, seventeen, eighteen . . . nineteen, twenty, twenty-one . . . twenty-two, twenty-three, twenty-four!"

"Hooray for Rini!" the rest cheered.

But Rini remained standing with a serious expression that made everyone else fall silent.

"I'm the last at something else too," the slender lad said. "I've listened to everyone tell their stories, but I haven't told mine. Every time someone tells about how they got into slavery, it makes my stomach all twisted into knots, especially the girls dealing with . . . you know. My story is very different. I chose to be a slave."

Looks of shock and disbelief came to almost everyone. Only Ilika didn't seem too surprised.

"I wasn't very old when I realized I didn't want to be like other people. Everyone around me, even my parents and my brothers and sisters, were hurting themselves, using each other, and abusing all the wonderful animals and plants. Everywhere I looked people were taking beautiful things and making them ugly . . . taking truth and changing it into lies . . . and making good into bad. It made my stomach twist up just like your stories do.

"I began walking into the woods and the hills, as far as I could go. At first my father would whip me when I got back. But I kept going, walking for hours, then all day, then several days. My father finally gave up when he realized I wasn't taking any food with me, just finding things in the wild.

"One day I met a man. He told me what it was like being a slave, since he had been one. I knew I didn't want to be a slave all my life, but I decided it might help me understand people. So I became a slave and it taught me many, many things. But now I'm really happy I'm with all of you."

When Rini fell silent, he looked around and saw everyone looking back at him with respect, almost wonder.

"Thank you Rini," Ilika said. "Now that we have all shared our stories, I want to point out something. If your lives had not unfolded as they did, including the poor family lives most of you had, and the slavery all but one of you endured, I would not have found you, and we would not be together now."

✷

At dinnertime, good appetites greeted a tasty shellfish stew. With some hesitation, the innkeeper wandered by the table.

"The wife and I were noticing that you're getting travel gear, and wondered if you'll be heading out soon."

"A few more days, maybe a week," Ilika replied. "Boots should be done tomorrow, and then we can start walking around the city a bit more."

"Mosa made a pudding for you tonight . . ."

"Yum!" several voices said at once.

". . . and she'd like to make a special meal for your last day here."

Ilika smiled. "That would be wonderful, Doko."

"I'm learning how to add and multiply numbers!" Sata told her father with pride.

Doko smiled at his daughter with pride. "Maybe you can come back someday and teach your hopeless brother!"

✳

Up in their room, nobody let Ilika forget about their book.

The first paragraph, which described the green forests and snowy mountains where the story took place, was figured out a word at a time by candlelight, each word by a different student, Ilika right there to help with problems. Each sentence was then read by each and every student. Finally the entire paragraph was read over by Ilika.

That one paragraph of half a dozen sentences filled their minds for the rest of the evening. They repeated parts of it to each other as sores were tended. They discussed it as hair was combed. They imagined being there as shoulders were massaged.

No doubt those magical woods and mountains filled their dreams after everyone was ready for bed and the candles were blown out.

✳ ✳ ✳

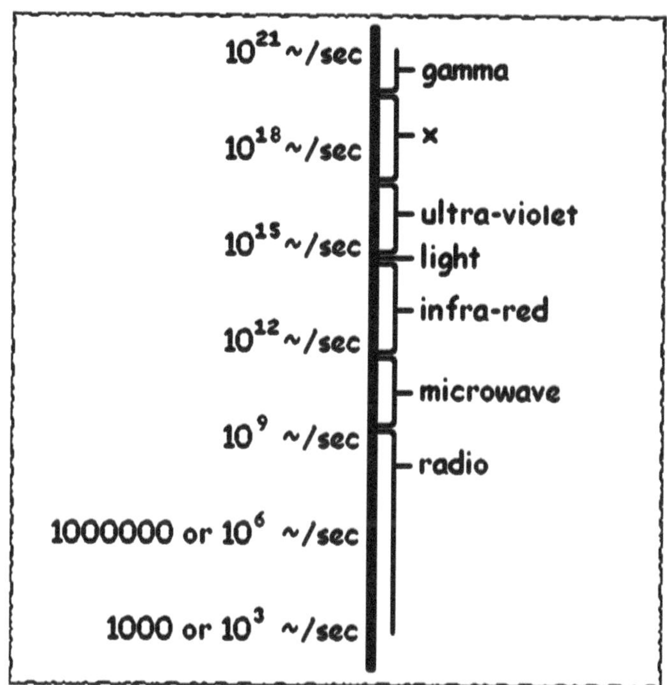

Chapter 31: Learning to Walk

"Why do we need sun hats?" Buna asked the following morning after the hatter had come and gone.

Ilika started drawing on paper. "The light and heat and other energy from the sun has different qualities depending on how fast it vibrates. The light we can see is just a tiny slice, out of this whole range of energy vibrations. Too much light can blind us, and when it hits our skin, it changes into heat. Also, the energy with vibrations a little slower than light, called infra-red, we can't see but it also changes into heat when it hits something.

"The energy that vibrates faster than light is the most dangerous because it can cook us without ever making us hot. Ultra-violet will tan our skin. X-radiation can go right through us, make us very sick, and if we get too much, we'll die."

All their faces were bleak.

"There are many unseen, but very real things out there, and the crew of my ship will have to understand them, and deal with them all the time."

"Um . . . ten to the twenty-first power . . ." Sata said with wide eyes. "That's more than a million, isn't it?"

"A million is only ten to the sixth power, way down here near the bottom."

"So . . . the faster they vibrate, the worse they are?" Boro proposed with a thoughtful look.

Ilika nearly did a double-take at Boro's insight, then smiled. "Yes, although the danger also varies with their strength."

"And the hats will protect us?" Mati asked with hopeful eyes.

"Hats and other clothes protect us from the visible light, infra-red, and ultra-violet," Ilika explained, returning to his drawing. "The air protects us from most of the high frequency radiation, and the low frequency energy isn't a problem.

"The important thing to remember is that you all have long, exciting lives ahead of you. You now have very good reasons to protect yourselves from all dangers, and too much solar radiation is just one small danger in a world of many dangers.

"You are no longer cheap labor. I have spent more than a year of my life preparing to come here and find you, I will spend half a year with all of you, and then years more training five of you to be my crew. You are important. You are worth protecting."

They could barely hold in huge grins of pride.

"I'm going to wear my hat!" Buna asserted with her squirrelly expression while putting it on.

Toli snatched it off her head. "It doesn't help in here!"

She crossed her arms. "I'll wear it if I want to. Put it back on my head, or no massage tonight."

Everyone snickered as Toli carefully replaced the hat on Buna's head, adjusting it just the way she had it.

✷

The innkeeper's knock rattled the door, and the bootmaker entered the room sideways, pole across his shoulders from which ten pairs of boots dangled. His profile, combined with his animated personality, made them all laugh.

"Hello again, hello! You all have socks, I hope?"

"Yep!" they cried and dashed to their beds to put them on.

"Let me see, who is Kibi?"

She presented herself, and he directed her to a stool.

"See, I etched your name onto your boots right here. You have rather wide feet. Point your toes and pull up on the bootstrap . . . yes. That looks like a good fit. Mati?"

She hopped over from her bed.

"I made yours myself. One boot for your left foot, one moccasin to keep your right foot clean and dry. But you should take it off every night, right along with your boot, so your poor little footsie doesn't rot."

"I will," she promised, laughing at his words.

"Who is Kodi?"

Complete silence filled the room.

"He's no longer with us," Ilika said with a hint of sadness. "I'll pay for his boots, but you can keep them and give them to someone his size who needs them."

"Okay. Who is Boro . . ."

Everyone had fun receiving their boots from the kind and humorous bootmaker. When he finished getting them all familiar with their new footwear, he told a few more jokes, bowed to them all, and said good-bye.

Ilika went to the table and opened the book. Nine pairs of booted feet scrambled to find places, some stumbling or getting tangled up with other booted feet. Ilika waited until all was quiet.

The second paragraph spoke of the birth and childhood of Godi in a village at the edge of the mountains. Ilika continued with each person working through a word they didn't already know. At one point Sata was able to read four words in a row before coming to a new word that needed sounding out.

As before, each sentence was read by each student, then the entire paragraph was reread, this time by Kibi.

*

While they ate lunch, they plotted and schemed.

They had all been thrilled by the plan to take gifts to Pica in Cobble Town. Some of them thought they should take tarts, one for each of them and several for the artist.

A few said candy would be better.

Rini suggested that Pica would like some real food, bread and cheese and such. He had heard that artists didn't make enough money to buy food.

Ilika's eyes gleamed as he saw an opportunity. "The majority is in favor of tarts."

"Yeah! So we're getting tarts!" Toli snapped.

Ilika continued. "But a majority ruling is just power politics, and that often makes people lose sight of the real goal. What is the important thing we're trying to do today?"

"Say thank you to Pica for helping you find us," Neti said confidently.

"Saying thank you is speaking from your heart. Groups sometimes try it, but they aren't very good at it. Only individual people can really speak from the heart."

"So . . ." Boro began thoughtfully, "we should each say thank you to Pica and give her a gift that we've chosen."

"Yeah!" several others agreed.

Toli looked a bit dejected.

"But in any group celebration," Ilika added, "there's a place for something that everyone shares."

Toli brightened.

"So I'll get tarts," Ilika said, "and each of you may spend a few coppers on a personal gift of your choice."

They quickly finished their lunches.

"Even though you are making individual purchases, I want you to stay in pairs. That way, if anything nasty happens, one of you can help the other, or run for me. Keep your money in your pouches until you're paying for something. We meet at the bakery in half an hour."

*

Ilika chatted with Tori while his charges fanned out into the wagons and carts of the marketplace. Rini and Boro soon returned with a small wheel of cheese and a bunch of flowers. Buna and Toli acquired candy and a leather pouch. Miko and Neti bore two different sizes of paint brushes. Last came Kibi, Mati, and Sata, who had pooled their coppers to get a big basket of fresh fruit.

Tori assembled a wooden platter of tarts as Ilika spoke to his students. "Cobble Town is for middle and upper-class people who live there or have business there. You are students in training for highly skilled professions, and you are visiting a friend. You have every right to be there, so carry yourselves as such. Slaves hurry. Students take their time and learn from everything they see."

They began their journey into streets once forbidden to all of them, except occasionally Sata. Ilika came last, keeping an eagle-eye out for problems. In good spirits, all the students laughed and talked about their gifts.

At each street corner, Kibi glanced back at Ilika, who gave her hand signals for direction. Mati and Sata came close behind Kibi. The rest proudly carried their gifts for the artist who witnessed their last day of slavery.

Kibi, at Ilika's direction, rounded a corner.

A city guard came striding down the street directly toward them.

Somehow Kibi sensed the importance of what she said and did in the next second or two. "Good day, sir! A piece of fruit for you?"

"I'm in a hurry," the guard said, "but thank you, I haven't eaten lunch yet."

Some of the students mirrored Kibi's attitude, complimenting the guard on his handsome uniform as he made his selection from the basket. Others just stood proudly in their clean clothes and new boots.

Ilika's heart filled his throat when he saw the situation, but he forced himself to stroll to the other side of the street to look at some herbs growing in a planter. A couple of students joined him there.

"Mmm. Nice and ripe," the guard said. "Thank you, I must be going."

"Bye!" Kibi and the others said cheerfully, waving.

As soon as the guard's back disappeared around a corner, Ilika went to Kibi. "Very good job, everyone."

"I almost wet my pants," Kibi mumbled under her breath.

Ilika nodded while others snickered.

They resumed their journey, and were soon at the bottom of a narrow wooden staircase that ascended the outside of a building, ending at a small door at the attic level.

"These stairs may not be strong enough for more than one or two at a time," Ilika said, glancing at his students. He climbed, platter of tarts in hand, while the others waited.

Pica greeted him and saw the others below. "Come in, my friends! Come in!"

They started climbing, one at a time.

"Rini, will you help Mati go up?" Sata asked, looking at the wooden steps with a frown. "You both together weigh about what I do."

Mati began the climb with the slender boy at her side. Rini warned her about a knot hole in one step, and she carefully placed her crutch to avoid it.

Soon they all gathered inside the artist's attic room. A simple bed and a small table took up one wall, two easels stood with the only window behind them, and a big, round, tattered rug covered most of the floor. Pica found a stool for Mati, and the rest got comfortable on the rug.

"So these are the lucky ones," the artist said with a big grin, looking them over. "I remember all of you, and I might have guessed Ilika would pick you."

"There was one more," Neti said, "but he tried to steal a gold piece from us, so we kicked him out."

Ilika smiled at Neti's choice of words. Others were soon talking about their new clothes and the lessons they were doing.

"I . . . I am happier than I have ever been before," Mati announced, her voice full of joy, "and you helped to make that possible, so me and Sata and Kibi got you this basket of fruit!"

"Sorry there's a piece missing," Kibi said with a hint of guilt. "I bribed a guard on the way here." She reached out to embrace the artist, but Pica grabbed her arms.

"It's okay," Ilika promised. "They're all lice-free now."

"Oh, good!" Pica said and hugged Kibi.

Everyone laughed.

The cheese came forth, followed by the flowers and the leather pouch, all of which were rewarded by kisses on the cheek. Then came the candy and the paint brushes.

Only Ilika was left. "I couldn't have done it without you, Pica. I couldn't have found these excellent students. Thank you for all your help." He let her choose the first tart, then the platter went around the circle.

They ate in silence for a few minutes, smiling eyes feasting on their bond of friendship.

Once the tarts disappeared, Pica invited them to gather around her easels to see what she was painting. She talked about the materials used to make her paints, including, she said with a glance at Ilika, the poisonous metal lead. She explained how she could only paint a little at a time because the paints took so long to dry, which was why she always had at least two things on her easels, even if one was just for practice.

"Is it hard to learn to paint?" Buna asked.

"Yes . . . and no. You're learning to read. Is it hard?"

"Not really."

"That's because Ilika only picked people who could learn new things, and wanted to. Do you remember the boy named Tiko?"

"Sort of," Buna said with a shrug. "I didn't know him very well."

"He hated the idea of learning new things, thought he already knew everything. For him, learning to read might have been impossible. Painting is like that. If you really want to, and you have a spark inside you for it, you can do it. It still takes lots and lots of hard work."

"Reading's like that for us too," Boro explained. "We have to work at it, but we love it."

"I'm glad," Pica said, nodding. "Me, I can read and write my own name, and that's about it."

Most of the students looked surprised.

"You guys can stay and talk if you want, but I have some paint I have to blend before it dries."

As evening was approaching, Ilika and his students said good-bye. The artist promised painting lessons to anyone interested on their next visit.

*

After descending the staircase, Ilika asked Miko and Neti to lead them back to the inn. The evening was warm and pleasant, Neti found the way back flawlessly, and Miko kept watch for any problems.

* * *

Chapter 32: Learning to Run

The sun was setting as the group, with Neti and Miko in the lead, rounded the last corner into the plaza. Eight city guards and one high priest, spread out in front of the inn, awaited the students and their teacher.

The captain of the guard stepped up to Ilika while the rest of the guards encircled the group. "I hereby execute this warrant for your arrest, as well as those with you."

Ilika could almost feel time slow to a crawl as the crisis penetrated deeply into his mind and heart. Countless lessons he had been taught over the years paraded before his mind's eye, lessons about keeping himself and his charges safe and free at all times. As he breathed slowly and struggled to clear his mind of the guilt that threatened to overwhelm him, his right hand moved toward the bracelet on his left arm.

Then he remembered the many other tactics he was supposed to try before doing anything drastic. Courage began to replace fear as he breathed deeper, stood taller, and held his head higher. He began to recall facts about this kingdom he had studied before arriving.

One more deep breath helped to spread the courage throughout his body as he faced the captain of the guard with his hands on his hips. "On what charge?" he demanded loudly, slowly, and firmly.

The captain was silent for a moment, not expecting this question, although he knew it was allowed. "On the charge of subverting the established order by freeing and educating slaves who have not earned their freedom."

The high priest's face held a huge, self-satisfied smirk.

The captain continued. "These charges were made to the Magistrate of the Plaza yesterday, who issued this warrant." He reached out to take Ilika's arm, and the other guards moved to do the same with his students.

"WAIT A MINUTE!" Ilika demanded.

The captain hesitated.

"The common law in this kingdom is that a man may treat his slaves any way he wants. The Slave Protection Decree was signed by the king's grandfather fifty-three years ago. It limited that right only in that a master may not kill or maim a slave. It set no limits on how nice a master could be to his slaves. The king affirmed all previous decrees at his coronation eight years ago."

The smirk disappeared from the high priest's face.

"Therefore," Ilika went on in the sternest voice he could muster, "I hereby CHARGE this priest with subverting the laws of the kingdom, and attempting to replace them with the doctrines of his religious order. Further, because there is a high probability he will take refuge behind his walls, which are not subject to warrant, I petition for the immediate ARREST of this priest so that he may be required to answer this charge."

The high priest's blank expression quickly changed to a frown.

The captain of the guard folded his arms on his chest and pondered the situation. "As a city guard of command rank, I have the authority to hear and consider your petition for arrest. Do you understand that by making this counter-charge, the Magistrate will most likely show you no mercy if he rules against you?"

Ilika took another deep breath to counteract the sensation of teetering on the edge of a cliff. "I understand. I know the laws and I believe the charge against me to be improper, and the charge I have made to be sound. My petition stands."

The captain rubbed his chin. "I find the charge that has been made by this man to be worthy of a hearing by the Magistrate. I further find his grounds for immediate arrest to be sufficient. They shall all be arrested until the case can be heard by the Magistrate."

"WAIT!" the high priest barked.

The captain folded his arms again. "What now? Having made my decision, I cannot unmake it."

"Perhaps not," the high priest said. "But you can receive the dropping of charges if a party discovers that . . . new information has come to light and that he has been . . . hasty in his accusations."

"I can."

Ilika looked at the high priest. "Perhaps we have both been . . . hasty."

"Do I understand correctly," the captain said with narrowed eyes, "that both of you are willing to drop your charge if the other is also willing?"

"Yes," the high priest spat out.

"Yes," Ilika said calmly.

"So be it. You are all free to go. Men, you are off-duty."

The guards surrounding the students departed and allowed Ilika to see them for the first time since the incident began. They clutched each other for dear life in twos and threes, faces pale, eyes showing fear.

"Kibi, take them up to the room. I'll be right there."

Ilika turned to the captain. “Thank you,” he said while digging into his money pouch with shaking fingers.

“Just doing my job.” He received the small gold piece from Ilika with hardly a glance, and slipped it into his own pouch. “Knowing the decrees saved you. The high priest couldn’t get away fast enough. His mistake was going to a Magistrate, so the charge would have to be decided based on law.”

“What do you think he’ll do now?” Ilika asked.

“Well . . . he might go home and consider himself lucky. Or he might go to the king and ask for a warrant by special favor. In that case, there would be no defense, I couldn’t do anything to stop it, and no one else could either.”

Ilika thought for a moment. “If he went directly to the king, how long would it take him to get back here with the warrant and a guard?”

“Hmm. His Majesty usually eats dinner late on nice days, so he might see someone of that status right away. The high priest could have his warrant in as little as . . . an hour. You know, he’s been making noise around the Court for more than a week, but it was only a couple of days ago we started hearing of some bratty little slave who was bad-mouthing you and telling everyone where you were staying.”

Ilika cringed, but quickly recovered. “So . . . right now my students and I could walk out the gate and no one would stop us?”

“True. And my lieutenant went that way, so the gate guards will know that the charge against you has been dropped. But . . . if you leave by the gate, we’ll know, and if another warrant comes out, we’ll have to search the countryside.”

Ilika took another deep breath. “Thank you for your good decisions and your insights. I should go and comfort my students.”

“I need to log this incident and find something to eat.”

*

When Ilika entered the room, he ignored everyone and immediately went to the loose piece of wallboard where he kept his supply of gold coins. He had never before opened it with anyone else in the room. This time he emptied it.

At the table, with the help of his own money pouch, he made nine stacks, each containing one great gold piece and a few smaller coins. “Everyone, put one of these stacks in your pouch, and keep it there unless need forces you to bring it out.”

Most of their hands shook as they picked up the coins.

“Sata and I are going downstairs for a few minutes to talk to her family. The rest of you . . . pack.”

Sata was immediately on her feet heading for the door, with Ilika close behind.

When he passed Kibi, he paused, pressed something into her hand, and said in a soft voice, “Pack this.”

Kibi looked at the small tube in her hand, of some soft material that allowed her to glimpse what was within. Judging by the light orange color that showed through, the heavy weight, and the length of the tube, she guessed she was holding about fifteen great gold pieces. Her entire body suddenly became hot and sweaty as she realized the great value of what she held, and the immense trust Ilika was placing in her. She quickly plunged the tube to the bottom of her saddlebags.

*

With dinnertime approaching, Sata's family was at work in the kitchen when Ilika and Sata entered.

"It wasn't any of us!" the innkeeper declared, fear showing in his eyes.

"Relax, Doko, I know who it was. It was Kodi."

Mosa and her son turned their attention to Ilika, though they continued to slice cheese and stir the stew pot. "Sata already told us what happened outside," Mosa said.

"Good. So you know I'm not a criminal. We're leaving tonight, going to stay with an artist friend in Cobble Town."

"Oh, goodie!" Sata said with a smile.

"I think I'm caught up on my regular bills," Ilika said, "but I want to give you those bonuses you earned for your confidence." He laid four small gold pieces on the work table.

"We shall make you a very special feast as soon as we serve the other guests!" Doko declared.

"Sorry. We must go now," Ilika asserted. "Say your good-byes, Sata, you won't have another chance."

Sata hugged her mother, who was silently crying, then her father. When she came to her brother, she took his hands in hers. "I'm not taking my gold piece. I want you to keep it, and when you get married, it's for your wife."

The lad was speechless.

"Okay . . . we must go," Ilika said firmly. "We'll visit when we can."

Sata hugged her mother one last time, then followed Ilika back to their room.

*

Sata hurried to pack, and Ilika did likewise as he spoke. The others gathered near his bed.

"I am very sorry that I didn't see this danger coming. I plan to be much more careful in the future, and do everything necessary to keep us all safe and free."

"It's okay," Neti said with a soothing tone. "You were wonderful out there, knowing all the laws and stuff."

"I had to read them before I came here. But we don't have much time, so I need to get right to the point. Do you all trust me enough to do exactly as I say?"

They all affirmed with words and nods.

"There must be no talking until we're safely at our destination, unless necessary to deal with something. We shall go a very round-about way. You all need to be like shadows, invisible, seen by no one. That means do nothing to attract attention — no running, no laughing, no talking."

He looked at them. They all seemed to sense the danger. "Sata and Mati will go first, out the back door, through the plaza, and will wait in the alleyway behind the bakery."

Mati nodded.

"Rini and Boro will go next, out the front door, and will wait silently in front of the woodworking shop."

"I know where that is," Boro said.

"Toli and Buna, back door, then wait at the corner by the hatter's shop on Market Way."

They nodded.

"Neti and Miko, do you remember that seamstress a block from the bakery?"

"Um . . . yes," Neti said, nodding.

"When you see me or Kibi walk by, say nothing. Just quietly follow a little way behind. Boro, take Mati's bags, and Miko, take her bedroll. Any questions?"

"What is our meeting place in case we can't find each other?" Toli asked with a shaking voice.

"I . . . haven't decided," Ilika replied after a moment of thought. "We will find each other, I promise."

He waited another moment. "Okay, Sata and Mati, head out."

Everyone else strayed to their beds, except Kibi who sat down close beside Ilika.

He took a piece of paper and started drawing a plan of the plaza and the nearby streets. Kibi paid close attention. He marked all the places where the pairs were going to wait. Then he put a star at one more street corner, deeper into Rumble Town, and pointed to it. Kibi nodded her understanding.

Ilika went to the candle, lit the paper, and tossed it into the fireplace. "Rini and Boro, time to go."

As soon as the two boys were out the door, the rest started getting on cloaks and saddlebags.

"Toli and Buna, your turn."

Ilika looked around the room one last time. The only thing remaining was excess paper that Doko could use.

"Neti and Miko, go."

Only Kibi remained, still close beside him. Ilika put his arms around her, and they held each other tightly for a minute. "Go out the front, get Mati and Sata behind the bakery, Toli and Buna at the hatter, then meet me at the place I marked, which is near a dentist."

She nodded, rose, and slipped out as silently as a ghost.

He waited another minute, blew out the candle for the last time, and left by the back door.

* * *

Chapter 33: Kibi

As Kibi crossed the plaza, she could still feel Ilika's arms around her, still hear his heartbeat, and still smell his scent. She thought she had been in love once before, but being a slave made it impossible to find out if it was anything more than passing feelings.

Seeing the happiness between Miko and Neti made her smile, but she knew that Neti's deepest dream was to have a house and children. Kibi, during the last few years, had come to realize that she wanted something different.

Although her feelings for Ilika were growing stronger every day, she did not yet know if she could love him without losing her dreams. She was willing to live her life alone if that was the price of remaining free . . . both of slavery, and of anything that felt like slavery.

The problem was . . . she couldn't yet see clearly what she wanted. She felt certain it wasn't here, in this kingdom, but she couldn't name a place where it might be found, or even point in a direction she should go.

Ilika had told them nothing about his country. Kibi sensed he couldn't tell them, that they just wouldn't understand if he tried. But as she listened to him talk, and watched him teach his students, she became convinced that his country was a place where people could do much more important things than keep house and raise children. And the only way she knew of getting there was to earn a place on his ship.

As she crossed the nearly-empty plaza, every step she took was a step on the path to her dreams. She vowed to learn and do everything necessary to continue that journey.

*

When Kibi wandered slowly behind the bakery, Mati and Sata rose from where they sat on a crate and silently followed.

As she approached the corner by the hatter's shop, she heard Toli whispering some concern to Buna. She hadn't realized a person could whisper and whine at the same time. He fell silent when she passed, and they followed. No longer needing to be recognized, Kibi put up her hood.

After going around three more corners, she approached the meeting place just past the sign in the shape of a tooth, now silhouetted against the evening sky. Ilika and the others were not yet there, but two men stood talking in the street. She quickly made the decision to keep walking right on past.

Not knowing the meeting place, her two pairs of followers thought nothing of it.

Suddenly Kibi realized this was an example of something Ilika talked about. Following his directions was important, but doing that mindlessly could be just as dangerous as not doing it at all. If her dreams were going to come true, she would have to be willing to improvise when unexpected things happened. So far, like earlier that day with the guard and the piece of fruit, her instincts had served her well.

Right now she had to decide how long to lead her little troop away from the meeting place. She figured there was no hurry, now that they were far from the inn. This part of the plan would be best carried out slowly and carefully. Since she did not want the two men to see them coming back, she decided to continue on for a few more minutes.

They passed a couple of lads carrying baskets of bread and vegetables, a girl leading a sheep, and a bit later an aged peasant woman entering a doorway. Kibi decided it was time to turn around.

As soon as she reversed their direction, Toli began whispering again. Kibi hoped Buna would do something about it, and the girl seemed to be trying, but Toli wasn't responding. Instead, he was getting louder.

Kibi remembered the firmness Ilika had used earlier to get them ready and out the door. She wondered if she could find that kind of strength inside herself. As Toli started talking out loud, she knew she had to find it or they could be in trouble.

Kibi spun around, strode up to Toli, and looked him right in the eyes. "We are all scared," she whispered firmly. "I have to get us to the meeting place, and I won't let one person ruin it. If you're coming with us, you need to do it *silently*."

"Yeah!" Buna whispered.

"Yeah!" Sata and Mati agreed.

Kibi could see he was close to tears. "Buna," she whispered, "hug this boy until he feels safe."

Buna was quite willing to do what Kibi asked. They all stood in the middle of the dark street, and by the light that lingered in the sky, could see fear flashing in Toli's eyes, but somehow Buna's embrace gave him the courage to remain silent.

Several minutes passed and Buna continued to hold Toli with all her might. Kibi and the others waited, all huddled closely around the entwined couple. Only one old man came by, muttering something to himself and paying no attention to the silent group.

Finally Toli sniffled a few times and whispered his willingness to go on.

Kibi led the way. Buna held Toli's hand tightly while Mati and Sata came behind.

When they got back to the meeting place near the dentist, the two men were gone, and Kibi recognized the five shadows waiting on the corner. She breathed a deep sigh of relief.

*

Ilika began to silently lead them deeper into Rumble Town. Kibi dropped back to the end of the line. Just enough light remained so she could make out the pairs — Sata and Mati by the unique motion of the crutch, Boro and Rini because of the contrast in their profiles, and Toli and Buna due to Toli's height. The remaining pair, also holding hands, must be Neti and Miko.

Soon they could see the outer wall of the city, higher than all the rooftops. Ilika guided them around another corner, then stopped in front of a doorway. He knocked and waited.

The little window opened.

"We request sanctuary," he said softly.

* * *

Chapter 34: Sanctuary

The door quickly opened and Doti ushered them all inside.

As soon as they were in, she stepped outside and opened her senses to both the visible and invisible forces around her. After about a minute, she stepped back in and locked the door.

Following Ilika's example, they all removed their boots in the entry room, then stacked their saddlebags and bedrolls in the larger room beyond. They found places to sit on stools at the work tables, or on the rug that covered most of the floor. A tall candle glowed on one of the tables, illuminating several ceramic jars and a mortar and pestle.

Doti came in, lit another candle from the one already burning, and looked them over. Then she disappeared through a doorway and returned a minute later with a loaf, crock of butter, board, and knife, setting it all in front of Buna.

"There is one of you missing."

"Kodi . . ." Ilika began.

". . . is a slave again," Doti completed the thought. "And if I read the signs correctly, he is the reason you are now on the run."

"Partly. Some of it is my fault." Ilika went on to share his feelings of guilt for not anticipating the danger.

The healer frowned, then said, "I did not see it coming either, and if I could not see it, it was well hidden, I assure you. Cast your guilt to the wind."

Buna began passing out slices of buttered bread.

"Ilika was great with the guards!" Boro proclaimed, and went on to describe the defense and counter-charge with admiration.

Ilika added the information he received from the captain of the guard after the students went inside.

"I was just wondering," Sata began with a wrinkled brow, "what happened to the idea of going to stay with Pica?"

"That was dis-information, Sata," Ilika explained. "It allows your family to give an answer if they are pressed, but leaves no trail to us. It's another example of how a lie is not always a bad thing."

Sata struggled with mixed feelings.

"It's late and you are all tired," Doti observed. "I shall make a tea that will help you rest and heal. We will talk more tomorrow."

They got their bedrolls and began arranging themselves on the floor. Ilika noticed that Buna and Toli immediately claimed spaces side by side. Kibi was somewhere near the kitchen door.

Soon Doti returned with a tray of mismatched cups. They all gathered around, and the warm tea seemed to relax the stomach and calm the mind. They all sat in silence, unwinding from the excitement and danger, until they could no longer keep from yawning.

*

After Ilika made sure everyone else was comfortable, and was just about to crawl under his blankets, he noticed Neti standing over him.

"I need to talk to you," she asserted in a serious tone.

He got up and followed her through the heavy curtains into the entry room.

"You asked a lot of Kibi today. She had to deal with something big. I don't know the details, but she's exhausted, and really needs to snuggle with someone tonight. You know who that needs to be."

"I . . . like her very much, but . . . I don't want her to feel like I'm pushing anything . . . and she always seems to prefer sleeping on the other side of the room . . ."

"That's because she needs you to *ask* her. She's a heart person, even though she's very smart. Your lessons aren't enough. You have to take care of her heart too . . . or you can't keep asking her to help you lead."

Neti went back through the curtain and crawled into her bedroll beside Miko.

Ilika followed slowly. He sat on his blankets for a long time, a variety of conflicting feelings coloring his face and posture from one moment to the next. Eventually he took some deep breaths for courage, stood up, went to Kibi's bedroll, and seated himself on the floor.

She wasn't asleep, and immediately raised her head.

"Kibi, would you like to sleep next to me?"

The smile that flashed onto her face told Ilika all he needed to know. Without further words, they worked together to move her bedroll to the free space beside his.

Suddenly the room was filled with clapping, as no one else had been asleep either.

* * *

Chapter 35: In the Eye of the Storm

As morning light crept into the sky, Doti tiptoed about the house opening curtains. Soon steam was rising from a tray of cups in the middle of the room, and a bright, fruity aroma filled the air.

Ilika peeked out from under his blankets. Kibi was still asleep close beside him, almost more under his blankets than her own. He gently stroked her shaggy black hair, and she slowly opened her eyes and began to stretch.

Others were already up, sitting on the ends of their bedrolls sipping tea, or going back and forth to the toilet room. Doti brought in a kettle of porridge and a stack of bowls. She got a stool and sat with them.

"Tibo has gone to Port Town for a couple of days to buy herbs. I was starting to get a little lonely, but now I have a house full of people!"

"We are grateful to you," Ilika said.

"I know who my brothers and sisters are, and I'm not talking about those religious orders where they call each other 'brother' and 'sister' all the time. I've seen the high priest who made the charge against you. He's so full of himself, he wouldn't know a god if one bit him on the nose."

Most everyone laughed, including some trying to drink their tea.

Ilika chuckled. "Do you know if there's any way out of this city . . . that the guards don't know?"

The healer thought as she sipped her tea. "I believe so. It hasn't been used for a long time, and may take great courage."

"We've got lots of that!" Rini said with a toothy grin.

Ilika smiled. "I want to get the best possible map of the kingdom before we go."

"I will do your shopping," Doti asserted. "You should not step outside my door until you have a path before your feet, and darkness to hide you."

"Thank you."

"When I go out, I'll see if a new warrant has been posted, and if just for the city, or kingdom-wide. Usually only serious criminals are sought beyond these walls."

Ilika puffed himself up. "That's me, serious criminal, freeing and educating slaves!"

Miko grinned and looked at his teacher with intense eyes. "We are all your partners in crime!"

Ilika chuckled and bowed his head to Miko. "I am honored, fellow criminal."

*

When Doti went out, Ilika began a shopping list. "Let's do the dishes and clean up any messes we've made. Remember, our freedom, maybe our lives, depend on our friends right now."

A kettle was soon heating over the kitchen hearth, and several students teamed up to handle the dishes. Boro found two brooms and tossed one to Miko, who swept the entry room.

When they all returned to the large room, Ilika was sitting on the floor making a chart of many numbers. The students looked at it with wonder, as if it was straight out of a wizard's box.

"Life on a ship is very much like this," Ilika explained, looking up at them. "Sometimes there's an emergency, and when it's over, you take a moment to unwind, then go back to the routine things that need doing. I need to teach you how to multiply numbers."

For the next three hours, the nine students learned everything about multiplying single digits. They drew rectangles of dots to represent the problems, then counted them. They practiced counting by twos, threes, fours, and fives. With some hesitation, they learned to use the multiplication table. Finally, they did as many problems in their heads as they could.

They also learned the commutative property that allowed them to do the problems in either direction, and the special cases of multiplying by zero and one. By lunchtime, they were all mentally exhausted, begging Ilika to let them chop wood or carry water.

*

"There most certainly is a new warrant out for you," the healer told them when she returned. "I spent a little silver and learned that the high priest tried very hard to get it kingdom-wide, but the king just laughed. So the high priest has made it a standing rule in his order that all priests and monks must inquire for news of you any time they are out in the countryside, which is often. If he gets word of you, he will ask the king to send guards."

Ilika thought for a moment. "If we don't stay in one place very long, then they'll always come too late. Hopefully the king will get tired of that."

Doti nodded, then spread out the map she had purchased. Most of the students had never seen one and gathered around, their eyes wide with fascination.

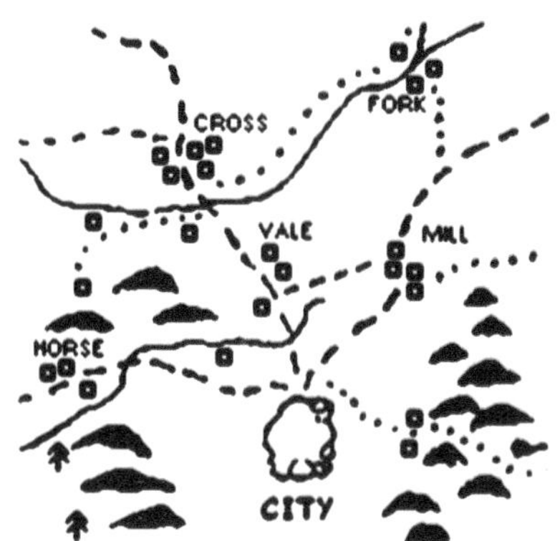

Doti pointed out the capital city and surrounding countryside. "The nearest horse trader is just a few miles down the western road," she explained, "but I think it might be closely watched. I recommend you get your horses from farms, one here, two there. Most farms have old horses they will sell for a few silvers."

Ilika looked thoughtful. "I'd really like to get a mount under Mati as soon as possible."

"I know of a donkey for sale," Doti responded, "a mature jenny. Also, a friend is looking into the condition of the old tunnels in the walls. They were originally built for the city guards, but later abandoned and only used by smugglers. It will be a dark and dangerous way, and you must come out at night and make your way into the wilderness before morning."

The students sparkled with interest, but some also looked fearful.

"I'm putting lantern and shovel on the shopping list," Ilika said as he wrote.

"Flint and steel knife," Miko added.

Ilika looked puzzled, but wrote what Miko requested.

"Don't worry about food when you get outside," Doti said. "Any farmer's wife will gladly feed you for a few coppers."

Having reminded herself of food, Doti listed the roots and herbs that could be found in her kitchen, and told them to make a stew. She quickly ate some bread and cheese, then ran around gathering supplies, explaining that she had a baby to deliver.

"Open the door to no one. Tibo has a key if he should return early. He will be interested in your story, as he has no more love of the religious orders than I."

She departed with her bags of potions and tools, and let the door lock behind her.

*

"So . . ." Ilika began, looking at his students, "who knows how to make a stew?"

"I think," Kibi said, "Sata should be the leader of this project."

Sata grinned. "I want two helpers, one for the fire, and one for vegetables."

"Choose."

"Um . . . Boro and Neti."

As soon as the stew was simmering, Ilika gathered everyone and explained many things about the map. They learned how to place it to match north on the map with true north. The symbols for hills, mountains, forests, rivers and springs, and towns and roads, all like little pictures, were easy to remember.

"This map doesn't have a scale, but I happen to know your kingdom is about fifty miles wide." He laid one edge of a blank piece of paper across the middle of the map, then made marks on the paper until it was divided into fifty equal sections. "It looks like about half an inch on the map is a mile on the ground."

"So you can measure the distance between things by looking at the map?" Sata asked with wide eyes.

"Roughly. If I put my scale between the capital city and Port Town, I can see they're about twenty miles apart."

Nine pairs of eyes counted the marks, just to be sure.

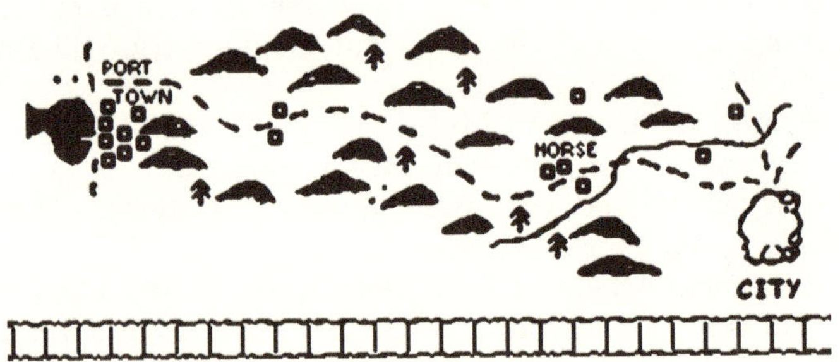

"Neat!" Toli said, fascinated by the process.

"But it could be sixteen, and it could be twenty-four," Ilika warned, "because this map wasn't drawn to a perfect scale. Also, I have measured a straight line, as the bird flies. It could be thirty miles by road."

Sata and Neti had to tend the cooking pot, so Ilika sat back while others tried measuring distances on the map.

"So you think the scale could be off by . . . two tenths either way?" Rini asked.

Ilika blinked in surprise. "That's my guess, Rini."

When the cooks returned, he went on. “I’m going to divide the kingdom into sections,” he said, making light pencil lines, “and the one we’re in goes from the hills around the capital city, up to the forest in the north. Each section will have an emergency meeting place in case we get separated. It doesn’t matter how we get there, or how long it takes. Some of us might take a day, and some might run into problems and take a week. See this little village in the forest? It’s small and unimportant.”

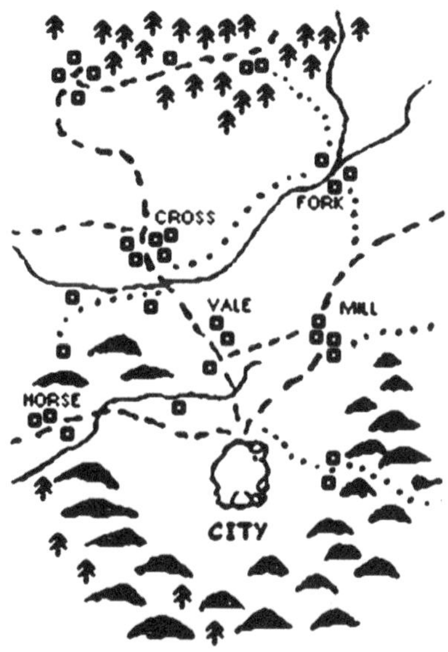

Once everyone memorized the meeting place, Ilika put away the map and everyone got ready for lunch.

*

“This is terrible!” Buna declared with her squirrelly expression as soon as she tasted Sata’s stew.

Sata bravely held back the tears.

Ilika cleared his throat. “Since this is Sata’s first time making a meal, we should give criticism gently.”

“I’m sorry,” Buna mumbled.

“It’s okay,” Sata said with a frown after swallowing several times. “I can taste it too.”

“Something . . . slightly bitter,” Neti said thoughtfully, rolling the bite of stew around in her mouth.”

“I think I know what it is,” Sata said with a guilty tone, looking at Neti. “I think one of the herbs got more bitter as it cooked.”

“Well, it’s not anything that will hurt us,” Miko said in defense. “I’ve tasted spoiled food many times, and this is way better!”

Rini chuckled. “And when you compare it to having nothing to eat, it’s pretty good!"

Many heads nodded from personal experience.

"I have an idea . . ." Ilika pondered aloud. "May I try something, Sata?"

"Sure."

Ilika disappeared into the kitchen, and returned a moment later stirring something into his bowl. He sat back down and turned to Kibi. "Tell me what you think of this, please."

Kibi took a spoonful of his stew. "Wow! It's great! What did you do?"

All eyes were on Ilika.

"I remembered that often bitter and sweet together make a good flavor. Have you ever tasted chocolate?"

Only Sata nodded as she disappeared into the kitchen, returning a moment later with the honey pot.

"I just used a little, about a quarter of a spoon," Ilika said.

Sata scooped, stirred, and tasted. "Yes! Thank you, Ilika!" The honey pot was quickly passed around.

"Well," Ilika said with a slight smile, "you do have to know a *few* things to become a ship's captain."

*

After the dishes were done, Ilika got out their precious book and they tackled some new paragraphs. Godi grew quickly and learned everything he could about travel and adventures. He was much less interested in farming and other aspects of settled life.

The girls were excited when Tima was introduced. The Elf child was born high in a great oak tree, and had the birds of the sky for her earliest playmates. By the time she was three, she loved running in the forest, and would have gone hunting with the older youth if they had allowed it.

Ilika noticed Kibi doing something that made him smile. "You're starting to figure out new words without sounding them out. That's wonderful, but I need you to teach them to the others."

"Oops. Um . . . forest . . . f-o-r-e-s-t."

*

When everyone took a break from lessons, Toli and Miko went snooping around in the kitchen. They didn't find sweet biscuits or tarts, but soon created a plate with thin slices of bread, each one buttered and dribbled with honey.

"Mmm, good!" Neti complimented.

"Neti, you have just introduced our next lesson."

She suddenly looked guilty. "I have?"

"It's all about good . . . and bad. Right . . . and wrong."

Neti shrugged. "Um . . . I don't know very much . . ."

"Actually, you know a lot more than you think."

"What about Kodi?" Kibi asked, her head tilted slightly askance.

"Good question. Is Kodi bad? Let's see if we can figure that out."

As the plate was now empty, Ilika had their undivided attention.

"The words 'bad' and 'wrong' are vague. We have to break them down into two different ideas. The first is when we make a mistake, like Sata did this morning — she put too much of some herb in the stew. But she didn't make the stew bitter on purpose. It was an accident, an error.

"The other idea is when we *know* something is wrong, and choose to do it anyway. I can't get inside the high priest's head, but I'm pretty sure he knows I didn't commit any crime or hurt anyone. Yet he chooses to use his power to seek my arrest. Where I come from, that's called evil."

"So if Sata had made the stew bitter on purpose, that would be evil?" Rini proposed.

"Yes. And if the high priest honestly thought I had committed a crime, then he would be making a mistake, but wouldn't be evil."

"I think . . ." Mati pondered, looking at the ceiling, "that Kodi didn't know he was doing something wrong. He hadn't gotten it through his head that you weren't a master."

"So in your opinion, he made a mistake, but is not evil."

"Yes."

"I disagree!" Miko burst out.

"Miko?"

"Kodi is not stupid. We all knew five minutes into the test day that you weren't a master."

"Okay, we have two different opinions, each one has some possible merit, and there's no way we can ever decide this for sure. Now comes the really interesting question. How do we know something is good or bad, right or wrong?"

"Sometimes we just know from experience," Miko said, "like that bitter herb shouldn't go in a stew . . . unless we add honey."

"Sometimes there's a law, or a rule our parents make, that tells us," Sata proposed.

Most of the former slaves frowned, unable to relate to Sata's idea.

"We can ask someone who knows a lot, like you," Boro said.

"Some things are good because everyone does them, or bad because no one does them," Neti said.

"Our hearts can tell us," Kibi said softly.

Everyone was silent and thoughtful for a moment.

"Which way is right?" Mati asked.

Ilika smiled. "They all are. Some are better in some situations, others at other times. The one I can teach you is called logical reasoning. Without it, you can't make good decisions no matter what you know."

They looked interested and confused at the same time.

"Logic starts with things we know from life, just like Miko said. For example, we know that when it rains, the ground gets wet and muddy. So let's say you hear the rain pounding on the roof all night long. When you get up in the morning, are you going to put on sandals or boots?"

Buna burst out laughing. "That's so easy!"

"I agree, that one's pretty hard to miss. Here's what the logic looks like. R is for rain, and W for wet."

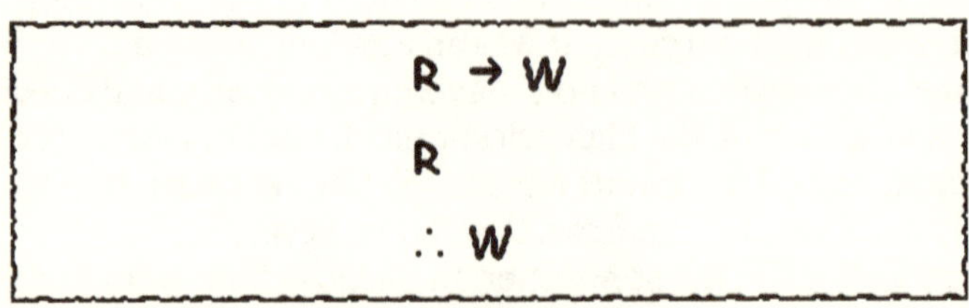

$$R \rightarrow W$$
$$R$$
$$\therefore W$$

"If we know that rain causes wet, and we know it rained, then we also know it will be wet. It's called Modus Ponens."

The students repeated the mysterious name to themselves while gazing at the symbols. "Makes sense to me," Miko said after a minute of thought.

"We can also use it in reverse. Let's say you were asleep all night in the house and don't know if it rained or not. You get up in the morning, go outside, and everything is dry and dusty. What would you think?"

Kibi laughed.

"These are so simple!" Toli said.

Ilika smiled. "Oh yes, but when the situations get complicated, it's easy to make mistakes. Here's what this one looks like."

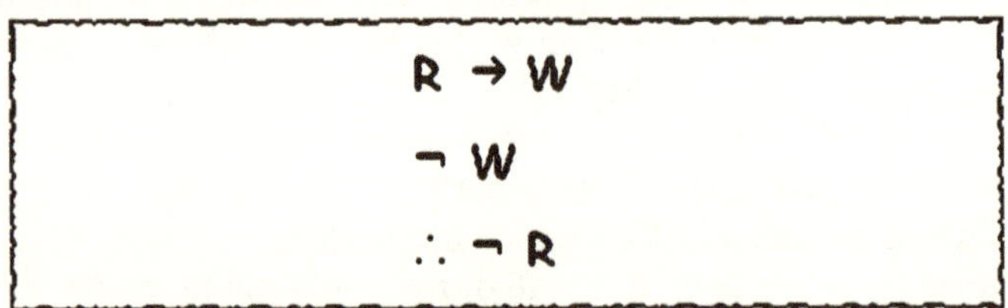

$$R \rightarrow W$$
$$\neg W$$
$$\therefore \neg R$$

"If we have the same relationship between rain and wet, and it's not wet, then we know it didn't rain. It's called Modus Tollens."

"That one makes sense too," Boro said.

Sata's hand went up. "Bitter herb causes bitter stew. No bitter herb, at least next time, therefore no bitter stew!"

Ilika smiled. "Sorry, Sata. It doesn't work that way. You just fell into a very common logic error, called a fallacy."

Sata frowned. "I did?"

"Yes. It doesn't work because there are *other* things that can make the stew bitter."

"Like burning it?" Toli suggested.

Ilika nodded. "But I want you to understand, Sata, there's nothing wrong with your idea. It's just that you can't assume the stew will be okay that way."

"I think I understand," Sata said, her face scrunched in thought.

"I don't," Neti said with a blank expression.

"Let's try that fallacy with the first example. You slept outside so you know it didn't rain. Are you going to sit down right beside an overflowing water trough?"

Neti laughed. "Okay, I get it. If the ground is dry, you know it didn't rain. But if it didn't rain, the ground might still be wet!"

*

Sata and Neti worked with the entire pot of stew, adding a little honey at a time, until it was just right. As the sky darkened outside, Ilika and his students sat in a quiet circle on the rug in the healer's house, spoons scraping bowls. Miko apologized for the lack of dessert.

"During the next few months," Ilika began, "we will sometimes have hot food and cold drink, cheeses and desserts. At other times we will have a dried up crust to share, and not know how far it is to the next farmhouse or inn. But we will always share alike in our fortune or misfortune. That's what being a team is all about."

"I'd rather share a crust with you guys than be a slave in a palace," Mati said with deep feeling.

After eating, candles were lit and it didn't take long for the bowls and other dishes to be washed. Buna poked Toli until he carried several armloads of wood from the storeroom to the wood box. Suddenly a key was heard in the lock, and Doti stepped into the entry room.

"I'm glad you're still awake," she said, setting down her bags. "I have news, but first I must find something to eat."

Everyone finished what they were doing, and a minute later the healer came out of the kitchen with a bowl and spoon. "This stew is delicious! I will have to get the recipe from you."

Sata and Neti smiled at each other.

"First of all, there is a new baby boy in the world, and his name is Zeno."

"Hurray!" all the girls cheered.

"There's an apprentice midwife staying with them tonight, and I will check on them tomorrow. Also, I have to help you get ready, because you must leave tomorrow night."

"We've been studying the map," Toli announced proudly.

"Good. Fact is, the person who can get you into the old tunnels has to leave on a journey in two days, so it's tomorrow night, or you're stuck here for a long time."

"If you can buy us a few things, we'll be ready," Ilika assured her.

"You have to get lice treatments also, or the eggs will hatch and you'll have bugs again. I'll show you the process, and then you can do each other. You'll have to keep the fire going and water heating all day long."

"We can handle that," Miko said, nodding at Boro.

"And I have something for Mati. About a mile down the western road, you will find a faint trail on the right just past a large oak tree. Down that trail is an old ruined shack and a little corral. Tomorrow night, a donkey I have purchased will be delivered to that corral."

"I don't know anything about donkeys," Mati said, "but I think I'm going to learn!"

* * *

Chapter 36: Departure

All of the students, save Mati, bounced around the house with excitement on the day their adventure would begin. Doti was out the door early to check on her patient, but promised to be back soon and reminded them to heat all the water they could fit in her kettles.

While they waited, they rolled up their bedrolls and tied them tightly. Ilika was amazed at the care they took packing, almost caressing their extra socks and underwear before tucking them lovingly into their saddlebags.

Doti returned by mid-morning, saying all was well with the new mother and child.

"Kibi?" the healer called.

"Madame?"

"Have you felt anything walking around on your head?"

"Just Ilika's comb and fingers."

Several of the girls snickered.

The healer began looking through Kibi's hair. "I'll treat you first. I bet your hair takes forever to dry."

"Twice that long," Kibi said with smiling eyes.

Ilika, Sata, and Neti watched as Doti carefully worked the soapy lice potion into every bit of Kibi's hair and scalp. Then they left her with a pot of warm water to rinse her head and finish her bath over the drain in the corner of the toilet room.

*

As noon approached, Tibo returned from Port Town. The couple spent some time in the kitchen seeing what herbs he had found and catching up on news, including Ilika's escape plan. As Tibo had no patients that day, he took Ilika's shopping list and went out. Doti left soon after to stock up on food from the marketplace.

An hour later the healer returned with carry-bags full of food. Neti got a board and knife, and they all gathered in the main room to eat.

"I found some rich fruit and nut cakes in the market that come wrapped in waxed cloth," Doti said. "I got you several for your journey, and some small cheeses."

Soon Tibo returned with a good rope, a small shovel, and a piece of red flint. He ate some bread and cheese, then went out to continue his shopping. Ilika handed the flint to Miko.

All afternoon, student after student emerged from the toilet room with wet, clean hair. As afternoon was turning to evening, Kibi approached Ilika with a smile and a bottle of lice potion. He laughed. Her strong fingers worked the potion all through his hair, and he enjoyed every minute of it.

*

When Tibo returned, two oil lanterns emerged from the box he carried, followed by a good knife in a leather sheath. Neti grabbed Miko and they helped the healer prepare their last meal together. Evening was deepening into night as they all ate hearty soup, bread, and soft cheese. As they ate, Doti spoke.

"The friend who will lead you to the tunnels is old, but he is the only one I could find who has been through, and still knows where an entrance is hidden. He will only be able to get you started, not go with you. The guards have tried to find all the entrances and seal them, but one or two remain. The tunnels are in very poor condition. Needless to say, do not trust old timbers or ropes. There may still be booty in there from the days when things were smuggled into the city. Beware old food and drink, for they will surely be poison after all these years."

"How long ago was the smuggling?" Ilika asked.

"Fifty years or more. He says it gets very wet and slimy in there, so don't be surprised if you need baths again when you come out."

For the last time, they washed the bowls and spoons, then Ilika passed out the wax-covered cakes and wheels of cheese. Several of the students packed the items with sparkling eyes but shaking hands.

*

A knock was heard upon the door.

Doti looked, opened the door, and an elderly sage peered out from under his dark, hooded cloak. He came in and carefully looked over the assembled group with keen eyes.

After a long silence he spoke. "I do not know if you can get the crippled girl through the tunnels."

"We'll carry her if we need to," Ilika said with certainty. "We will not go without her."

"So be it. I see much strength, and some fear." After peering into their hearts and souls for another long minute, he tapped Boro with his walking stick. "This one will lead. His courage will see you through."

Boro swallowed, then looked at Ilika with questioning eyes.

Ilika nodded and smiled.

"He will come with me," the sage continued, "as he can turn the key in the lock. My old fingers are no longer so strong. Come as silent shadows. When you arrive at the doorway, speak no word, make no sound, just enter quickly. These lanterns are your lives while in the tunnels. Think nothing of losing all your money, but lose your lanterns and you will surely die in there."

They all took a moment to absorb his words of warning.

"Rini, make a trio with Toli and Buna," Ilika said. "Kibi and I will come last."

Ilika placed a great gold piece in the healer's hand. "Will this cover all your expenses and trouble?"

"Very well. Thank you."

The students shared hugs with Doti, handclasps with Tibo, and many soft words of thanks.

Cloaks were tied tightly, saddlebags lifted, and bedrolls taken up. Boro and Rini grabbed Mati's burdens without being asked. Ilika put the coil of rope over Toli's shoulder, and handed the shovel to Miko.

Doti lit the lanterns and adjusted them, handing one to Boro, the other to Kibi. "The half moon will rise about midnight to guide you to the shack."

The healer opened her door. The sage and the large fourteen-year-old made their way out into the street at the pace of a walking stick.

About every minute, a pair or a trio went out.

When Ilika and Kibi were the only ones left, Doti looked at both of them with penetrating eyes. "The gods be with you. You will need them to get through those tunnels."

Ilika smiled.

The captain and his companion silently slipped out.

After seeing her friends disappear into the night, the witch closed and locked her door for the last time that evening.

* * *

Chapter 37: The Dark Way

The old sage led the group along a slow and winding route through the quiet streets and alleys, sometimes closer to the wall, sometimes a little farther away, but always generally northward toward the old Peasant's Gate.

Finally, after inching silently down a narrow walkway between two dark wooden warehouses, he stopped and motioned with his walking stick toward a pile of straw lying against one of the walls.

Boro scooped the hay back from the wall with his hands, and found a small wood and iron door, no more than two feet square, with a rusty padlock.

The old man handed Boro the key.

It fit in the lock, but took all Boro's strength to turn. At last he felt it click, the lock opened, and he was able to swing back the little door with a creaking sound that made his bones tingle.

The sage said nothing, but motioned with his stick for Boro to enter with the lamp.

The next pair came forward out of the darkness. Mati frowned at the size of the door. With Sata's help, she lowered herself to the ground and scooted in. The pain that shot from her knee brought tears, but she remained silent. Sata brought in the crutch.

Rini could feel the frustration in Toli and the fear in Buna. When they came to the little doorway, Toli got out half a word before he was silenced by a sharp poke in the ribs. The tall boy managed to hold his tongue as he twisted himself through the opening, having almost as much trouble as Mati. Buna came next but was breathing rapidly. Rini slipped in after.

Neti and Miko nodded their thanks to the sage who stood silently by the opening, and crept in toward the light of Boro's lamp.

Kibi looked into the elderly man's eyes and could feel the wisdom there. She kissed him on the cheek and climbed through the little doorway behind

Ilika.

The sage slowly pushed the door closed. They could hear him fumbling with the lock, and for several minutes they hardly dared breathe. Finally it clicked, and they faintly heard the straw being pushed against the door once more.

Then there was silence.

*

"I don't like this," Boro said softly.

Ilika looked around. All ten adventurers crowded close together in the first few yards of a rough tunnel about four feet wide and just as high, with stone and mortar walls, a heavy wooden floor above, and uneven dirt below. It continued straight across under the building into the darkness. Boro, at the far end of the line, had one glowing lantern, and Kibi the other. "I don't like it either," Ilika began, "but it does seem to be the path we must follow. And someday, perhaps a story will be written about our adventures, and students will pay two great silver pieces to purchase a copy to learn to read."

Ilika's prediction brought smiles to many faces in the near-darkness.

"Are you going to teach us to write?" Buna asked with renewed courage and determination. "Writing down our own stories would be so wonderful!"

"Yes, I am, Buna." After a moment of thought, he continued. "I think I know why this entrance was not discovered and sealed. It's not in the city wall itself, but the width of a large building away. Clever." He looked down the line of students. "Boro, even though the sage had great faith in you, I want you to lead us very slowly and carefully, and stop so we can all talk when you come to anything dangerous or strange."

"No problem," Boro agreed. "Heroes die too young, seems to me."

Sata chuckled.

"Rini, I'd like you to join Boro in the lead now," Ilika said. "Mati may need Sata's strength, and maybe yours also, Boro. Toli has the rope?"

"Yep!"

"Miko has the shovel?"

"Sure do!"

"Everyone remember — there's no hurry. We're not going a great distance, so even if we crawl the whole way, we'll get through. If we get tired and decide to spend the night in here, we'll be okay."

"Oh, I hope we don't have to do that," Neti said with a slight whine.

"Me too," Buna mumbled.

Boro and Rini crept forward into the darkness, leading the group to one side of the passage or the other to avoid sharp rocks or muddy places.

Since the tunnel was not high enough to allow her to stand, Mati was reduced to scooting along backwards with two hands on the ground and her bad leg dragging behind.

The others crawled, but with the saddlebags, bedrolls, and other burdens they carried, they could move no faster than Mati.

*

After what seemed like an hour or more, Boro came to a thick stone wall pierced by an irregular hole. He looked through with the lantern while waiting for the others to gather.

"Wall about three feet thick," he said softly. "Inside is an old stone stairway that goes down to the left, up to the right. Littered with rocks and old cement."

"Sound? Light? Smell? Signs of recent use?" Ilika asked from the end of the line.

"No, nothing."

"Thoughts, anyone?"

"Since we're at ground level, we don't know if we should go up or down," Toli said with a hint of despair.

"Okay, Boro and Rini, go through and report."

The lead pair had no trouble getting through the hole, Boro thrusting himself through with sheer strength, and Rini slithering like a snake. They looked around as best they could with the flickering light of their lantern. Walls of rough stone blocks supported a ceiling of rotting wooden planks, with crumbling rock sometimes sifting down onto their heads. The squeaking of rats echoed from somewhere in the distance.

"Down is completely blocked with rubble only about ten feet from here," Boro reported, poking his head back through the hole. "Up looks free, but we'll have to go slow with all the junk on the steps."

"Looks like we must go up. Any other thoughts?"

"I think we should poke at the rubble down there with the shovel, just to see if it's solid," Kibi suggested.

"Good idea. Miko, when you get through, you and Boro try that."

Several anxious minutes passed while Mati struggled to navigate the hole. Toli, waiting behind her, opened his mouth to say something, then shut it when he saw her silent tears and clenched teeth. The rest had little trouble after passing their bedrolls and saddlebags through.

Ilika and most of the others busied themselves scraping rocks off the steps so they could all sit down. Miko went with Boro to look at the rubble.

"It's solid," Miko announced. "Clearing it would take as long as it takes Kibi's hair to dry."

Kibi laughed. Miko and Boro took seats others had cleared for them.

"Adventure, phase one, completed," Ilika announced.

Buna snorted. "Our adventure started the day the guard told us someone wanted to test us for work as porters on a long voyage. We knew something was weird because they were calling out girls, and skinny boys, and Mati."

Ilika smiled. "I guess my adventure began when my teachers told me I had to find and train my own crew, and I had to do it in a city I'd never been to, in a far-away land, speaking a language I'd never heard before. That was more than a year ago."

"Did it take you that long to sail here?" Kibi asked.

"No, it took me most of that time to learn your language."

Boro yawned. "I think we should keep moving so we don't fall asleep."

"Yeah . . ." Sata said, unable to hold in her own yawn.

"The danger now is this loose stuff on the steps," Ilika pointed out. "Same order, staying close together so we can support each other if someone slips. Find a solid place for each footstep before you take the next."

The passage barely allowed two to walk side by side. Boro and Rini began slowly working their way up the ancient stairway, making sure they didn't get too far ahead of Mati and Sata. Each step seemed to take half a minute or more. Clearing a place for a foothold was easy. Doing it without tumbling rocks down onto everyone else was nearly impossible. Curses were heard below, apologies above. Water trickled down the slimy walls onto the steps, adding to the danger.

*

After many long minutes of climbing, Ilika heard the lead pair talking. "Let's keep the lantern away from it," Rini said.

"What do we have, Boro?" Ilika asked from below.

"Small window on the city side, about a foot square. Looks like we're almost above the rooftops. Steps end, level passage ahead. Lots of junk, old crates and barrels and stuff."

"We'll rest at the window," Ilika said.

They gathered at the top of the steps, and each person wanted to take a peek out the window, set deeply in the thick stone wall. They could make out the shapes of a few rooftops and chimneys, but little else in the darkness.

Buna clapped her hands together when she looked out. "This is so wonderful! I've never been this high up before!"

Ilika almost choked on some private thought, but managed to hide it.

"I think we're right over the old Peasant's Gate," Miko said excitedly. "I've worked near here."

Mati's eyes were wide. "I always thought these walls were solid rock. I never dreamed I'd be creeping around inside them."

"I just hope it goes all the way through," Toli mumbled with concern.

"The sage said he'd been through," Neti pointed out.

"I believe him," Ilika said, "but I also worry that things may have changed since then."

* * *

Chapter 38: Old Timbers and Ropes

Ten slices of fruitcake quickly disappeared as the nine students and their teacher discovered how hungry they could become while having adventures in forgotten dark tunnels.

When they again had their saddlebags on and their bedrolls in hand, Boro carefully led them along the level passage littered with the remains of the smuggling trade. Boxes and bags once contained food, but rarely did they see any trace of the original contents. Everything edible had been replaced by bugs, bug droppings, bug webs, and the husks of old, dried bugs.

Even unbroken jugs and bottles had been violated as insects ate through the corks. Rini found one bottle that still contained liquid, but it had separated into a cloudy murk and a scum sticking to one side of the glass. No one was tempted to open it.

For many minutes they moved slowly along the stone corridor, talking about the crates, barrels, jugs, and bottles, and what they may have once contained.

"Ohhhhhhh, shit!" came Boro's voice from the front of the line. "Everybody stay back! Let Ilika through."

"What do we have?"

"Hole in the floor. Bigger than I can jump. Couple of old timbers."

Ilika arrived at the edge. The floor was completely broken in from wall to wall, the opening a good six feet across. Two rough timbers, less than a foot wide, showed several long cracks and numerous rotten places.

"Everybody have a seat," Ilika said. "We'll lower a lamp and see what we can see."

"I can jump that!" Miko said suddenly, getting ready to make a running start.

Neti closed her eyes tightly.

"Whoa!" Ilika yelled, blocking his path. "Have you looked at the ceiling,

Miko?"

Miko shrugged. "Um . . . no."

Neti opened her eyes and breathed again.

"Most of us could jump that," Ilika explained, "if the ceiling was higher. But jumping requires some vertical space for an elliptical trajectory. Your head is almost touching the ceiling now, Miko. If you tried to jump across, you'd hit your head about half-way across and fall down, down, down . . ."

Miko, rapidly turning red, sat down beside Neti and tried to hide his face.

"What's an ellip . . . tical . . . something?" Sata asked.

"We'll get to that in geometry lessons, I promise. Rope?"

Toli came forward.

"Kibi, pass your lantern up," Ilika said. "We need to keep one near the edge so we don't forget where it is."

Boro tied the end of the rope to the handle of his lantern.

"Try to keep it from swinging and hitting the walls," Ilika counseled, crouching beside Boro at the edge.

Boro carefully lowered the lantern. His frown grew as the light passed ten feet and continued to descend. Old ropes and rusty chains dangled from spikes driven into the stonework. As the lantern passed twenty feet, the bottom remained hidden in darkness.

"How long is the rope?" Rini asked from somewhere behind them.

"I haven't measured it, but it looks like about a hundred feet," Ilika said.

Finally, more than forty feet down, the lantern made a slight clink as it touched a rock. Boro pulled back up slightly to keep it level.

Ilika and Boro beheld jagged rocks, broken crates, and shattered human bones. Dark stains splattered the rocks near the bones. Something small scurried out of sight.

Boro gazed at the scene with round eyes. "I don't see any doors or holes. No way out of that pit." He turned to Ilika with a grin. "It's a *dead*-end."

Ilika grinned back. "I think the bones agree. Okay, come and look, one at a time, Rini first."

Rini took in the sight calmly, as did all the other former slaves. Sata, however, shriveled her face at what she saw. Buna noticed and put her arm around the innkeeper's daughter.

"Everyone get settled," Ilika said as Boro pulled up the lantern. "We have two old timbers to work with, and a rope. As you all saw, lowering ourselves into the hole wouldn't accomplish anything."

"But the healer said not to use old timbers!" Toli reminded everyone with a shaking voice.

"We have to cross," Boro said firmly, "and if they'll hold me, they'll hold any of us."

"Maybe so," Ilika began, "but I don't want to lose you that easily. You'll be on a safety rope."

"A loop under my arms?" Boro suggested.

"It's too easy for a single loop to tear your arms off, or crush your ribs."

"Ouch!" Boro said, his face scrunched in pain just thinking about it.

Ilika sat down and worked with the middle of the rope, making two leg loops, then a chest loop a little farther up. Everyone watched as best they could in the dim light and cramped quarters. "Now the leg loops will take most of your weight. If you fall, hitting the wall could knock the wind out of you, but that would be nothing compared to plunging to the bottom."

Boro nodded and Ilika helped him put it on.

"Yeah, this is good. I'll sort of be sitting in it if I fall," Boro said as he examined his make-shift harness. "My arms won't get torn off."

"I like you better with arms," Sata said with a worried look.

Boro smiled at her, then coiled one end of the rope and tossed it across.

"Now we need to arrange our anchors. We don't have anything to tie onto, so first me, then Miko, then Toli, then Sata are your anchors. Each of us must have some cloth to protect our hands."

All four dug out hats or tunics.

"The anchors all sit down," Ilika said while demonstrating. "The rope goes around our backs, is held in front with the cloth-protected hand, then goes to the next anchor. Boots are wedged against the walls as best we can. Boro pulls the rope through freely, but we watch him like a hawk, ready to stop the rope if he falls."

The anchor people cleared the floor of junk and got into position. Everyone else moved back behind them. Miko had recovered from his embarrassment, and Sata beamed with pride as one of the anchors.

Boro adjusted the placement of the timber that looked strongest, then turned to see if everyone was ready.

Ilika glanced at the other anchors and nodded.

Boro stepped onto the timber, keeping one hand on the wall for balance, and began inching across.

When he arrived at about the middle, suddenly a cracking sound filled the air, Boro went down, and both halves of the timber plunged into the abyss.

"No!" Sata screamed.

Ilika clamped the rope tightly with his cloth-covered hand, and the others did the same. Seconds ticked by, but no one felt any weight on the rope. They all strained to see in the dim light, eyes wide with fear for their friend.

Eventually they saw Boro's hands clinging to the other timber. A moment later, he began to slowly pull himself onto it.

"Anchors, stay where you are," Ilika commanded, "and slowly take up the slack. Kibi, move the lanterns out of Boro's way, but don't try to help him. He's safe while roped. You're not."

Kibi squeezed by and cleared the way for Boro.

"Ilika," Boro said, finding his breath and swinging a leg onto the timber, "I think . . . I figured out . . . which timber . . . is good."

No one could keep a straight face, and several chuckled. Even Sata smiled through tears of worry.

"But you know," Boro continued, straddling the timber, "since I'm half-way across, I think I should go on over. We need someone on the other side to anchor the rope for other people, don't we?"

Ilika thought for a moment. "How are your hands and arms?"

"A little scraped, but I'm okay."

"Okay. Anchors, play out slowly."

Boro scooted the rest of the way across, taking his time. Finally he reached the far edge and took a deep breath.

"Hurray for Boro!" everyone cheered.

The large lad breathed deeply for a minute, hands on his knees, then climbed out of the harness.

*

"Can you see anything over there?" Ilika asked.

"Just more broken stuff. Some old rotten rope . . . I can tear it with my hands."

"Mati, come up here. Let's talk."

With Sata's help, Mati joined Ilika at the edge.

"We can put the timber however you want, but I think it'll be safest if you go alone."

Mati swallowed her fear as she gazed across the black hole. "The timber is near the wrong wall. My left hand will be free. Will I . . . have the rope thing on?"

"Yes, and there will be anchors on both ends, so if you fall, you won't even hit the side."

"I think I can do it. We know the timber is strong enough to hold Boro. I . . . I have to do it," she said with a shaking voice, looking into Ilika's eyes with a mixture of desperation and trust.

"Let's start by getting Rini and Toli across. Then we'll have plenty of people on each side."

Ilika pulled the harness back over while Boro held one end of the rope. Rini smiled slightly as he got into the harness, then pranced effortlessly across the timber.

Next came Toli, obviously holding his breath and shaking, but he managed to cross without needing the services of his anchors.

Ilika and Boro then moved the timber for Mati.

"Hey!" Kibi said with a burst of inspiration. "We should tie a short rope to the crutch so it can't fall into the pit."

Ilika nodded.

Miko found the knife in his saddlebags and cut a length from the far end of the rope.

The anchors on both sides got into position. Mati stepped up to the timber and took a moment to figure out where to place her crutch. Those watching were not sure she was breathing, and they knew for a fact they weren't.

Mati looked across at her destination. Rini was the second anchor on that side, his bright eyes and contented smile waiting for her. She stepped onto the timber.

"The weird part is, I have to put my crutch in front of me, instead of on the side."

"Take as long as you need," Ilika said in a reassuring voice.

Angled nearly sideways, she took several small steps, slowly and carefully, and then another, arriving at the mid-point. She glanced at Rini again, patiently taking in the rope. Another few steps.

No one else made a sound.

Another step. The far side was getting very close. Two more steps. With her entire body trembling, Mati stepped off the timber onto solid stone.

The nearly forgotten tunnel, somewhere inside the old city wall, echoed with clapping and cheering until they saw Ilika holding up his arms for quiet.

*

Buna, Neti, Kibi, and Sata crossed without incident. Ilika and Miko worked together to rope across the saddlebags, and toss the bedrolls over one at a time.

When Miko crossed, Ilika was his only anchor on that side, but he too was sure-footed.

Ilika looked around for anything they had left, and found someone's hat. He coiled his end of the rope and put it over his head, took up the lantern, and worked his way carefully across.

Kibi's embrace helped him release all the fear and tension he had been feeling ever since they first looked into the gaping black pit with its silent bones.

* * *

Chapter 39: The Way Down

Most of the students were poised to dash along the passageway and distance themselves from the miserable black pit, but Ilika sat down with Boro and opened a jar of ointment. When they saw how badly Boro had scraped his hands and arms, they muttered apologies and found places to sit.

"I had a hunch Boro was worse than he realized," Ilika said as he applied the softest ointment. "It's easy to ignore pain for a while when things are happening quickly."

"Miko does that too," Neti said with fondness.

"It's good to be able to do that, as long as you take care of yourself as soon as possible," Ilika added.

"That feels a lot better," Boro said. "They were starting to sting."

"Accurate reporting is more important now than ever before," Ilika said as he looked around the group. "This isn't a classroom. This is real. Mistakes can get us killed. Any other problems?"

"I'm still shaking inside a little," Mati admitted. "But I think I'll be okay in a few minutes."

*

About a quarter hour later, they all felt truly ready to move on. The level passage, with its collection of old smuggling booty, allowed the group easy walking for about fifty feet. Another small window revealed the half moon in the eastern sky. From that point, a stairway led steeply downward, but was covered with even more rubble than the first.

Boro and Rini tried to lead very slowly and carefully, but most of the students, and even Ilika, were repeatedly slipping and scraping themselves. Mati found her crutch nearly useless, and soon had to let Boro steady her while Sata carried the crutch. Rini took the lantern and the lead, announcing whenever anything dangerous was underfoot, from broken steps to rusty spikes in old boards.

Toli and Neti fared the worst. Buna wasn't strong enough to keep Toli from falling. Miko would have carried Neti if he hadn't been having almost as much trouble himself. Only Rini and Sata seemed to be okay.

Suddenly a number of changes caused them to halt. The rubble they were constantly kicking loose came to rest a moment later.

Buna shivered. "It just got colder."

"And the walls are made of smaller rocks," Toli added.

"And they're dripping wet," Kibi said, touching some yellow slime with a finger.

"I think we're below ground level," Ilika speculated, looking up at the rotten wood and crumbling stone on the ceiling.

Sitting would have been nearly impossible, so after a moment to examine everything they could see or touch, Rini continued to lead them down into the earth.

*

"Something ahead!" Rini called a few minutes later. "A doorway. We're coming to a room, I think."

"Take it slow," Ilika said from the end of the line. "Report as you can see."

"Loose rock floor that slopes down, and . . . oops! . . . a pool."

As the others entered the room, they spread out to the sides when they saw Rini holding the lantern at the edge of the dark water, one of his boots wet.

When Ilika finally arrived, he raised his lantern. The room was a square about twenty feet on each side, the walls rough stone blocks with no other doors or openings to be seen. The dark pool covered about a third of the floor, going all the way to the far wall.

Boro took the lantern from Rini and walked as much of the outside edge of the room as he could, then returned to Ilika and Kibi. "No other way out," he said.

*

After eating a piece of cake, Ilika looked around. All his students were tired and sore. Some were trying to get comfortable on the sloping rubble, without much success.

Boro wandered over to where Sata was sitting. He could see Buna, not far away, putting ointment on Toli's scrapes and cuts. Neti handed them pieces of cheese, and Boro gladly ate one.

He was gazing across the room, starting to feel sleepy, when something caught his eye. At one point on the edge of the pool, a little stream of water came from somewhere under the rubble. The stains on the rocks, however, showed the level of the pool to always be about the same.

Boro patted Sata on the back and rose to investigate. After making his way around the pool to the little inlet, he sat down to think about the situation.

Ilika noticed Boro's thoughtful look and joined him.

"If the water's coming into the pool all the time, and the pool isn't getting any deeper, where's the water going out?" Boro pondered aloud.

"Could be just cracks in the walls," Ilika said with a slight shrug.

Boro looked across at the place where the pool touched the far wall. "I'm a good swimmer. I'm gonna find out."

"Let's tie a rope around your waist so I can follow you if necessary," Ilika said.

Boro stripped off most of his clothes while Ilika got the rope from Toli. By now everyone was sitting up, watching. Ilika secured the rope around Boro, who entered the frigid water slowly.

"Be careful, Boro!" Sata called after him.

When he came face to face with the stone wall, his head and shoulders were still above water. He glanced back. Ilika was playing out the rope, Kibi beside him. Sata was down at the water's edge. He turned back to the wall, took a deep breath, and went down to his knees.

After blinking to get his eyes used to the water, a dim grayness loomed before him, rough to the touch. He felt farther down, and the wall ended with a jagged edge. He felt for its limits, finding it roughly circular, about three feet across.

Pulling himself into the opening, Boro guessed the wall to be about two feet thick. He pulled himself through, then felt above him. His hand broke the surface, so he pushed off the bottom.

Breathing deeply of the cold air, he strained to see, but found only darkness all around him.

Then, as time passed and his eyes got used to the darkness, he sensed a tiny bit of green light coming from under the water, from the submarine hole in the wall. It failed to illuminate anything in the room, but showed the way back to his friends.

After breathing for another minute, he went down and aimed himself back through the hole, pulling on the rope to speed himself along.

✷

"Wow! You sure can hold your breath a long time!" Sata said with admiration.

"I wasn't holding my breath," Boro admitted as he sloshed his way out of the pool. "I was in the next room over. Only problem is, it's pitch dark in there."

Ilika untied the rope and listened to Boro's report of the size of the opening and the thickness of the wall.

"How far under is the top of the opening?"

"Only about a foot."

Boro dried off with a piece of clean clothing Sata handed him. Then he looked at Ilika, who seemed to be lost in thought. "How can we get a lantern over there?"

Ilika was silent awhile longer. "That's exactly what I was wondering. I can see how we can get everything else through without too much damage. But getting the lanterns through that pool while lit . . . or in any condition to be relit . . . doesn't seem possible."

Boro remained silent, but his face showed intense frustration that his discovery had been for nothing.

* * *

Chapter 40: Ultimate Trust

After a few more minutes pondering the situation, Ilika closed his eyes.

Boro put his tunic back on, then received a piece of fruitcake from Kibi.

Suddenly Ilika opened his eyes and began to strip down to his shorts. "Boro, will you be on the rope for me?"

"Sure."

"I'll return within a quarter hour." Ilika secured himself, entered the water, and went under.

Boro played out the rope, but wore a puzzled look. Soon the rope went slack.

Sata could see Kibi frowning. She sat down and put her arm around the black-haired girl. "Don't worry. Ilika is very strong and smart."

"I know," Kibi said, worry still coloring her voice.

*

The next ten minutes seemed like ten hours as the students waited in the dark, cold, underground room for their teacher to return. Some tried to get comfortable again, but the anxiety in the group grew thicker as the minutes slowly passed.

Finally Boro took off his tunic and started breathing deeply. Before he even stepped into the pool, something broke the calm of the water's surface. A moment later, Ilika emerged.

"There's light in the next room now, and the way out is not far. We have work to do. We need to repack our stuff so it will stay as dry as possible. The food needs to go down at the foot of a bedroll cover. Kibi and I will do the same with the book and paper. Other than that, most everything will get wet, and we will dry it as soon as we can. Our goal right now is to get out of these tunnels."

Kibi noticed that the dark metal bracelet Ilika always wore on his left arm was missing.

Almost everyone went into action. Ilika and Kibi worked together to wrap the educational materials in as many layers of waxed canvas as possible. Everything else was packed securely.

When all was nearly ready, Ilika noticed Toli coaxing Buna to help, but she just sat, hands around her knees, hiding her face. "Buna, we're about to leave," Ilika called. "What's wrong?"

She said something too softly for Ilika to hear.

"She says she can't go under the water," Toli repeated.

"The opening is only about a foot down."

"I know, but she says she can't put her head under."

"Talk to her, Toli. I'll get the others through."

Toli nodded.

"Boro, you and Sata go through. I'll hand off stuff to you right at the hole, you pass it up to Sata, she sets it on the rocks to drain. The first bundles will be the papers and food."

Toli pleaded with Buna, but she wouldn't budge.

The others stacked the bundles and saddlebags as close to the transfer point as possible. Miko added the shovel.

Boro coiled the rope, went under, and a moment later Sata followed.

Buna began snapping at Toli, telling him to leave her alone.

Ilika entered the water, waded to the wall, and ducked under to look. Silhouetted against the light that now filled the other room, Boro's hands were ready.

Kibi handed him the first bundle, the one that contained their precious book.

Ilika took a breath, went down, and within seconds had it in Boro's hands. He saw Boro immediately lift it clear of the water.

After Toli put his and Buna's bags with the others, he sat back down, but gave her some space.

When the most important bundles were through the hole, Ilika started moving faster, and all the saddlebags and bedrolls were quickly moved to the other room.

"Should we take off our boots?" Neti asked.

"There's no point," Ilika said. "They'll get wet either way."

Toli had given up on Buna and was getting ready to go through with the others.

"Okay, line up! First person through will meet Boro's hands, ready to toss you up to Sata like a bundle."

Rini grinned. "I'll go! I'm small enough to toss."

Almost everyone laughed. Ilika even thought he saw Buna crack a tiny smile for a moment.

Rini . . . Neti . . . Miko . . . each swam through the hole.

Ilika scanned the room for anything they had forgotten. In addition to those students ready to cross, he only saw two flickering lanterns and one fourteen-year-old girl.

"I'm taking the crutch through," Kibi said, "then I'll be underwater to help Mati."

Ilika nodded. "I'll help her on this end."

Kibi went through.

"You ready for this, Mati?"

"Sure. My knee works better in the water than anywhere else."

Ilika went down with her, but was hardly needed.

Toli was the last one lined up to go, and he looked frustrated, almost disgusted. Ilika made sure he was safely through, then slowly came out of the water and sat down beside Buna.

✷

"Hi," he said.

"I can't put my head under the water! I'm sorry!" she snapped.

Ilika let some time pass. "Any idea what stops you?"

"I had a master's wife try to drown me when I was about nine. I was coughing up water for a week. I think I almost died." She buried her face in her hands and began to cry.

Ilika didn't say anything, just put his arms around her. Eventually the tears ran their course.

"Well, I'm not going to leave anyone behind in these tunnels."

Buna looked at Ilika. His face showed complete sincerity. "You'd . . . stay in here with me?"

"If I had to."

"But . . . we don't have anything to eat . . . and there's no other way out."

"That appears to be true."

"If we went all the way back and pounded on that little door, a guard would probably come and you'd be arrested!"

"Probably."

Time passed as teacher and student sat in silence together.

Suddenly Boro surfaced in the pool.

"We all talked about it, and thought of something that might help. I was chosen to do it because I'm leading right now." He went to one lantern and blew it out, then to the other and did the same. Without a word, he returned to the pool and disappeared.

The room was now completely dark, except for the greenish-blue glow coming through the underwater hole in the wall.

Ilika smiled to himself.

After getting over her surprise, Buna started crying softly. "Now we can't go back . . ."

"It would be very hard. We'd have to cross the timber over the pit by feel."

They both fell silent again, sitting side by side in the darkness. A faint squeaking sound came from somewhere behind them. Buna shivered.

"How . . . long does it take?" she asked in a tiny, shaking voice.

"About ten seconds, at the most, underwater. The wall is only two feet thick. You can see now exactly where the opening is."

"Yeah. It's not very far down," she said with a little more hope in her voice.

"No."

"And when you're through, you can go right up?"

"Yes. The wall is straight up and down on the other side, just like this side."

She was silent again for a long minute. A tiny rustling sound came from somewhere under the rubble.

Finally Ilika heard a very soft voice in his ear. "When I go under, I want you to push me through that hole. I don't care what I'm doing, you have to push me through. Promise me."

Ilika was silent for a moment. "I promise."

She got up and took several tortured steps until she arrived at the edge of the pool. Ilika stayed right at her side.

"The water sure is a pretty color with that light coming through. Where is the light coming from?"

"My bracelet. It's sitting on a rock in there."

"Wow . . . a magic bracelet."

"Yes."

"I'd like to see that," she said with a tiny grin.

He took her hand and they walked into the water together until they were facing the wall.

"Just hold your breath, close your eyes, and let me do the rest," Ilika said in a reassuring tone.

She took a breath and went down. Ilika was right with her, and immediately clamped her arms against her sides and shoved her through the opening.

Boro grabbed her and pulled, and most of her body was through the hole before panic set in and her legs started thrashing wildly. Ilika received several hard kicks to his head before he was able to get clear.

He tried to find the surface, but was dazed and confused, and his lungs were screaming at him to take a breath. An instinct told him to go toward the light, and he started to, then remembered the light was not toward the surface. He stopped himself, went a different way, and slammed into a rock.

✷

An unknown amount of time later, a strong arm grabbed Ilika and pulled him up. He gasped and sputtered and coughed for a long time, but the strong arm held him steady, and eventually his breathing and balance returned to normal.

"When you weren't right behind Buna," Boro said with wide eyes, "Kibi knew something was wrong and made me come back for you. I'm sure glad I did!"

Ilika looked at the young man who had just saved his life. "Me too!"

✷ ✷ ✷

Chapter 41: Freedom Without Walls

Ilika rested a few more minutes, then went through the underwater passage for the last time. Boro followed.

As soon as Ilika surfaced, he saw Buna, still shaking like a leaf, in Kibi's arms.

When Buna saw Ilika, she jumped back into the water and nearly knocked him over. "Thank you! Thank you so much! You could have just left me over there and I would have died in the dark . . ." Her words faded away into sobs.

"No one gets left behind," Ilika said while he held her, "if there is any way to bring us all out safely."

When Buna was finally ready to let go, Ilika looked around at his students. They all looked at him with deepened respect and admiration, but at the same time they all looked like sleepy drowned rats. He noticed Toli sitting as far away from Buna as possible, and not looking in her direction.

Ilika's bracelet remained on the large rock, casting a bright beam of light onto the ceiling. This room was very similar to the first, except that the pool went right to the doorway on the far side, slowly overflowing across the slimy stones.

Ilika stepped out of the water and stood facing Kibi.

"Thank you," was all he said as he put his wet arms around her. They held each other silently for a long time.

"Ilika . . ." Boro said between deep breaths, "I'm . . . exhausted. Could . . . someone else . . . lead now?"

Ilika and Kibi sat down with the others.

"Of course, Boro. My brave students, let's make a decision. The way out is a short walk from here. I've seen it. Then we have to cross some open grass, at night, without any light but the moon, and get on the western road for about a mile. We can do that now, or we can rest in here tonight, all day tomorrow, and go tomorrow night. Either way, we have to do it at night."

"Everything's wet," Neti said in a pouting tone while shivering, "and we're so cold we wouldn't get much sleep."

"Nothing's going to dry in here," Sata added. "We need air and sunshine."

Everyone else merely nodded agreement.

"I want everyone to understand that we have to do this stretch silently. If the guards in the towers hear us, they'll start looking for us in the countryside, and that's what we went to all this trouble to avoid."

"There's a little good news," Rini announced.

Ilika looked at him.

"The book and papers stayed dry."

"Fantastic! Thank you, everyone, for finding the courage to get through these old tunnels. Miko, you seem fairly awake. Want to lead us to that shack?"

He suddenly sat up taller and straighter. "Sure!"

Everyone was soon ready. Kibi placed herself beside Buna, who looked grateful. Ilika asked Toli to bring up the rear with him.

"Are we going to walk by the light of your magic bracelet?" Buna asked with a gleam in her eyes.

Ilika replaced the bracelet on his left arm. "Yes, as far as the tunnel goes."

They entered the passageway on the far side of the room. Ilika had the only source of light, so he shined it toward the ceiling ahead of him.

Miko moved slowly down the wet, slimy passage. It turned twice, passing three side tunnels choked with rocks and broken timbers. Finally, a small stone doorway covered with vines and weeds stood before them.

"I've never seen this side of the city," Ilika said. "Anyone know the lay of the land?"

"It's grassy," Rini replied, "with some little gullies. I bet this water goes into one of them."

"If we don't go straight," Boro proposed, "but zigzag instead, the guards won't be able to tell where we came from."

"Or where we're going," Mati added.

"Yeah!" Miko agreed. "And we can angle down to the road as if we're going toward the gate!"

"Good ideas," Ilika said. "Let's take our time and do it right. This is the last stretch."

Rini worked beside Miko to make a way through the vines, and as they did, Ilika made his light dimmer and dimmer. It was no brighter than a stubby candle as they all filed through into a small muddy ditch. From there, Miko led them up onto the grass.

Ilika turned off the light and exited last. He took a moment to pull some vines back over the opening, then followed the others.

They passed like ghosts during the last hour of the night, back and forth across the grassy slope, none of them caring about the wet, dewy grass in their drenched condition. They finally joined the western road and floated along like shadows, two by two, never any faster than a girl with a crutch could move. Slowly they crested a shallow rise and rounded a bend.

✷

When the guards changed shift at first light, the new guard in the western watchtower looked out over the stretch of grass where no settlement was allowed. He could faintly see a meandering path of trampled grass that looked like a horse had gotten loose and grazed for a few hours. But the animal appeared to be gone now, so he didn't even bother to report the incident.

✷

"We can talk softly now," Ilika said.

"Are we safe?" Sata asked.

Boro sighed with relief. "The danger of the wall is behind us."

"Now we have the danger of the road and the woods," Kibi pointed out.

"I'm happy with that change!" Rini said, jumping up and down. Seeing him, Buna giggled and danced in a little circle in the growing light.

"Now we have to find that oak tree, and the path," Miko said in a serious, leader-like voice.

Ilika looked around at the trees on both sides of the road. "I hope someone knows what an oak tree looks like."

"Don't *you?*" Toli asked with disbelief.

"No. There aren't any in my country."

Mati smiled. "You'll like them. They're big and strong."

"Are we going to do lessons today?" Buna asked excitedly, somehow full of renewed energy.

Ilika yawned. "I don't think so, Buna. I think everyone's going to sleep all day."

A quarter hour later, in the growing dawn light, Ilika gazed up in wonder at the towering oak tree. Then he looked around at the faces of his nine students. Even though they were all sopping wet, cold, and tired, he could tell they were ready for adventure.

* * * * *

About the Author

Born in the Mojave Desert, J. Z. Colby now lives and writes deep in a forest of the Pacific Northwest.

He has studied many subjects, formally and informally, including psychology, philosophy, education, and performing arts, but remains a generalist. His primary profession as a mental health counselor, specializing with families and young adults, gives him many stories of personal growth, and the motivation to develop his team of young critiquers and readers.

All his life, he has been drawn toward a broad understanding of human nature, especially those physical, emotional, mental, and spiritual situations in which our capacity to function seems to reach its limits. He finds fascinating those few individuals who can transcend the limits of our common human nature and the dictates of our cultures.

In his spare time, he flies helicopters and airplanes.

He may be contacted at the email address listed on the internet site www.nebador.com.

www.ingramcontent.com/pod-product-compliance
Lightning Source LLC
Chambersburg PA
CBHW020614310726
48979CB00008B/1475/J

* 9 7 8 1 9 3 6 2 5 3 0 0 5 *